"You're Going to Have to Know Me Better

before you can make an accurate assessment of what will or won't please me. Making a home is an . . . intimate . . . process," Cain said.

"Not that intimate," retorted Shelley.

Cain smiled slightly. *"I'll behave, little mink. I promise. It will be business and only business, unless you say otherwise."*

"Mink?"

"Soft and wild," Cain explained helpfully. *"Mink."*

"Is this your idea of business?" she asked in exasperation.

"Am I touching you?" he countered.

"No, but you're reaching me!"

ELIZABETH LOWELL
lives in California with her journalist husband and their two children. Her beautiful marriage is responsible for her strong belief in romantic love. That belief, combined with her imaginative power and sorcery with words, makes her a favorite with romance readers.

Dear Reader:

There is an electricity between two people in love that makes everything they do magic, larger than life. This is what we bring you in SILHOUETTE INTIMATE MOMENTS.

SILHOUETTE INTIMATE MOMENTS are longer, more sensuous romance novels filled with adventure, suspense, glamor or melodrama. These books have an element no one else has tapped: excitement.

We are proud to present the very best romance has to offer from the very best romance writers. In the coming months look for some of your favorite authors such as Elizabeth Lowell, Nora Roberts, Erin St. Claire and Brooke Hastings.

SILHOUETTE INTIMATE MOMENTS are for the woman who wants more than she has ever had before. These books are for you.

Karen Solem
Editor-in-Chief
Silhouette Books

Traveling Man

Elizabeth Lowell

Silhouette Intimate Moments

Published by Silhouette Books New York

America's Publisher of Contemporary Romance

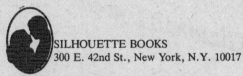

SILHOUETTE BOOKS
300 E. 42nd St., New York, N.Y. 10017

Copyright © 1985 by Ann Maxwell

Distributed by Pocket Books

ISBN: 0-373-07097-7

First Silhouette Books printing June, 1985

10 9 8 7 6 5 4 3 2 1

America's Publisher of Contemporary Romance

Printed in the U.S.A.

Books by Elizabeth Lowell

Silhouette Desire

Summer Thunder #77

Silhouette Intimate Moments

The Danvers Touch #18
Lover in the Rough #34
Summer Games #57
Forget Me Not #72
A Woman Without Lies #81
Traveling Man #97

For
Jayne Ann Krentz,

a pleasure to talk with
a pleasure to read

a pleasure indeed.

Chapter 1

TO THE WEST THE LAND SLOPED STEEPLY DOWN TO THE sea. Beneath a restless wind, tawny grass shivered and swayed, bleached beneath southern California's hot August sun. The Pacific Ocean presented a burnished blue surface to the world, mirroring a flawless summer sky. The view of water and wind and land was unfettered, almost untamed, except for the elegant homes astride the hills.

Shelley Wilde stood inside one of those homes, wishing that she could walk to the partially drawn drapes and throw open the sliding doors that led to a redwood deck overlooking the sea. If Shelley had been given a free hand in decorating Ms. JoLynn Cummings's rented house, she would have used the view itself as an objet d'art, a compelling sweep of primary color and primal force.

JoLynn, however, had felt differently. Despite man's best efforts, the Pacific didn't wear a designer label sewn neatly along the seam where land met sea. If an object wasn't labeled, JoLynn didn't know what to think of it. So instead of the Ellsworth Kelley oils and the Saarinen furniture Shelley would have chosen, JoLynn had required that the gilded curves of Louis XIV grace the multileveled, ultramodern glass house. From that choice had followed a host of others. One of them was heavy velvet draperies shutting out the magnificent view. Another was the rented crystal chandeliers that looked rather startling against the open-beamed ceiling of the dining room.

With a sigh, Shelley set aside her notebook and catalogs of rare objets d'art. She didn't need to make notes on subtle signs of personality and use those notes to puzzle out the best choice in finishing touches for the room. There was taste in abundance around her, but no originality. There was great beauty, but no individuality, nothing to give her a clue as to the unique combination of education and experience, hopes and fears that made up JoLynn Cummings. If there were anything more compelling than insecurity beneath JoLynn's lovely surface, she wasn't giving out hints. Everything she had rented from Brian Harris could have been taken intact from a museum.

Shelley caught herself yawning as she went to yet another part of the house. There was nothing out of place, even in the maid's quarters. Gilt and grace, elegance and gilt, a blue and white and gold fragility that was almost suffocating. Not that the decor or furniture itself was at fault—the furnishings were as exquisite as everything Brian rented to his wealthy clientele—but the unrelieved perfection around her made Shelley itch to put in accents that would subtly remind the occupant that this was a home, not a museum.

With another yawn, Shelley abandoned that particular fantasy. It was obvious that JoLynn didn't have enough confidence in her own taste to survive any ripples in the perfect surface Brian had created. For Shelley, people like JoLynn were the easiest and least satisfying kind of clients. Give them a room straight out of the last museum they had seen and they were content. Less individuality and sense of adventure than a clam.

Shelley looked over her shoulder, but saw no one. Brian and JoLynn were still out in the garden discussing lawn furniture and statuary. Skirting the large, flawlessly furnished living room with its chiffon-and-velvet framed view of the wild sea, Shelley went into the east wing of the Pacific Palisades home. She pushed open a door that had recently been repainted white with gilt trim. The room beyond made her take a quick breath. She smiled and then began laughing softly.

Someone in the house was fighting a battle for breathing space amid all the perfection. Here, Louis XIV replicas were buried beneath an eclectic onslaught that fairly shouted of unusual pursuits. Posters of barbarians in full sword-and-sorcery regalia were tacked to the eggshell walls—crookedly. The hem of the velvet drapes had been ruthlessly stuffed over the top of the curtain rod, effectively nullifying any attempt to shut out the view. A turtle as big as a dinner plate was sunning itself in a muddy terrarium perched atop a gilt table. On the floor in a dark corner there was another terrarium with the lid askew. Inlaid dresser drawers were partially open, allowing folds of socks and T-shirts to creep out into the light. The canopied bed was gloriously unmade. Its powder blue velvet bedspread had been kicked onto the thick white carpet in a huge pile that was held in place by a pair of battered, grass-stained running shoes.

Still smiling, Shelley looked around the room, feeling excitement quiver in her blood. It was always that way when she encountered anyone who met life head on, nothing held

back, no need for uniforms or labels or evasions. There
were so few people like that, no matter what their age—and
it was obvious that whoever inhabited this room was
somewhere between twelve and eighteen.

Shelley approved of the spare yet functionally graceful
lines of the computer that overran the dainty desk. Boxes of
software were stacked on top of piles of comics and science
fiction books. The closet door was jammed open with a Star
Wars light-sword that had been scratched and bent in
cosmic battles. The television sprouted video games in a
tangle of wires and cassettes.

But the crowning defiance was a stereo with black
speakers powerful enough to be heard on Jupiter.

Mentally, Shelley began a list of the accents she would
love to add to the room. First, a framed poster of a famous
ad showing a young man in black seated in front of two
huge stereo speakers. He was hanging onto the arms of his
chair with casual strength, for the force of the music
pouring out of the speakers had whipped his tie over his
shoulder, blown his hair straight back, and sent a lamp and
a martini glass teetering on the instant of falling over.

Shelley also had in her home a modern painting of Saint
George and the Dragon that would fit beautifully amid the
barbarian posters and science fiction books. The painting
radiated power and mystery, good and evil, life and
death—all the bloody absolutes that fascinated teenagers.
The dragon itself was enough to raise the hair on anyone's
neck. The beast's powerful muscles rippled and gleamed in
a hammered metallic gold, its eyes were as brilliant as
diamonds, its teeth and claws glittered with lethal edges.
Clearly, St. George was in for the battle of his life. It would
be a perfect painting for this room. The Louis XIV furniture
would have to go, though. Period. The blue, white and gold

color scheme could be shifted from French elegance to barbarian splendor by intensifying the colors and giving the gilt a metallic, high tech finish.

This was one room and one personality that it would be pure pleasure to work with.

Smiling, feeling refreshed, Shelley walked back down the short hallway to the living room. Voices filtered through, telling her that she was no longer alone in the house. She recognized the cultured, drama school tones of her partner, Brian Harris. The other voice was that of JoLynn Cummings, divorced from more money than Midas ever dreamed of. Breathy, light, somewhere between a whisper and a sigh, JoLynn's voice was a perfect match for the house.

Shelley passed the huge, gilt-framed mirror at the end of the hall without a glance. She didn't need a mirror to tell her that her mink brown hair was neatly coiled at the nape of her neck, or that the jewel-toned tapestry pantsuit she wore fit her slender figure without a wrinkle. She knew that her emerald silk blouse brought out the green in her hazel eyes and heightened the healthy glow of her lightly tanned skin. She also knew that if she looked in the mirror, she would see intelligence and humor rather than provocative beauty. While Shelley considered herself a reasonably attractive woman, she doubted that she had ever stopped traffic in her life, except for the time her car had died in a busy intersection at rush hour.

After twenty-seven years of living, Shelley had no illusions about her appearance, herself or other members of the human race, including men. Especially men. After her divorce five years before, she had taken stock of herself and life, decided what she had wanted from both and pursued it. She had achieved what she sought. She was in control of her own life, a life she had built through her own skill and discipline, owing her success to no one. Most particularly, to no *man*.

"There you are, Shelley," said Brian, smiling at her. "JoLynn was just telling me about some Grecian statues she saw at the Louvre."

Brian was taller than Shelley, slender and had the natural ash blond hair that some women spend their lives trying to find at the bottom of various dye bottles. His eyes were almost startlingly blue against his tanned, clean-shaven features. He had the classic beauty of a recently fallen angel and business instincts that could easily rule over hell. Shelley had become fond of Brian, particularly after he finally had accepted that she was more of an asset to him as a business partner than a bed partner.

"Sarah Marshall," continued Brian, "convinced JoLynn that you have an absolute genius for matching people with just the right objets d'art for their homes."

Shelley smiled professionally. Mrs. Marshall had been one of her favorite clients—intelligent, confident and highly individualistic. "Sorry if I kept you waiting, Mrs. Cummings. I was looking at your house. As usual, Brian has done an excellent job of interpreting his client's wishes."

"Oh, call me JoLynn, please. When I hear 'Mrs. Cummings' I think of my ex-husband's mother. Awful woman."

"JoLynn," murmured Shelley, shaking the small, surprisingly strong hand the woman had automatically extended when she saw Shelley approach.

JoLynn's hard hand was the only surprise about her. She was exactly what anyone would expect after having seen the house. JoLynn's appearance had little relationship to anything about her but her former husband's bank balance. Her hair, trendy clothes, makeup, nails, hose and shoes were all perfect; and as sterile as the back side of the moon. Shelley had always chosen her own clothes for timelessness rather than trendiness. Her wardrobe would go out of style the same instant good taste, fine materials and quality workmanship did. JoLynn would be out of style when she sat down to breakfast and opened the fashion section of the *Los Angeles Times*.

Yet the woman was stunningly beautiful. Red-blond hair, creamy skin, jade green eyes and a body that would make a showgirl weep with jealousy.

"Cain," said JoLynn, "this is—" With an exasperated sound, JoLynn looked around, realizing that there was no one in the room with her but Brian and Shelley. "Where has that man got to now?" she muttered. Then, loudly, "Cain?"

Shelley stood quietly, waiting to hear an answer from another part of the house. Nothing came. Then JoLynn's eyes widened as she looked over Shelley's shoulder.

"There you are," breathed JoLynn. "You are the most impossible man to keep track of."

"So I've been told," said a deep voice behind Shelley.

Startled, Shelley spun around. She had heard nothing, despite the fact that the floor behind her was polished hardwood rather than plush carpet. Even more surprising, the man wasn't wearing soft-soled tennis or running shoes, but knee-high, lace-up boots of the type used by rough country hikers.

"Cain," said JoLynn, "this is Brian's partner, Shelley Wilde. Shelley, Cain Remington."

Automatically, Shelley held out her hand. The hand that enveloped hers was as surprising as the man's soundless approach had been. Strong, scarred, callused, yet very clean, Cain's hand belonged to a man who was the antithesis of what she had expected to find with the recently divorced JoLynn. Cain was neither a too-young Adonis supported by a wealthy older divorcée, nor was he an overweight, overage businessman supporting a much younger woman.

In fact, Cain Remington did not fit into any category Shelley could think of. Though casual, his clothes were excellent. His voice was deep, almost rough, and his face was too hard and too male to be labeled good looking. Though tall and well built, he didn't appear to be a product of Century City gyms. He was too . . . hard. Chestnut hair and aloof gray eyes, cleanly sculpted lips, a mustache that gleamed with bronze highlights and a smile that went no further than the serrated edges of his teeth.

In all, Shelley decided that Cain Remington was very much his own man. He looked on the world with the detached amusement of a well-fed predator. If Cain had been the dragon of myth, St. George would have been in terminal trouble. Cain didn't look shallow enough to be satisfied with JoLynn's obvious but limited assets. On the other hand, Shelley's ex-husband had taught her all about the average male IQ when confronted with a D-cup bra and a breathy little-girl voice.

"Mrs. Wilde," said Cain, holding her hand for an instant longer than necessary, as though he sensed the slightly cynical appraisal behind Shelley's smile.

"Miss," corrected Shelley.

"Not Ms.?"

"If a man cares enough to ask," said Shelley with a thin smile, "I make sure to tell him I'm a member of a dying breed."

"Spinsters?" asked Cain, his gaze traveling over the gentle curves of Shelley's body.

The anger that flared in Shelley's hazel eyes passed almost too quickly for anyone to notice. Cain had, however.

His hard mouth shifted slightly in what could have been a smile. Beneath that civilized, jewel-toned exterior was spirit, and Cain approved of spirited things. He wondered if Shelley was half as intelligent as her eyes and expression promised.

"Define spinster," suggested Shelley, "and I'll tell you whether I fit your label."

"A woman who can't hold a man."

"Bingo," said Shelley coolly, but her eyes narrowed against painful memories. "In my case, the spinster is a divorcée who reclaimed her maiden name. I'll bet you're a bachelor. A man who can't hold a woman."

Brian stirred uneasily. "Shelley, why don't we—"

JoLynn, who apparently had had more experience with Cain's sardonic sense of humor, drew Brian off toward the end of the living room where sunlight filtered through chiffon curtains. Breathlessly, she began describing the marble statuary she wanted added to the yard.

Neither Cain nor Shelley noticed the discreet withdrawal. Both were intent on a moment of mutual anger. And discovery.

"Actually, I've always considered myself more of a connoisseur," said Cain.

"Ah, yes," murmured Shelley. "Of women, assuredly. Though you aren't handsome yourself, you doubtless require that your women be perfectly stunning, as objectively superb as any connoisseur could want. Your women have to be more decorative than Greek sculpture and ever so much more flexible in bed. They must also," she added in a cool tone, "be blessed with the intelligence and insight of a clam."

"Bright and beautiful too," said Cain, smiling a very male smile and leaving no doubt that he meant Shelley.

"To believe that compliment, I'd have to line up with the

clams," said Shelley. "I have, Mr. Remington, a rather exact appreciation of just how 'beautiful' I am."

"Call me Cain," he said, laughing softly.

"Wise of you to limit my options," said Shelley.

"In name-calling?"

"Yes," retorted Shelley. But she felt her irritation giving way to her own sense of humor and the laughter that she saw gleaming in Cain's no longer aloof gray eyes. "You're rather a renegade, aren't you?" she asked, smiling despite herself.

Before Cain could answer, JoLynn's high, piercing scream shredded the silence. As one, Cain and Shelley turned and ran toward the far end of the living room. At the same instant, they saw the dusty-rose-colored snake curled in a patch of sunlight on the floor. JoLynn shrieked again.

With a single clean motion, Cain lifted JoLynn and spun her out of reach of the snake. As he put her down he straightened and turned to deal with the reptile. Then he stopped in shock. Shelley was bending over the slender snake, picking it up as calmly as though it were a faded rose ribbon dropped by a careless child. Brian made a sound that in a woman would have been described as a tiny shriek.

"S-Shelley, what the hell!" stammered Brian.

JoLynn made indecipherable demands and grabbed at Cain's arms. Barely glancing aside, he handed her over to Brian. All Cain's attention was on the woman standing in a cataract of sunlight with a long snake coiled in her hands.

"It's all right, Brian," said Shelley. "This one's a pet."

"How can you be s-sure?" demanded her partner.

"It didn't faint when JoLynn screamed," offered Cain dryly.

Shelley fought not to smile. In the end, she gave up and bent her head over the snake. "It's all right, Brian. Really.

This specimen is a lovely, relaxed, well-fed rosy boa constrictor.''

Brian gulped audibly. "A *boa?* They eat people!"

JoLynn screamed. Casually, Cain clapped a large hand over her perfectly painted mouth.

"Only in bad movies about the Amazon jungle," said Shelley as she deftly draped reptilian coils around her arm. "This snake likes dry country and field mice."

She wrapped the last coil around her arm. One hand continued to hold the snake's head in a firm yet gentle grasp. A dark, forked tongue flickered out repeatedly, "tasting" her skin with the snake's unusual olfactory equipment. Reassured by her warmth and her matter-of-fact handling, the snake snuggled itself around her arm like the good pet it was. All it had wanted was a warm place to sleep, and Shelley definitely was warmer than a glass cage in a cold corner of a boy's bedroom.

"Where did it come from?" said Brian.

"The bedroom down the hall would be my guess," said Shelley, stroking the snake with her fingertip. Its body was smooth and supple, muscular and resilient. Whoever owned the snake obviously took good care of it.

JoLynn made emphatic, muffled sounds. Warily, Cain removed his hand.

"Billy!" rasped JoLynn. Nothing was left of her wide-eyed expression. Her skin was unnaturally pale, with only two hot spots of color high on her cheeks. "I'm going to kill that little brat! The turtle is ugly enough, but a snake—" She turned toward Cain. "Kill it! Kill it right now!"

Shelley backed up, automatically putting a protective hand between Cain and the snake. "That's not necessary," she began in a firm voice.

The front door slammed.

"Mother, I'm back from the beach," called out a boy's voice. The boy in question rounded the corner, clad in bathing suit and a generous coating of sand. He saw his pale mother. Then he saw his favorite pet wrapped securely around a strange woman's arm. His lips formed a word usually reserved for adults. "He won't hurt you," said Billy, hurrying into the room.

"I know," said Shelley, stroking the snake again, enjoying the subtle rose patterns illuminated by the late afternoon light. She looked up at Billy. "He has lovely manners. What do you call him?"

"Squeeze."

Shelley's sudden smile made Cain take an involuntary step forward, like a cold man walking toward a fire. The combination of intelligence, approval and humor in her face was electric.

"Squeeze," repeated Shelley, laughing softly. "He certainly does."

Gradually, realization dawned on Billy's face. He walked over and stared at Shelley. He was exactly at eye level with her, a tanned boy with light brown eyes, dark blond hair, and an expression too serious for someone so young. "You aren't afraid?"

"Disappointed?" asked Shelley with a wry smile.

Billy's brown eyes widened. Then he smiled back. "I'm Billy," he said, holding out his hand. "Who are you?"

"Shelley," she said, taking his hand with her left because her right was full of snake.

"Boy, your kids sure are lucky," said Billy, pumping her hand. "Can you believe it? A mother who isn't afraid of snakes!" He shook his head, awed at the possibilities.

"Cain," said JoLynn in a harsh, trembling voice, "kill it!"

"Aw, Mother," said Billy, turning toward JoLynn. "You don't mean that."

"The hell I don't."

The flat statement transformed Billy. He stared at his mother for a stunned moment, then at Cain's enigmatic face. Slowly, almost hopelessly, Billy turned toward Shelley. She raised an eyebrow and looked at Cain. Though she said nothing, her entire body made it clear that Cain would take the snake only if he was ready to drag it from her unwilling hands.

"It's only for two months, Uncle Cain," said Billy, his words for Cain and JoLynn, but his eyes glued to Shelley's sympathetic face. "I can't take him home because Dad is overseas and the housekeeper won't allow the snake there unless I'm there, too."

"I won't allow the snake at all," said JoLynn, her voice shaking. Her skin was sallow and she was sweating visibly. Obviously her reaction was not an act. She had a genuine phobia of snakes. "I want it *dead*." She shivered. "Slimy beast! How can you bear to touch it!"

"Its skin is drier than ours," said Shelley gently, accustomed both to snakes and to people who feared them. "Have you ever touched a snake?"

JoLynn made an odd sound and backed up, although Shelley had made no move toward her. Brian's arm wrapped soothingly around her.

"Kill it, Cain," pleaded JoLynn. "Kill it *now!*"

Billy glanced appealingly at Cain and started to speak.

"No," said Cain, watching Shelley closely.

Shelley stared at Cain for a moment, then nodded. Though nothing had been said, an agreement had been reached. She looked toward Billy. "Would you let me keep Squeeze for you until you move back in with your dad?"

"You wouldn't mind?" asked Billy.

"No."

"Squeeze only eats live mice," said Billy hesitantly, torn between honesty and a desire to save his pet.

"I know." Shelley's voice was as gentle as the fingertip that stroked Squeeze's relaxed coils.

"You do? How come? Do you have snakes?"

"No, but I grew up with them. My dad is a herpetologist," said Shelley, walking slowly toward Billy's room, drawing the boy after her and removing both of them from JoLynn's immediate view. "Do you know what that means?"

"Yeah. He studies reptiles."

"Especially snakes."

"Poisonous snakes, too?" asked Billy enthusiastically, walking beside Shelley.

Cain followed with a gliding, silent stride, listening as intently as the boy. Cain felt as he once had in wild country, when he had been expecting one kind of rock formation and found instead a glittering vein of gold.

"Mostly. Dad's fascinated by what he calls 'sand ecology,' or how reptiles adjust to the really dry places of the earth," explained Shelley. "Most desert snakes are poisonous. Very poisonous."

"Like the Mojave Desert?"

"And the Sahara, and the Negev, and the Sonora. We lived in most of the great deserts."

"Oh, wow! I've always wanted to live in a desert."

"You've got a leg up on it in southern California," pointed out Shelley as she walked back into Billy's bedroom. "Without our imported water, we wouldn't last a month."

"Really?"

"Really," said Cain, his voice deep and amused.

Shelley whirled around, startled by Cain's presence. She

hadn't heard him follow her down the hall. "For a big man, you're very light on your feet."

"You're rather surprising yourself."

She stood on tiptoe and looked over his shoulder. "Where's JoLynn?"

"Mother doesn't come in my room anymore," explained Billy as he patiently tried to unwrap the well-named Squeeze from Shelley's arm. "It makes her mad." He shrugged. "A lot of things make her mad. Especially Daddy." He tugged firmly. "C'mon, Squeeze, let go. It's time to go back in the tank."

Squeeze, well, *squeezed*, reluctant to give up the source of warmth.

"A snake after my own heart," said Cain, leaning close, speaking too softly for Billy to hear.

"A constrictor?" suggested Shelley tartly, yet she realized that she didn't feel confined by Cain's closeness.

"A connoisseur of warmth," corrected Cain.

"Squeeze!" said Billy in exasperation. "Let go!"

"Here," said Cain, bending even closer.

He took Squeeze's head in one deft, gentle hand and used the other to pry off one coil after another. The snake had absorbed enough of Shelley's body heat to become lively and surprisingly fast. Squeeze looped itself quickly over and around Cain's hard, bare forearm. The snake's dark forked tongue contrasted with the metallic bronze of Cain's body hair as Squeeze "tasted" its new perch. Cain sighed but didn't object.

"Hey, you're not scared either, Uncle Cain," said Billy. "Did you study herpetology too?"

"No, but I was once a boy who liked snakes."

Billy looked up at the hard man who seemed to tower over him. "That musta been a long time ago."

"Centuries," Cain assured him.

Shelley snickered. Then the laughter died when Cain switched his glance to her. His eyes were so close to hers that she could see the tiny flashes of blue and shards of black that gave contrast to the icy gray iris. She could also see the sudden expansion of his pupils as they dilated with interest. At the same instant she saw the tiny, sensual flare of his nostrils as he inhaled her perfume. Though he hadn't touched her, she felt all but surrounded by him. She felt the warmth of his breath caressing her lips, smelled the clean, sharp male scent of him, sensed the heat from his body like a promise given in silence. When his glance shifted to her lips, a shiver of awareness coursed through her.

"Shelley," said Brian from the doorway, "if you're serious about taking that damned"—he looked quickly at Billy—"er, creature with you, you'll have to get a cab. I won't have that, ah, *thing* in my car."

"No problem," drawled Cain softly, never looking up from the moist pink tip of Shelley's tongue as it nervously traced the line of her lower lip. "I'll take Shelley wherever she wants to go."

"That takes in a lot of territory," Brian retorted.

"So do I."

There was a taut silence, then Brian shrugged. "Great. I'll take JoLynn to the Gilded Lily to look over Shelley's stock. OK, Shelley?"

"Fine." Shelley tore her attention away from the light gleaming in Cain's hair and making his eyes as deep and mysterious as twilight lakes. "That's fine, Brian. Don't bother showing her anything that isn't in high school art history books. She won't be comfortable with it."

Brian's finely curved mouth shifted into a double-edged smile. "I'll be very soothing. She's had a rough day."

Shelley glanced up quickly at Cain, looking for traces of jealousy. There were none. Apparently he didn't hesitate to leave JoLynn trembling in Brian's well-dressed, sympathetic arms. Considering Brian's Olympian good looks, that meant either that Billy's "Uncle" Cain wasn't interested in JoLynn or that he was supremely confident of himself. Or both. That, coupled with his casual handling of Squeeze, intrigued Shelley. Despite the conventional wisdom that said only women were afraid of snakes, Shelley hadn't found many men who would approach snakes except to kill them.

"That's nice of you, Brian," said Shelley absently. "We'll meet you there after I get Squeeze set up in my house."

"Don't hurry," Brian said, searching Cain's face with the same intensity that Shelley had.

"We won't," Cain assured him.

Brian muttered something indecipherable and stalked down the hall.

"Boyfriend?" asked Cain very softly.

"Worse than that. Partner."

"As in bed?"

"As in business."

Cain hesitated. "Whatever you say."

"If you aren't going to believe me, why bother to ask?" Shelley turned away. "Billy, is that Squeeze's terrarium?" She pointed toward the corner, where a glass box sat with its lid askew.

"Yeah. I musta put the lid on crooked on my way out this morning. I was late," he added.

Shelley had a feeling that was a chronic condition with Billy. California's hot, burnished summer days gave her a case of wanderlust, too, reminding her of all the wild winds she had felt as a child, all the distant lands and unexpected people. Firmly she put away the memories and buried the restless longing that sometimes rose in her. She had made her choice when she was nineteen. A home. Security. Peace. The assurance that if she called out for help, the answer would come in a language she understood. The knowledge that there was one place on earth that was hers and hers alone. The certainty that her life was her own to roam or stay, as she pleased.

And she pleased to stay and build a home.

"OK, Billy," said Shelley in a crisp voice. "What's the feeding schedule?"

"Squeeze won't need anything for about five days. Better make it six. Otherwise he'll just ignore the poor mouse until I take it out and then I make a pet of it and have to buy another one when Squeeze finally starts acting hungry."

Shelley made a sympathetic sound. She always felt sorry for the mice, too. But then, she felt sorry for the wildlife that house cats preyed on, and the rabbits and opossums and skunks and domestic pets flattened on the road. Life was incurably messy.

"Right," she said. "I'll be sure that Squeeze is hungry. That way it will be quick and clean."

Billy brightened. "Thanks. I knew you'd understand." He sighed. "It'd be nice if you let your kids play with Squeeze a little, too. He likes to curl around me while I do my homework."

At the word "kids," Cain's eyes narrowed.

"I don't have any kids," said Shelley, "but I'll let Squeeze out to play once in a while. You can visit, too, if your mother will let you."

"Could I? Oh, wow! That'd be great!"

With a wide smile, Billy went to retrieve Squeeze's terrarium.

"That's going to be kind of awkward on a motorcycle," Cain said.

"A motorcycle?" said Billy, straightening. "Did you bring your motorcycle?" Then Billy's young face assumed blank lines, betraying neither enthusiasm nor longing. "I have a dirt bike, but Mother won't let me ride it while I stay with her."

Shelley looked at the hunger and hero worship in Billy's eyes as he watched Cain. She felt sudden, unexpected tears burning behind her eyelids. Her parents might have dragged her all over the face of the earth, but they hadn't put her through the special hell that comes to a child when his parents no longer love each other enough to live together.

"I know," said Cain, his voice gentle. "Dave and I decided that you'd need some company while he's in France."

"You're not here to, uh, see Mother?"

"No. I'm here to see you."

"Does she know that?"

"No."

"Don't tell her," said Billy bluntly. "She wouldn't understand. She hates anything to do with Dad."

Cain hesitated, trying to find some gentle words to counter the bitter truth in Billy's young voice. Finally, Cain put his hand on the boy's shoulder reassuringly. "We'll work out something. Until then, can we borrow that helmet?" he asked, pointing toward a motorcycle helmet that was barely visible beneath a sandy beach towel next to the bed.

"Sure." Billy snatched up the helmet and measured Shelley with a professional eye. "Should fit her just right if she takes that knot out of her hair."

Cain's left hand moved so quickly that Shelley didn't have time to evade or object. She felt the firm, seeking pressure of his fingers; then her hair spilled suddenly down her back in a rich, dark fall. Hidden beneath, his hand caressed her nape, then withdrew, leaving behind a shiver of unexpected pleasure.

Billy fitted the helmet over Shelley's head and nodded approvingly. He lifted off the helmet and stepped back. "Fits like it was made for you."

"What about Squeeze?" asked Shelley in a distracted voice, still feeling the aftershocks of Cain's hidden caress.

"How would you fasten a helmet on a snake?" asked Cain innocently.

Billy laughed. "Scotch tape?"

"That's a thought," murmured Cain absently, lifting the hand that had been buried beneath Shelley's hair. His nostrils flared slightly as he scented her perfume on his hand. He looked at her intently, wanting to feel the silky fall of her hair again, to taste deeply the sweetness of her mouth. He saw the emerald shimmer amid the tawny lights of her eyes, the very slight trembling of her lips as she watched him, and the dilation of her pupils as sensual awareness quickened in her. In that instant it was all he could do not to take her down to the floor and bury himself in her until a lifetime of hunger and loneliness was only a fading memory.

". . . carry Squeeze?" asked Billy.

Cain tried to gather his seething thoughts but could only think of the sweet instant when his body would become a part of Shelley's, held tightly within her satin warmth.

"Pillowcase," said Shelley. She closed her eyes, unable to bear the intimacy of Cain's look any longer. She forced herself to take a deep breath, trying to calm the frightening storm of sensuality that was electrifying her body. She had never been aware of a man like this, sensing his every breath, the metallic gleam of light caught in his thick hair, the tawny chestnut mustache curling against the most beautiful male mouth she had ever seen. Hard yet full, responsive to laughter, hungry. "Pillowcase," repeated Shelley, her voice husky, her eyes still closed. "I'll carry Squeeze in a pillowcase."

She turned away before she opened her eyes. With quick motions she removed the cover from one of the bed pillows. When she was finished, she looked dubiously at the lacy confection in her hand. The powder blue pillowcase looked more like lingerie than bed linen. When she turned around, Billy and Cain were struggling with almost four feet of lively, reluctant Squeeze.

"Here," she said, giving Billy the pillowcase. Working with both hands, she unwrapped the snake from Cain's arm. As she did she couldn't prevent her fingers from feeling his skin and the sliding, muscular strength beneath. It was his body heat that astonished her. He radiated vitality. "It's a wonder you didn't cook Squeeze alive," she muttered.

"Funny," whispered Cain against her sleek brown hair, "I thought the same thing when I pulled him off you."

In silence Shelley dropped the unwilling snake into the pillowcase and knotted the top. "Ready."

"I hope so," murmured Cain in a husky voice.

Shelley's head snapped up, but Cain was looking at Billy.

"We'll take good care of him," said Cain.

Billy nodded. Cain strapped Shelley's helmet in place again with a few practiced motions.

Shelley followed Cain down the hall and out of the elegant home. A stripped-down motorcycle was parked in the driveway. Powerful, lean, the bike reminded her of a black jungle cat. Cain mounted the bike in a single lithe motion. Shelley hesitated, then stepped on the peg and settled in behind him. The bike ripped into life, vibrating with leashed power.

Cain snapped his helmet into place and looked over his shoulder. His eyes gleamed like twilight ice. "Ready?"

No. But Shelley wasn't about to tell him that. She put one arm around his hard waist and held on.

Man, woman, snake and lacy blue pillowcase accelerated down the twisting road with a primal roar.

Chapter 2

SHELLEY WAS FEELING MORE THAN A LITTLE UNEASY BY the time Cain pulled into her driveway and shut off the motorcycle's powerful engine. Not that she had been afraid. She had enjoyed the ride. Cain had controlled the bike skillfully, always aware of the heavier cars around him and the unpredictability of drivers who believed that they were the only people on the road. What had made Shelley nervous was her own deep awareness of Cain, the hard warmth of his waist beneath her arm, and the rippling power of his back as he maneuvered the motorcycle.

Abruptly, Shelley realized that she still had one arm around Cain's waist even though the bike was quite still. She removed her arm as though she had been burned. If Cain noticed, he said nothing. With the same smooth, clean movements he had used to drive the bike, he removed his helmet and hung it over the handlebars.

Feeling awkward by comparison, Shelley climbed off the motorcycle. The pillowcase wriggled visibly with Squeeze's silent protests. One-handed, Shelley struggled with the unfamiliar fastening on her helmet. Strong, tanned fingers brushed hers aside. The back of Cain's hand caressed Shelley's soft throat as he slowly, very slowly, unfastened the helmet strap. He removed the helmet with equal care, watching her the whole time, holding her eyes in a smoky gaze. The intimacy of the moment was so great that Shelley felt as though she were being undressed by a lover. Without looking away, Cain hung her helmet next to his on the handlebars. When his fingers carefully tucked her tangled brown hair behind her ears, she didn't think to object.

"You don't scream at snakes. You don't sneer at motorcycles." Slowly, Cain lowered his head and whispered, "What other conventions do you ignore, Shelley Wilde?"

Sanity returned just before Cain's mouth touched hers. Shelley stepped backward. "I don't kiss strangers, if that's what you mean."

Cain's eyes narrowed in denial of her words. Then he relaxed, though the intensity of his gray eyes didn't change. "I don't feel like a stranger around you. And you sure don't *feel* like a stranger to me," he added, stroking her cheek with the back of his fingers.

Shelley took Cain's caressing fingers and wrapped them around the top of the lively pillowcase. "Pet Squeeze," she suggested forcefully. "He doesn't know strangers from fat shoelaces."

Unwillingly, Cain laughed. He took the pillowcase in one hand, Shelley's arm in the other, and walked toward her house.

From the front, little of the house was visible. Like many California hillside homes, it was oriented toward the view.

As the view was at the back of the house rather than the front, the architect had wasted little effort making the entrance impressive. From the street, the house looked like a rather long, single-story California version of a weekend retreat—fire-resistant shake shingles on the roof, huge panels of thermal glass, and natural redwood in between. The narrow yard was landscaped with unobtrusive, mani-cured plants that were very green against the backdrop of tawny wild grass and chaparral in as many shades of brown and gold as Cain's hair. The privacy of the side yards was guarded by six-foot-high redwood fences.

Not until Cain walked in the front door did he realize that he was only seeing the tip of the redwood iceberg. Built into the hill, the house dropped down in levels from the public entertainment area at street level to the privacy and retreat of the bedroom suite more than thirty feet below. There, the architect had taken advantage of a natural bulge in the hillside and had designed a pool, patio, barbecue pit and flower garden. The swimming pool sent up shimmering promises of coolness and pleasure. A faint breeze rising from the bottom of the wild ravine far below picked up the ravishing scent of flowers and spread it throughout the house. Southern California's incomparable light poured through every window in silent golden cascades.

Cain stood in the center of the first story and turned around slowly, realizing that he had never felt so much at home in any place on earth. Everything from the soft gleam of wooden floors beneath his feet to the smooth, cream-colored walls and high beamed ceilings, called out to his senses. The house was both civilized and subtly, deeply, wild. The wildness was there in the view that was a part of the architecture, hills so steep and thick with chaparral that even the land hunger of metropolitan Los Angeles couldn't wholly conquer them. Hills that would be called

mountains almost anywhere else. Hills where nothing
walked except animals that had never been tamed by man.
A few hundred feet from the road, the land hadn't really
changed since the day a Spanish sea captain mistook a
continental land mass for a fabled island and called it
California.

Shelley's house and those nearby were like carved gems
strung together across the ridge line, connected by the thin
ribbon of road that was visible far below. More glittering
necklaces were flung across the ridge lines of other hills,
marching in serried ranks from the ocean to the high
mountains further inland, hills broken by occasional long
valleys where cities clustered and crowded and consumed
the land. But not here, not on Shelley's hill. Here the land
breathed and flexed like the wild, living thing it was.

"Magnificent," said Cain, thinking aloud in a low voice,
his gray eyes intent as he absorbed the elemental harmony
of land and house.

Gradually, other things drew Cain's attention from the
sere, steep hills. The room itself had groupings of under-
stated furniture whose colors and textures complemented
the view. Scattered throughout the huge, light-filled room
were various objets d'art. Unlike JoLynn, Shelley had
chosen her furnishings and finishings for a congruence of
feeling rather than a perfection of form. A luminous
Kashmir rug glowed like a jeweled pool in one third of the
room. Smaller rugs appeared in the remaining area, an-
choring furniture into intimate groups. A superb nineteenth
century Japanese screen featuring eggshell white cranes
angled elegantly off to the right. Other, smaller screens
appeared throughout the room, dividing what could have
been an awkwardly large space into areas that were both
intimate and unconfined.

Shelley watched as Cain walked slowly through the room, the forgotten Squeeze dangling in the pillowcase from his large right hand. She wondered what he was thinking while he stood in front of the line drawing of a Balinese dancer suspended timelessly within a golden frame, femininity and strength captured in a few fluid strokes. Did Cain see beyond the primitive surface of the Eskimo carving of an old woman to the courage and serenity beneath? Did he see beyond the expensive gloss of an Arabian ivory chess set to the timeless celebration of intelligence and play? Did he see beyond the antiquity of the Egyptian scarab to the human fear and reverence?

When Cain paused, then stood rooted in front of a glass case, Shelley stopped breathing. Inside that case was one of her favorite possessions, a jaguar carved by a German master from a large piece of opal matrix. The opal was Australian, a never-ending shimmer of blue and green, blazing orange and shards of gold, a rainbow shattered and then caught forever in a translucent cloud of white. The artist had matched the mixture of matrix and gemstone with the jaguar's lines in a way that suggested the cat's immense vitality and yet acknowledged the animal's deadliness. The matrix itself was a very deep, lustrous gray, almost black, as though jungle shadows were falling over the cat, concealing its predatory beauty.

The carving alone was extraordinary, well worth its considerable cost. But what made the piece unique, and irresistible to Shelley, was the carved ruby butterfly that was perched on one of the cat's solid gold claws. Large wings half-spread, their veins a delicate network of pure gold, the butterfly was wholly at ease. And the jaguar? Somehow the artist had given the cat an expression of bemused pleasure, as though he didn't know quite how it had happened, but thoroughly approved of the scrap of beauty that had drifted down to quiver trustingly on his paw.

A slight motion caught Shelley's eye. She turned toward the movement. Gliding, stalking, every muscle poised, a Maine Coon Cat eased across the polished floor. The cat's gold eyes never looked away from the pillowcase wiggling so intriguingly beneath Cain's large fist. Shelley took two running steps and snatched the pillowcase from Cain, holding it above her head. Cain, who had glimpsed her out of the corner of his eye, turned suddenly and grabbed her, preventing her from banging into the glass case and sending it and its precious contents smashing to the floor.

Shelley steadied herself by putting her free arm around Cain. For an instant it was like being on the motorcycle again as she hung onto Cain's hard body. There was a difference, though. He was standing, facing her, pressed along her soft length. The difference was devastating.

"I wouldn't have dropped Squeeze," said Cain mildly, watching a wild flush climb Shelley's cheeks.

"Nudge," Shelley said. It was the first word that came to her mind.

"That was hardly a nudge you gave me," he pointed out, tightening his grip subtly, "but I'm not complaining."

"You don't understand," she explained desperately, knowing she couldn't evade Cain's beautiful mouth, which was coming closer with each breath, each instant. "Nudge was stalking Squeeze!"

Firm lips hesitated, then curved into a lazy, sensual smile. "Sounds like fun."

"What?"

"Nudge stalking squeeze. Kind of like push coming to shove, only sexier."

Shelley made a strangled sound that was halfway between despair and laughter. "Nudge is my cat."

"That explains it," said Cain gravely.

"It does?"

"Either that or you have a third leg that's playing footsie with me."

Shelley's eyes widened. She peered down at the floor. "That's Nudge."

"Claws is more like it."

"If you'll let go of me, I'll—"

"Don't bother," said Cain, lowering his mouth to hers, "I have nothing against claws."

Cain's kiss was like his smile, sensual and slow, an exploration of the joined possibilities of their mouths. Shelley felt like a ruby butterfly held within a jaguar's soft grasp. A quiver of pure pleasure shimmered over her nerves. She returned the kiss as gently, as thoroughly, as it was given to her. It had been a long time since she had allowed a man to kiss her so intimately. It had been forever since she had enjoyed a kiss half so much.

A warm, sinuous body wedged itself between Cain's and Shelley's feet as Nudge tried another approach to the lacy pillowcase. The cat's familiar pressure along her knees reminded Shelley of where she was, who she was and the things that she wanted from life. Casual kisses from a stranger weren't among them. Cain sensed the change in Shelley and released her reluctantly.

"Cain, I—" began Shelley.

"I know," he said in a husky voice. "You don't kiss strangers. I'm not a stranger, Shelley."

"But—"

"I know that you love things that are both beautiful and wild, civilized and unrestrained. I know that you're intelligent, independent and compassionate. I know that you're very much your own person, yet will share yourself with a boy you barely know who has just gone through hell. I know that you're warmer than my dreams, sweeter, more alive. And you're as elegant as a ruby butterfly trembling on a jungle cat's solid gold claw.'' His lips brushed over hers. "Am I a stranger, Shelley?''

"N-no." Then, almost afraid, she added, "But I don't know you, Cain.''

"You will," he promised.

Nudge bumped her head against Cain's knee. Cain glanced down. His eyes widened in surprise as he took in the size of the mottled cat.

"My God, that thing's as big as a lynx!''

"Almost," said Shelley, smiling. "Coon Cats and Himalayas are the biggest domestic cats.''

"Domestic?" asked Cain, eyeing Nudge, who was watching the wiggling pillowcase with frankly carnivorous intent. "You're sure about that?''

"Cats are always cats, no matter where they live.''

Nudge stood on her hind feet and reached playfully for the pillowcase. Shelley was still holding it out of reach, though her arm had begun to tremble with the effort. Squeeze was hardly as light as a shoelace.

"Allow me," murmured Cain, retrieving the pillowcase and hoisting it even higher. "Now, call off your cat.''

Shelley bent down, grabbed Nudge firmly and walked to the front door. With one hand she opened the door. With the other she launched the cat into the yard.

"Good-bye, Nudge. I'll call you for dinner.''

With a disgruntled twitch of her tail, the cat stalked off to find more accessible prey.

Shelley turned around and saw that Cain was surveying the room again, his gray eyes intent. She could see that he approved of what he saw. Despite their disparate origins, there was a harmony of line and emotion and excellence in the room and its contents that unified the whole. The room was neither masculine nor feminine, neither modern nor old-fashioned. It was simply very human.

"What, exactly, do you do for a living?" asked Cain, turning suddenly, catching Shelley's tawny hazel eyes as they watched him.

"Gild lilies."

A wry smile changed the line of Cain's mouth. "Care to be more specific?"

"My clients are the mobile rich, the people who are only in one place for a few months at a time but want that place to be more welcoming and suited to their personalities than an expensive hotel suite," explained Shelley. "Most of them don't want to buy anything, although I do finish some vacation homes." She turned away, indicating that Cain should follow.

"Most of my clients want to rent everything from the Oriental rug on the floor to the Picassos on the wall to the wall itself," she continued. "That's Brian's department. The walls and furniture. The basic lily, as it were. My job is to gild it. I have an inventory of various objets d'art, which I use to personalize rented homes, rented furniture, rented lives."

"But you don't live like that," Cain said, noting the changes in the house as he progressed from level to level.

"No. This is my home."

Her slight emphasis on the word *home* said a great deal about how Shelley felt on the subject.

"Still, you understand what it's like to be rootless and yet want to live in a place that feels right, even if you can't stay long," said Cain slowly.

"I spent my childhood wanting a home, a place of my

own, the certainty that if I called out in the night——''
Shelley stopped abruptly, realizing what she had almost
revealed. Her nightmare, the worst experience of her life,
when she had been sick and frightened and unable to
communicate with the people in camp because her mother
was sick, too, and her father was out in the field. "Yes, I
understand what it's like to hunger for something more than
a rented room."

Cain didn't ask any more questions about rented rooms
and homes. He sensed that Shelley wouldn't answer.

At the bottom of the stairs, the second level of the house
opened out. To the left was a suite of rooms that Shelley
ignored. Instead, she led Cain past a family room and
kitchen that had spectacular views of the hills and distant
cities. Pots of herbs stood three deep on a sunny window
ledge. A large white bowl heaped with fresh lemons was set
on the counter. A wheeled butcher block with a built-in
knife holder was in the center of the brick floor. Pots and
pans hung within easy reach over the stove. Their sides
were clean, but showed the patina that only came from long
use over heat. Obviously, Shelley preferred to cook in her
kitchen rather than to eat out at the multitude of restaurants
Los Angeles had to offer.

The further into Shelley's house Cain went, the more
personal the decor became. He sensed that few people ever
went below the street level, which, while very inviting, did
not have an aura of intimacy.

Stairs carpeted with a thick, rust-colored wool plush led
down to the third level. Pale, creamy walls were hung with
paintings which beckoned to Cain, but Shelley kept walking, giving him no time to linger. A room pleasantly
crowded with overstuffed suede chairs and a huge sectional
couch invited Cain to stop and rest, but Shelley never
slowed down. She didn't even pause at the door of what

appeared to be a library. The room was filled with racks upon rows of catalogs and art books, as well as novels and a stereo that rivaled Billy's. It was here that St. George and the golden dragon fought in deadly silence on the far wall.

Cain hesitated, then walked quickly into the room, drawn by the gleaming malevolence of the dragon. Sensing that she was no longer being followed, Shelley stopped and backtracked to her library.

"Cain?"

"A minute," he said, approaching the dragon. He stood in thoughtful silence, measuring the potent fascination of the battle. Reluctantly, he turned away. "I always wanted my own dragon," he explained, catching up with Shelley.

"That one is a bit dangerous for a pet," she pointed out dryly.

Cain's smile was very male. "That's a big part of the fascination."

Together Cain and Shelley returned to the hallway, walking toward the final suite of rooms. The smell of flowers was stronger here, and with it the herbal scent of cured grass and chaparral. The combination was piquant, opposite scents refreshing each other.

Cain stopped again, but it wasn't to admire a painting. The fragrances were coming through the louvered windows of Shelley's bedroom. There was so much glass on the western exposure that it was like being outside. A wall of mirrored, sliding closet doors reflected the grand view. The bed was covered in a vivid Jacobean-style bedspread that repeated the colors of the flower garden and pool. The bed itself was beneath a transparent skylight.

Beyond the room, wrapped in flowers and lush greenery that trailed down the hillside next to a rock stairway, an artificial waterfall tumbled into one end of a swimming pool that had been designed to resemble a natural body of water.

Potted plants and flagstone walkways and multileveled wooden decks surrounded the irregular shape of the pool. The sound of rushing water falling into the pool was both soothing and sensual, a murmured invitation to let go and float on the warm body of the water, drifting amid the heady scents of flowers, mint and wild chaparral.

Shelley walked quickly through the bedroom, slid open a large mirrored closet door, and began tugging at a huge aquarium she had stored in the bottom of her closet. Cain set the lively blue pillowcase on the bed and went to help her.

"Planning to raise sharks?" he asked mildly as he pulled the large, heavy glass box into the room.

"That's about all that could survive Nudge," sighed Shelley. "This was full of the most beautiful fish until the day Nudge went swimming. The fish that survived were never the same. I gave them to a neighborhood kid, siphoned out the aquarium and dragged it into the closet." She looked around the room. "Over there, I think," she said, pointing to the north corner where a deep bookcase held a selection of art books. "Warm enough but not too warm. Wouldn't want to cook the poor devil."

"Nudge?"

"Squeeze."

"My pleasure," said Cain, bringing Shelley to his side and squeezing her gently.

"Cain—"

"But you agreed we weren't strangers," he pointed out reasonably.

"That doesn't mean we're kissing cousins."

"You're sure?" he asked, nuzzling against her lips with his own. "Let's explore our family trees."

Just before Shelley would have objected more forcefully,

Cain released her. He picked up the awkward, heavy aquarium and walked across the room.

"Wait," said Shelley. Hurriedly she began pulling out books until she had cleared a space as long as the aquarium. "See if it fits."

Cain lifted the aquarium and slid it onto the middle shelf of the tall bookcase. There was just enough room at the top for Shelley to have access to the aquarium, but not enough for Nudge to go fishing.

"Perfect," announced Shelley. "Now for the sand and rocks."

Shelley opened one of the glass doors and went out and around to the side of the house, where the gardener had a potting shed. There she found a bag of sand. She filled a bucket with sand, began to lift it and had it taken smoothly from her hands.

"I'm the beast of burden, remember?" asked Cain. "You're the beauty who thinks up new ways to work me."

Without giving her a chance to reply, Cain went back to the patio. Shelley saw that he had brought the aquarium outside.

"Once it's filled with sand, won't it be too heavy?" asked Shelley.

Cain looked up from dumping sand into the glass box. "For the bookcase?"

"To lift."

The whispering flow of sand stopped. Cain's gray eyes narrowed thoughtfully. "You really are used to living alone, aren't you?"

"What do you mean?"

"You think in terms of what you can do by yourself. Like this aquarium. Empty, you could have dragged it into place somehow. Full, it would be too heavy for you. But for me''—Cain shrugged—''no problem. You didn't think of that, though, so you're used to not having a man around.''

Shelley hesitated, then turned away without saying anything, disturbed by Cain's perceptivity. She wasn't accustomed to being around people who saw beyond their own needs. She went out into the garden, returning in a few moments with several smooth, fist-sized ornamental rocks she had stolen from the garden. Wordlessly, she arranged the rocks on top of the sand. A pottery saucer filled with water and sunk flush with the sand completed Squeeze's home.

As Cain lifted the aquarium and fitted it into the bookcase, the strength in his arms and back became more apparent with each smooth shift of muscle and tendon. The sleeves of his pale blue shirt had been rolled up, revealing both the power of his forearms and the sensual shimmer of hair bleached gold by the sun. Shelley remembered the ease with which Cain had controlled the heavy, powerful bike, and the gentleness with which he had held her. His combination of strength and restraint was as compelling to her senses as the combined scents of chaparral and flowers. The temptation to run her fingertips over the shifting gleam of male hair and tanned skin was almost overwhelming.

Hurriedly Shelley switched her attention to the bed and the wriggling blue pillowcase. She unknotted it, opened it wide, and grabbed Squeeze just behind his weaving rosy-beige head.

''Gotcha,'' she muttered. ''Now hold still.''

Squeeze wasn't having any of it. He thrashed around, tangling himself in pale blue folds. He wasn't in the best of tempers, having been jostled repeatedly within the pillow-case. Shelley had expected Squeeze to be in a snit, however, and was careful not to provide the snake with a target for his displeasure.

In the end, she had to lift out the snake and let him thrash free of the dainty pillowcase. Cain caught the muscular coils. Together, he and Shelley gently stuffed Squeeze into his new home.

"Won't he crawl out?" asked Cain, watching the snake glide around the perimeter of the aquarium with supple, sinuous ease.

Shelley made a startled sound of agreement and went back to her closet. Two pairs of walking boots and a yellow rain slicker tumbled out, followed by a sleeping bag and a lightweight aluminum mess kit. All that was visible of Shelley was her nicely rounded bottom as she continued burrowing into the contents of her closet floor.

Cain leaned against the bookcase and enjoyed the view. The only problem was the temptation to find out if she felt half as good as she looked. With any other woman, he simply would have walked across the room and run his palms over the feminine curves. Shelley, however, was not any other woman. She was a woman who had lived alone for so long that it had become a fact of life as deeply embedded in her mind as her own name. Though she had responded to his kiss in a way that made blood gather heavily in his body, she also had retreated in the next breath, shock and surprise clear in her hazel eyes.

Like her house, Shelley was a tantalizing balance of opposites—civilized, yet with a wildness just beneath her surface that called to Cain's male senses like nothing he had ever encountered in his life. As he watched, appreciating the graceful line of her legs, Shelley turned, her oval face slightly flushed and a rectangle of thick glass held triumphantly in her hands.

"Found it," she said.

Cain smiled lazily, watching Shelley's supple movements as she came to her feet. For a moment he let himself wonder what it would be like to be locked in a glass cage with Shelley, her legs wrapped around him and his body deeply joined with hers. The thought did nothing to cool the gathering heat of his blood. Nor did the realization that her bedroom was very much like a glass cage with a soft floor to ease the sensual impact of flesh meeting flesh. Cursing silently, Cain turned his thoughts in a less provocative direction, stilling the thick beat of blood in his veins and the growing heaviness of his body.

Carefully, Shelley eased the glass rectangle into place on top of the aquarium. A narrow strip of the glass was hinged on one side to allow access into the aquarium without removing the entire lid.

"How did Nudge ever get to the fish?" asked Cain. "Did you forget to cover the aquarium?"

Shelley grimaced. "No. She flipped up the hinged part, hooked her claws under the rest and dumped the lid onto the floor."

Chestnut eyebrows climbed in silent admiration. "Strong cat. Smart, too."

Shelley's response was blessedly unreadable.

Cain laughed. "Well, she won't be able to get to Squeeze in the bookcase."

"That was the whole idea." Shelley packed a few books around the aquarium, securing it snugly on the shelf. Then she stacked the rest of the books on the floor to one side, stepped back to look at the aquarium and began laughing softly. "Can you believe it? A rosy boa sandwiched between *Netsuke Through the Ages* and *Shades of Tiffany: A Study of Glass Art.*"

"Having met you," murmured Cain, "I can believe anything."

Shelley gave him a look out of startled hazel eyes. She began to ask what he meant, then thought better of it, deciding that you didn't ask Cain questions unless you were very sure you wanted the answer.

"We'd better get back down the hill," said Shelley, turning away. "JoLynn will be wondering what I've done with you."

"Brian looked like he could answer any questions JoLynn might have," said Cain smoothly, "and then she could give him a few answers of her own."

"I doubt it." Shelley's voice was wry, but beneath it was the certainty that when it came to sex, Brian had asked all the questions and gotten all the answers long ago.

"Then Brian and JoLynn are well-matched. Like us."

Shelley looked away from the sensual certainty in Cain's smoky eyes. "Right," she said quickly, "the only two snake-handlers in L.A."

"That wasn't what I meant."

"Cain—" she began firmly.

"Don't look so wary," he said with a crooked smile. "I'm not going to wrap myself around you and squeeze until you can't say no. Remember?"

She remembered the gentleness of his kiss, the restraint that had held the male strength of his body in check. A flush crept up her cheeks.

"What I meant," he continued smoothly, "was that I'm in need of gilding, and you're the best gilder around."

"You don't look like a lily," muttered Shelley.

"You noticed," said Cain, pushing away from the bookcase.

Reflexively, she retreated. He didn't come any closer to her, however. He simply stood and waited for her to realize that she was safe.

"See?" he said. "Harmless."

Shelley's hazel glance took in Cain's six-foot three-inch height, the width of his shoulders, the decided swell of muscle beneath his shirt, the blunt strength of his large hands, the lean length of his legs. "Harmless," she repeated carefully. Then she smiled, "Oh, Cain, if you could only see yourself. *Harmless.*"

"I don't look harmless?" he said wistfully.

"No."

"How about trustworthy?"

She started to say no, then hesitated, sensing the emotion behind his apparently light question. She realized that despite the fact that she was alone in her bedroom with a rather large not-quite-stranger, she wasn't afraid. Her instincts told her that Cain, while he had a primitive male interest in her, would pursue that interest in a civilized fashion.

"Yes," she said finally.

"Good. People who do business together should trust each other."

Shelley blinked. "Business?"

"Of course. You're gilding my lily, remember?"

"Er, no."

"I'll tell you all about it while I make some fresh lemonade for us. Those were lemons in that bowl upstairs?"

Bemused, she could only stare at him. "Lemonade?"

"Unless they're grapefruit." Cain held out his hand. "Ready?"

Shelley stared at his hand, remembering its strength and callused warmth. The scars on his knuckles showed as a lighter shade of brown beneath the gleaming sun-bleached hair. "No," she said, her voice low and distinct.

Gray eyes narrowed, then Cain's face relaxed. "Is it all men or just me?" he asked quietly.

She stared at him out of wide, tawny eyes flecked with green. "Cain, I'm not—I don't—"

"You don't do business with men?" asked Cain. "Funny, I could have sworn Brian was a man beneath all those designer labels."

"Business, yes. The rest, no."

Cain smiled slowly. "Whatever you say."

Shelley closed her eyes. She knew, she *knew,* that he was remembering the kiss they had shared. And it had been a sharing. She hadn't been passive in his arms, waiting for an unwanted embrace to end. That was what frightened her. She hadn't felt anything for a man in years. Nor did she want to. She had fought a long time for the security she had. She didn't need some hard stranger sweeping in and turning her home and her heart upside down.

The sooner Cain Remington was out of her life, the better.

Shelley opened her eyes to tell him so, but found herself staring at his retreating back. He climbed the stairs in long, powerful strides. His voice came floating back down.

"When life gives you lemons, you make lemonade. Didn't your daddy ever tell you that?"

"Only when life gives you sugar, too!" called Shelley in exasperation.

Cain halted. There was a moment of silence followed by rich, male laughter. He looked over his shoulder at Shelley. "As long as you're around," he said, "sugar will be no problem at all."

Chapter 3

"LET ME," SAID CAIN.

Shelley started to refuse, then gave in. After a long motorcycle ride in the hot sun, the black helmet was both heavy and stifling, and the chin buckle was beyond her. She stood patiently while Cain's long fingers coaxed the stubborn leather free of the buckle. The clean scent of fresh lemon oil drifted up from his hands, filling her nostrils. Cain hadn't bothered to use a juicer on the fresh lemons; he had simply squeezed the liquid out of the fruit with a speed and power that had startled her. Shelley didn't consider herself a weakling, but Cain's strength was a constant revelation to her.

Cain eased the helmet from Shelley's head, disentangling silky tendrils of her hair as he went. He could have removed the helmet more quickly, but he enjoyed the texture and warmth of her hair sliding over his hands. His nostrils flared, savoring her scent. Mixed with her understated perfume was a haunting drift of lemon. The lemonade had dried and left a faint silver line along Shelley's upper lip. He smiled, knowing that if he licked the silver residue, it would be sweet. Sugar sweet, and tasting of woman.

A frisson of sensation went over Shelley when she saw Cain's smile. She looked away quickly, rummaging in her purse for a hairbrush. When she glanced up again, Cain was matter-of-factly hanging her helmet next to his on the handlebars. For a moment Shelley paused, realizing how incongruous the black bike looked parked next to Brian's silver Mercedes 450 and a scarlet Ferrari that probably belonged to JoLynn. The motorcycle's tires were large and rough, designed for off-road as well as highway use. Cut-away fenders and the absence of chrome added to the outlaw appearance of the motorcycle. Like the man, there was nothing superfluous on the bike. Its power, endurance and speed needed no flashy embellishments.

"Is this where you gild my lily?" asked Cain, looking from the elegant Beverly Hills store-front to the equally elegant woman with hair as dark and satiny as melted chocolate.

"A bike like that doesn't need gilding. It is what it does—beautifully."

Cain turned and stared at Shelley. "I've been looking for you for a long time," he said finally.

"You should have tried *Architectural Digest*," she said crisply, putting away her brush after a few quick strokes. "I'm a regular advertiser."

Cain laughed softly, enjoying Shelley's quick mind. He knew his frankly male interest made her uneasy; he was learning that there was nothing specifically personal in her wariness of him; and he suspected that he had gotten further inside her defenses than any man in a long time.

*What happened to you, Shelley Wilde? Who taught you to
mistrust yourself and men?*

But the questions went no further than Cain's mind. He
sensed that he had pushed Shelley as far as she was going to
go at the moment. If he pushed any further, she would
simply smile professionally and slide through his fingers
like sunlight, leaving only darkness behind.

"I should have thought of that sooner," said Cain,
following Shelley to the glass-fronted shop that looked
more like a gallery than a store.

"What?" said Shelley, glancing up from the stubborn
lock on the front door, a distracted look on her face.

"Checking the ads in *Architectural Digest*," Cain said
evenly. "I would have enjoyed L.A. a lot more."

While Shelley was occupied with the lock, Cain admired
the subtlety of the electronic burglar system. The windows
had a nearly invisible border of hair-fine wires and glass
thick enough to survive a determined hammer. Elegant
calligraphic script announced the name of the shop. Beneath the name was the discreet warning: By Appointment
Only.

Cain followed the gentle swing of Shelley's hips into the
Gilded Lily. The interior of the shop was both restrained
and fascinating. An eclectic selection of objets d'art were
displayed throughout the area much as they would have
been in a private home. The furniture, too, suggested a
residence rather than a commercial establishment, with
casual conversational groupings.

Shelley watched Cain's reaction to the various items in
the room. Silently he went from one display to another,
pausing over soapstone carvings of birds from Baffin Island
and a Landsat photo of the Sahara. The photo showed the
desert reduced to its essence, a purity of line and light and

shadow that was almost surreal. Other displays Cain passed by with little more than a cursory glance. Minimalist art did not interest him, nor did the more avant garde experiments in mixed media or warring colors. Works of *trompe l'oeil* drew little more than a raised eyebrow.

Just when Shelley had decided that Cain had an aversion to abstract art, he stopped in front of a large free-form wood sculpture. The wood was smooth. It had a soft satin gleam rather than a hard lacquer finish, and was marked with long, curving dark lines. The shape of the sculpture was utterly abstract, resembling nothing in the real world. Yet the flowing curves and satin texture somehow cried out to be touched. For several moments Cain did just that, running sensitive fingertips from one fluid curve to the next and finally letting his palms smooth lightly down the sculpture's satin sides.

The sensual appreciation implicit in Cain's reaction made Shelley's breath thicken and then stop. When he turned and glanced back at her, he saw her watching the slow movements of his hands over the gleaming wood. For a moment, hunger darkened his gray eyes. Then he looked away before she could glance up from his hands, see his reaction to her, and become even more physically wary of him than she already was.

As Cain looked down, he saw the title of the sculpture: *I Love You, Too*. He threw back his head and laughed with delight. The sound of Cain's laughter freed Shelley from her trance. When he looked toward her, she grinned in response. The sculpture was one of her personal favorites, a combination of sensuality and humor.

"Is this for rent?" asked Cain.

Shelley hesitated, for the sculpture was very useful to her in assessing clients' reactions. Many of her clients had specifically requested it. She had always refused and substituted a similarly tactile sculpture.

"I keep it here," she temporized, reluctant to refuse Cain. "It requires a lot of petting. That's what its special glow comes from."

The corner of Cain's mouth turned up in a slow smile. His sun-streaked chestnut hair gleamed as he bent closer to the inviting, polished curves. "Like a woman," he murmured approvingly, smoothing his palm over the sculpture again.

"Don't men like to be petted?" asked Shelley tartly.

"You're a woman, you tell me," he said without looking up from the gleaming curves.

Shelley forced herself to appear to consider the question. Her former husband hadn't wanted to be petted. At least, not by her. Busty barflies were a different story entirely. With the ease of long experience, Shelley concealed the painful memories beneath a cool expression of indifference.

"You're asking the wrong woman, remember?" she said. "I'm the one who can't hold a man."

Cain looked quickly at Shelley. Her hazel eyes were aloof, as watchful as a cat that has known more curses than kindness. "And I'm the man who can't hold a woman, remember?" he said, trying to soften the cutting edges of the remark he had made to her when they first met.

"I doubt that you ever wanted to," said Shelley, turning away, dismissing the subject.

"Have you?" asked Cain, quickly closing the distance between them, pursuing the subject because her withdrawal angered him.

"What?"

"Ever wanted to keep a man."

"Once. The cure was quite effective."

"What cure?"

"Growing up," said Shelley, a hint of savagery in her voice and in the metallic gleam of gold in her eyes.

"What does that mean?"

Abruptly, Shelley turned and faced Cain. "It means that I am my own person now. I have furnished my home and my life to suit myself."

"And there's no room in it for anyone else, even on a temporary basis?"

"Especially on a temporary basis," she said in a flat voice. "Rented rooms, rented people, rented lives. No thank you, Cain Remington. I'm not for rent."

"Are you for sale, then?" inquired Cain politely.

"What?"

"Marriage. An outright purchase until death do you part."

"Or divorce, whichever comes sooner," retorted Shelley. "And we both know which comes sooner, don't we?"

"So that's it. Your husband dumped you."

"Tactful to the core, aren't you?"

"Did he?" demanded Cain.

"Did he what?"

"Dump you."

"Like a handful of dirt. Satisfied?"

"No," said Cain, his expression changing as he looked at the taut, angry lines of her face and the curving feminine lines of her body, a living sculpture crying out to be stroked. "I'm not satisfied."

"I'll find JoLynn," said Shelley, turning on her heel. "I'm sure she comes with a money-back guarantee."

A large hand clamped around Shelley's wrist. "I don't want JoLynn. I want you."

"You can't afford me," said Shelley in a clipped voice.

"Name a price," shot back Cain, angry again.

She listened to the cold, confident voice and felt anger

uncurl hotly in her mind. Her former husband had been confident, too. And he, too, had been wrong. "Love, not money, Mr. Remington."

Emotion showed for an instant on Cain's hard face; then all expression faded into a polite mask. "Love is an elusive commodity," he said quietly.

"So that's it," she said mockingly, echoing Cain's earlier words. "You loved a woman and she dumped you."

"Tactful, aren't you?" retorted Cain, giving back her own words.

"To the core." Pointedly, Shelley looked down at the large hand wrapped around her wrist. "Excuse me. I have a lot of work to do."

"So do I," he said rather grimly. "Your husband burned you but good, didn't he?" Cain asked.

As he spoke, he caressed Shelley's inner wrist with the ball of his thumb. The combination of his hard fingers and gently caressing thumb distracted Shelley. When she spoke, her voice vibrated with suppressed emotion.

"My ex-husband taught me the price of sharing my dreams."

"Disillusionment?" suggested Cain.

"Was that what happened to you?"

Cain's mouth flattened. "You could say that I was disillusioned, yes." His voice was deceptively mild, but his eyes were the color of winter ice. "You could also say that I was mad enough to kill."

Shelley's eyes widened. She had the distinct feeling that she wouldn't want to be on the receiving end of Cain's unbridled rage. "Did you?" she asked before she could stop herself.

"I was mad at myself, not her. She wasn't worth killing for."

Another question came to Shelley's lips, but she said

nothing. Beneath Cain's anger she had seen a flash of old pain. "Neither was my husband," she admitted. Then, "I'm sorry," she said, touching his arm. "I had no right to pry."

The corner of Cain's mouth turned up in a wry smile. "I had it coming. I've been chipping away at your civilized veneer since I saw your cynical little smile when you looked from JoLynn's cleavage to me." His thumb moved over the inside of Shelley's wrist with slow, gently searching strokes. "When I saw you pick up that snake and hold it as carefully as though it were a kitten, I wanted to know you. I wanted to know how a woman who spent her life surrounded by the finest products of civilization had learned to handle snakes and lonely children. And then you calmly stepped onto my bike in your silks and stylish heels, carrying a boa constrictor in a Spanish lace pillowcase."

Cain's voice paused. His warm thumb kept up its slow, mesmerizing rhythm against the pulse beating beneath Shelley's soft skin. "When I walked into your house, your civilized and deeply wild home, I realized that I *had* to know you, but you kept retreating. You're still retreating. Don't. Please. I don't want to hurt you or frighten you. I just want to know you." His clear gray eyes searched her face. "Truce?" he asked in a deep, quiet voice.

Shelley felt the tug of Cain's words on her mind as deeply as she felt the lure of his sensuality on her body. She had no doubt that he was telling the truth. "Truce," she agreed softly.

Cain lifted her wrist and pressed his mouth against the soft skin that his thumb had been caressing. The feel of his lips and the silken brush of his mustache awakened every nerve ending in Shelley's body. Nerves that had slept for a long time. Nerves that she had forgotten. Nerves that she had never suspected existed.

"What do you want to eat for dinner tonight?" he asked, feeling her pulse accelerate beneath his lips. "Seafood or French food? Portuguese? Thai? Mexican? Chinese?"

"Cain, I don't—"

"Eat?" interrupted Cain. He shook his head. "Don't be ridiculous. Of course you eat. Besides, how else are you going to find out how to gild my lily? I'll tell you right now, Shelley, I won't tolerate any of the garbage that JoLynn has. I want something as individual as I am, not some decorator's silly idea of ancient or recent trends in room furnishings."

"Do you really have a house that you want me to work on?" demanded Shelley.

"Of course. What did you think I meant when I said I wanted you to gild my lily?"

Shelley caught herself just before she would have apologized for misconstruing Cain's intent. There he stood calmly caressing her wrist with his lips and at the same time acting indignant over having his intentions misunderstood. The fact that he had almost gotten away with it was an indication of just how lethal his particular brand of charm was to her defenses. He was indeed what she had called him. A renegade.

Cain's expression of injured innocence gave way to a very male smile as he saw the slight flush beneath Shelley's skin. For a moment she tried to ignore him, then she burst into laughter that was both sweet and unrestrained.

"How can I resist gilding a renegade lily?" she asked, her eyes alive with laughter and challenge and the feel of his lips against her soft skin.

Cain's smile changed, more intimate now, as warm as the slow pressure of his mouth sliding over her pulse. "I'm usually quite well-behaved," he murmured. "You and your half-civilized smile have a disastrous effect on my temper."

"You and your sharp tongue have a similar effect on mine," she retorted.

"Sharp? Are you sure?"

Delicately Cain ran the tip of his tongue over the veins of Shelley's wrist, his gray eyes smoky as he watched her. The intimacy of the moment and the gesture disturbed Shelley more than she wanted to admit to anyone, even herself. Especially herself.

"Cain, if you don't stop, the truce is off and so is the gilding."

He assessed the determination and fear that underlay Shelley's quiet words. His long fingers opened, letting her hand slide through his in a release that was also another kind of caress.

"Have you decided where you want to have dinner yet?" he asked calmly.

"It isn't necessary."

"You're wrong."

Cain's flat statement surprised Shelley into silence.

"I meant what I said," he continued. "You're going to have to know me better before you can make an accurate assessment of what will or won't please me. Making a home is an . . . intimate . . . process."

"Not *that* intimate."

Cain smiled slightly. "I'll behave, little mink. I promise. It will be business and only business, unless you say otherwise."

"Mink?"

"Soft and wild," explained Cain helpfully. "Mink."

"Is this your idea of business?" she asked in exasperation.

"Am I touching you?"

"No, but you're reaching me!"

Cain's laughter was no comfort to Shelley's ruffled

nerves. "And you're learning about me, aren't you?" he asked. "That's business." He grinned, showing a clean curve of white beneath his golden brown mustache. "I'll pick you up at seven."

Shelley stood and watched Cain stride out of the Gilded Lily. Even through the thick glass, the motorcycle's primal roar had the ability to make her shiver. Not with distaste, she admitted. Like the man, the motorcycle made no attempt to conceal what it was and was not.

It was definitely not civilized.

"Awful machine," said a breathy voice next to Shelley's ear. "The man is something else, though."

"They're one and the same," Shelley said. "Uncivilized."

"Like you," said Brian, coming up behind JoLynn.

"Me?" said Shelley, glancing in surprise toward her partner. But it was JoLynn who answered.

"Darling," explained JoLynn, "no *civilized* woman would hold a slimy snake."

"Darling," said Shelley, turning toward JoLynn, "fish are slimy. Snakes are not."

JoLynn shuddered. Shelley smiled. Brian cleared his throat.

"Ah, Shelley, why don't you have JoLynn show you what she found in the catalogs?"

"Only if you've washed your hands since you touched that snake," said JoLynn in a clipped voice.

Shelley looked down at her slender hands and counted to ten. It wasn't high enough. "I haven't washed them since I touched Cain," she said musingly, "and he felt just like Squeeze. Strong and warm and hard." She looked at the other woman with wide hazel eyes. "Do you think I should wash?"

JoLynn made a strangled sound.

"You're right," agreed Shelley. "I probably should."

Even hours later as she dressed for her dinner with Cain, the memory of JoLynn's expression made Shelley's mouth curve in a smile that was considerably less than civilized. It had taken Brian a few minutes to soothe the red-headed JoLynn into a businesslike frame of mind. By the time Shelley had returned—ostentatiously drying her hands on a paper towel—JoLynn had been ready to point out the type of objets she wanted to finish her house with. Predictably, she chose nothing that didn't have an analog in a famous museum.

Shelley paused as she reached into her closet. Cain hadn't told her where they were going, or whether the motorcycle would be their means of transportation. To be on the safe side, she pulled out her favorite what-am-I-going-to-wear black slacks. The roughly woven silk was strong enough to take a motorcycle ride, discreet enough to eat hamburgers in and elegant enough for a fancy restaurant. A summer-weight wine silk sweater met the same requirements as the pants. Black high-heeled sandals completed her outfit.

Automatically, Shelley began to pull her hair into a smooth knot at the base of her neck. She remembered that the hairstyle wouldn't fit beneath a motorcycle helmet. She hesitated, then began sectioning off her hair for a sleek French braid. Instead of wearing the necklace of tiny carved jet and amethyst beads she had set out, Shelley wove the glittering jewelry into the rich darkness of her hair. When she was finished, her hairstyle matched her clothes, under-stated yet elegant.

The sound of chimes drifted down from the upper level. Shelley crossed the room to the intercom, depressed a button, and said, "Yes?"

"Glad to find you in such an agreeable mood," said Cain's voice, its deep tone unmistakable even through the intercom.

Shelley pushed another button, releasing the electronic lock on the front door. "Door's open. I'll be right up."

She grabbed a deep maroon summer jacket and ran lightly up the two flights of stairs. Cain was just inside the front door, squatting on his heels, rubbing his strong fingers down Nudge's back. The cat arched and preened in the manner of all felines no matter what their size. Her purr sounded like a very large hummingbird. Smiling, Cain stood up. Nudge bumped her head against his knee, demanding more petting. He laughed softly.

"If you say 'Just like a woman,'" muttered Shelley, "I'm going to sic Squeeze on you."

Cain's lips shifted slightly as he tried not to smile. Shelley watched each subtle movement, realizing again what a beautifully formed mouth he had. Neither too blunt nor too slight, the shape of his lips would have done credit to Michaelangelo. The temptation of Cain's mouth shouldn't have fit with the unyielding planes of his face or the thick, uncompromising sweep of his hair, yet it did. Perhaps it was the lively intelligence in his gray eyes that drew everything together, balancing the sensuality of his lips with the angular lines of his face.

"Is my mustache on crooked?" asked Cain with a lazy smile.

Abruptly, Shelley realized that she had been staring at him as though he were an objet d'art she was considering acquiring. "Sorry," she murmured. "You have an unusual face."

"Unusual?" He laughed briefly. "Is that a polite way of saying ugly?"

Startled, Shelley said the first thing that came to her

mind. "Good God, Cain, the last word I'd use to describe you is ugly. You have the most beautiful mouth I've ever seen on anyone, man or woman."

It was Cain's turn to be startled. His eyes widened as he realized that Shelley was being neither coy nor flattering. She had told him the truth as she saw it.

"Thank you," he said simply. Then he smiled again, a slow, wicked gesture that sent warnings down to Shelley's very feminine core. "I'd tell you what I thought of your mouth, but you'd accuse me of being unbusinesslike."

Shelley didn't disagree.

"So I'll show you instead."

With no more warning than that, Cain gathered Shelley into his arms and lowered his mouth over hers. He fitted his lips to hers exactly, gently, then the tip of his tongue traced her mouth in a caress that told her more about the beauty of her lips than any compliment could have. At first Shelley stood stiffly, wondering what kind of game Cain was playing. Then she felt the tremor of desire that went through him, heard the deep sound he made when his tongue probed the moist warmth of her inner lips. Whatever Cain was doing, it didn't come under the category of gamesmanship. He was as caught in the sensual moment as she was.

"Cain—" Shelley's voice was more husky than protesting, though she hadn't meant it to sound that way.

Cain took advantage of Shelley's parted lips to slide his tongue into her mouth, expanding the kiss until he had sampled every texture from the tiny, sharp serrations of her teeth to the slight, sensual roughness of her tongue and the creamy softness of her inner lips. He knew he should stop before he frightened her, but the taste and feel of her was simply too enticing. The kiss deepened until he filled her mouth completely, slow movements of his tongue sliding over hers, her body flowing over his, her softness fitting against his strength as perfectly as his mouth fit over hers. He felt the tremor that took her, heard a sound come from deep in her throat, a sound that was balanced between fear and desire. Not wanting fear to gain ascendancy, he lifted his mouth.

"Before you yell at me for being unbusinesslike," said Cain, dipping his head between words for small, brushing tastes of her mouth, "think how much you just learned about me."

Shelley was glad that he didn't want her to say anything. Her thoughts were more than a little scattered. The taste and feel and scent of Cain filled her senses. And he was right. The kiss had told her a lot about him. He was a man of shattering sensuality. Physically, kissing him was more intimate and exciting than anything she had discovered in or out of marriage. Mentally, kissing Cain was a kind of sharing that had no analogs in her experience. He had given himself to the kiss with a completeness that first surprised and then inflamed her, yet he had been so restrained in his expectations of her that she hadn't felt either crowded or angry.

And despite his gentleness, he was more than strong enough to support her weight when her body had decided to turn into warm honey and flow all over him.

In silence, Shelley allowed Cain to lead her to the black Jaguar XKE parked in the driveway. The car's classic, sinuous lines appealed to her in much the way Cain himself did. It was restrained without being at all tame. Though the engine was nearly two decades old, it started at the first turn of the key. The sound the car made fit its name perfectly. Jaguar.

"Have you been keeping this in a time capsule?" asked Shelley as the car devoured the twisting, narrow hillside road with the gliding ease of a jungle cat.

"Close," said Cain. "When I'm out of the country, I leave the Jag in storage with a classic car nut."

Out of the country. The words echoed and reechoed in Shelley's head. She should have expected it. Everything about Cain proclaimed it.

"You're a traveling man," said Shelley flatly.

Cain looked over, his gray eyes briefly searching Shelley's expression before focusing again on the road. Her face was like her voice—withdrawn, remote, shut down. She was sitting within arm's reach but she was light-years away, retreating further with each breath, each instant of time.

"You say that like a curse." Cain's voice was soft, yet it hinted at the surprise and anger that Shelley's retreat had caused in him.

"It's a fact. Like death."

"Life is also a fact," he countered evenly.

Shelley shrugged, pulling her composure around herself like a shield. Which it was, a shield against Cain's potent attraction for her. She had watched her mother grow old trying to make a home for a traveling man. Shelley hadn't learned her lesson, though. She had married a traveling man herself, believing that if she provided an inviting enough home, her husband would no longer wander.

She had been wrong. Traveling men were incapable of appreciating homes or the women who made them and waited, hoping, until hope died.

Shelley dug into her oversized leather purse, pulled out a notebook and slim gold pen and settled back in the comfortable seat. In quick, neat strokes she wrote *Cain Remington* across the top of one page.

"How long are you usually in the country?" she asked, her voice wholly professional, utterly neutral. It was not the voice of a woman who had just melted and run like honey beneath the sensual heat of a man's kiss.

With a smothered curse Cain downshifted suddenly. The Jaguar gave a full-throated roar, a powerful, angry noise. To the right of the road there was only brush climbing up the old road cut. To the left there was more brush, a thick growth of chaparral dropping steeply away into a canyon that had no name. The tires made a high, wild sound as Cain took the car through a tight curve.

Shelley looked up from her notebook, but she wasn't alarmed. Cain handled the powerful car the same way he had handled the bike—with ease, skill and control combined. She realized that he was angry, and knew that he had sensed the finality of her retreat. Quietly she cursed his perceptivity; it wouldn't make her job any easier. And that was what it came down to. Her job. Cain was going to rent some personal touches to gild his temporary residence. She was not going to be one of the touches that he rented.

Chaparral went by in a brown and gold blur.

"What do you have against traveling men?" said Cain finally, his voice as hard as the steel color of his eyes.

"Not a thing," murmured Shelley. "Without them, I'd be out of business." *Rented homes, rented people, rented lives.* "How long will you be in the country this time?" The question was all but uninflected. It said more clearly than words that she was inquiring for business rather than personal reasons.

Cain did not answer. For long moments the silence stretched as the black Jaguar consumed the road, the car's power held in check by Cain's strong, skilled hands. Evening light poured into the interior, turning Cain's features into a golden brown study of planes and angles softened by velvet shadows. Gold burned incandescent in his hair and mustache, but none of the warmth reached his eyes when he glanced at Shelley. Like ice, his eyes took the rich light and transformed it into translucent shades of blue and gray, eyes as still and deep as an Arctic twilight.

Suddenly the Jaguar swooped into a turnout at the edge of the dropoff into the brush-choked canyon. Cain turned off the ignition and faced Shelley.

"I'm not a mercenary." Cain's voice was like his eyes, clear and very cold.

Startled, Shelley half-turned in the seat to face him. "I didn't think you were."

He paused as though examining her words for truth. Finally, he nodded. "All right. What *do* you think I am?"

Shelley blinked, not understanding why Cain was angry. "A traveling man, that's all."

Cain's impatience showed in the tightening of his hands on the wheel, and the curtness of his words. "A lot of men travel in their work. What's so dishonorable about that?"

"I didn't say it was—"

"The hell you didn't!" interrupted Cain. "When you heard that I traveled, you shut down. No warning, no explanation, just good-bye, Cain Remington."

Shelley wished Cain were less perceptive. Most men wouldn't have noticed her mental withdrawal or have questioned her about it if they did.

"Since when do good-byes bother traveling men?" she asked. "Tonight, tomorrow or two months, it's all the same. Good-bye, so long, see you around." Shelley's voice was cool, calm. Too calm. But she knew if she let her control slide just one fraction of an inch, she would be yelling at Cain, and neither one of them deserved that. It wasn't Cain's fault that he was so damned attractive to her and at the same time the worst possible man for her. Traveling man. He would be here today and gone tomorrow, but her emotions would not. They would stay with her, eating her alive. "What's so new about good-bye?" she asked, her voice calm. "Or is it just that you're not the one saying it this time?"

Cain took a long breath and a better grip on his temper. What Shelley was saying was reasonable. He was accustomed to good-byes. And, he admitted to himself, he was used to being the one to say good-bye.

Score one for sweet reason.

But he was not ready to say good-bye to Shelley Wilde. He would not. Which meant that he had better walk very carefully for a time, business and business only, no more of the wild honey of her kiss, no more of her womanly softness flowing over him and teaching him how hungry and alone he had been, no more heat and heavy need gathering inside him, tightening his body until he ached in time with the thick beating of his heart.

Sweet reason could take a flying leap off the nearest cliff.

Cain took a second long breath and started the Jaguar again. Its powerful, subdued sound was soothing. "You're right," Cain said, his voice an uncanny echo of the car's primal purr. "I'm used to good-byes."

Smoothly, he let out the clutch and turned back onto the road. Guided by hard, restless hands, the Jaguar resumed its tireless prowling through the gilded evening light.

Chapter 4

THE RESTAURANT CAIN CHOSE WAS THE INTIMATE FRENCH type that L.A.'s West Side did so well. Le Chanson wasn't one of those tiresome watering holes like the Polo Lounge where rude tourists demanded autographs and Hollywood hustlers paid the maitre d' to page them for nonexistent phone calls from important people. Le Chanson served nouvelle cuisine, aged wines and haute checks. The civilized gleam of linen, silver and crystal provided a perfect backdrop for the equally civilized murmur of patrons who discussed books and art and the theater as often as they discussed Dow-Jones, real estate and the IRS. Of course, that could have been because books and art and the theater were also businesses, ones in which Le Chanson's patrons invested income as well as intellect.

"Do you live in L.A. often?" asked Shelley as she opened her menu.

Cain looked up sharply, but she hadn't taken out her

notebook again. It was just as well. Beneath his smooth outer surface, he was still seething. It had been a long time since anyone had made him quite so angry as Shelley had by withdrawing behind her seamless business facade. The reappearance of her notebook might have been the death of his uncertain hold on his temper.

"I live in L.A. whenever I can."

"Do you like it?" asked Shelley, real curiosity in her voice instead of the implacably neutral tones she had used since she had discovered Cain was a traveling man.

His mouth turned up slightly beneath the tawny brown of his mustache. "Yes. Unfashionable of me, isn't it?"

Shelley couldn't help smiling. Getting people to admit that they liked L.A. was almost impossible. It was de rigueur to hate Los Angeles. All the trendy folks did, and were proud of it. Cain, of course, wouldn't give a damn about trendy or not, in or out, up or down. She had known that the instant he had called her a spinster, and then pigeonholed her as a woman who couldn't hold a man. Rude, yes, Cain was that.

And accurate.

"What do you like about L.A.?" she asked.

"Freedom. Technology. Fine food. Bookstores. The ocean. The endless rivers of cars."

"What don't you like about the city?"

He shrugged. "The usual things. Traffic jams when I'm in a hurry. Smog when I want to see the mountains. People when I'd rather be alone. Noise when I'd rather hear silence."

"And then you leave."

It was more of an accusation than a question.

"Some people run away by staying in one place, Shelley. It's called hiding."

"I'm not working for 'some people.' I'm working for you. You run away in the usual manner." Shelley heard the echo of her own words in her mind. Not very businesslike at all. "I'm sorry," she murmured, smiling her best professional smile. "That came out rather badly. Everyone needs variety. Men more than women, I'm told."

Shelley set aside her menu and reached for her leather-bound notebook. Cain reached for his temper. The tiny *click* of her slim ballpoint pen seemed very loud in the silence. His teeth came together with a small, feral sound that went no further than his lips.

"What are you doing?" he asked in a deceptively mild voice.

"Writing down your likes and dislikes," she said without looking up. "It will help refresh my memory when I go through my catalogs."

"I see." Then, savagely, "Here's something for you. I despise leather-bound notebooks and little gold pens that go *click.*"

Shelley's hand paused. She looked up, her hazel eyes wide and almost gold with the reflected gleam of candlelight. "Perhaps," she said carefully, putting away notebook and pen, "I'm not the person you need to add warmth to your home."

Cain laughed harshly. Need? Right now he needed her so badly that it was just short of pain. But if he said that, she would smile professionally, get up and walk out of his life. He sensed that as surely as he had sensed her anger when he called her a woman who couldn't hold her man. Although if she had kissed her husband with half the shivering passion that she had kissed him this evening, her husband must have been a brass-bound idiot to go looking for the "variety" that she had mentioned.

"Sorry," said Cain, smoothing the savage edges off his voice with an effort. "I'm never in my best temper when I'm hungry."

"Then we should order," said Shelley, retrieving her menu and studying it in silence.

Grimly, Cain looked at the menu. No matter how hard he searched, he could find no entree called "Shelley Wilde." With a sigh, he condemned himself to an undetermined time of hunger.

"Appetizer?" asked Cain.

"I can't decide between stuffed mushrooms and oysters on the half shell," she admitted, licking her lips in unconscious anticipation.

Cain watched the pink tip of Shelley's tongue leave a sheen of moisture over her lips. He remembered how warm and sweet her mouth had been. With a silent, searing curse, he turned his attention to the menu. When the waiter appeared, Cain had decided. And so had Shelley. As one, they chose baby salmon stuffed with bay shrimp.

"What was your second choice?" asked Cain. "Gulf shrimp in lemon butter with herbs?"

"How did you guess?"

"It was mine, too," said Cain dryly. To the waiter he said, "One baby salmon and one Gulf shrimp. We'll have the Kentucky lettuce salad and the New England chowder. For appetizers, bring an order of stuffed mushrooms and one of oysters."

"I can't eat that much," Shelley said.

"I can."

Shelley looked at the hard, wide-shouldered body of the man across the table from her. She had no doubt that he could eat his dinner, hers and then look around for dessert.

"I'm assuming you prefer dry wines to sweet," said Cain.

Shelley nodded.

"Chardonnay?"

"Please," she murmured.

"French or California?"

Shelley remembered that a "whisper" of garlic and a "kiss" of shallots had been mentioned in the description of both entrees. "California, I think. Some of the French Chardonnays are so light they disappear with anything but the most bland foods."

Cain ordered the wine, handed the menus to the waiter, and turned back to Shelley with a grin. "You can gild my dinners any time. It's like listening to myself order."

"Sounds boring," said Shelley lightly.

"Not at all." His voice was soft and very certain. "Sometimes I surprise the hell out of myself. And"—he looked caressingly at her mouth—"I think you do, too."

Shelley glanced down, letting her near-black lashes shield the luminous interest in her eyes. As she turned aside, the amethyst beads woven through her dark hair gleamed like a distant constellation glimpsed through midnight clouds.

"What do you do for a living, Cain?" she asked, her voice low.

She felt the intensity of his glance like a caress, disturbing her careful control. She licked her lips once, a gesture of nervousness that didn't help. She still tasted of him, slightly sweet, slightly salt, unique. A single kiss, and she couldn't touch her tongue to her lips without tasting him all over again.

"What do you think I do?" asked Cain.

The edge of hostility in his voice surprised Shelley. She remembered his hands, hard and scarred and strong, clean and gentle and sensitive. "I don't know. Whatever it is, though, I'm sure you do it better than anyone else."

It was Cain's turn to be surprised. "Why do you say that?"

"You aren't the kind of man who does things by halves," she said. *Even a simple kiss,* she added silently.

The waiter returned with the wine. Cain tasted it, defied convention by handing the glass to Shelley and waited. She sipped as he had, savoring the expanding flavor of the wine and the realization that his lips had touched it just an instant before hers. When she handed the glass back to him, her hand trembled almost invisibly.

Cain saw the tremor, though. His pale eyes missed nothing that Shelley did, not even the slightest hesitation in her breath. He accepted the glass from her, draining it with a quick movement that was quintessentially masculine. He nodded to the patient waiter.

"Tastes even better the second time," he said quietly as the waiter poured their wine. "Warmer."

Shelley knew he was referring to the fact that her lips had touched the wine, rather than to a good Chardonnay's marked tendency to improve in flavor with slight warming. But she could hardly accuse Cain of being unbusinesslike in his conversation without betraying the direction of her own thoughts. So much of what he said could be taken two ways—one utterly normal, one richly sensual.

"The best Chardonnay is like that," said Shelley, sipping the wine that had just been poured for her.

Cain looked up and smiled at her. The smile was like his conversation, filled with levels of meaning and invitation. He settled more comfortably in his chair, like a man who had made a decision and was going to follow it through to the end, whatever that end might be.

"I'm a geologist," said Cain, watching Shelley closely.

"Oil?"

"Everything but."

Shelley nodded as though he had confirmed something. "What does that little nod mean?" he asked.

"Most petrologists work for very large companies. You're too independent to do well working with a corporation." She smiled slightly. "Unless you owned it, of course."

"I do. It's called Basic Resources. We do mineral surveys, Landsat interpretations and mining consulting, as well as resource planning, projections and conservation." Cain's pale eyes narrowed. "And despite what dear JoLynn might have hinted, I'm neither a mercenary nor some kind of covert government agent."

Surprise showed for an instant on Shelley's face as she realized that it wouldn't have shocked her if Cain had been "some kind of covert government agent." He had the self-confidence, intelligence and physical hardness to survive very well as a lone wolf. "All JoLynn told me about you," said Shelley evenly, "was that the bike was awful but the man was something else."

Shelley's summation drew a reluctant smile from Cain. His tawny chestnut mustache shifted, making candlelight gleam in it like molten gold.

"Be grateful she didn't elaborate. She can be quite, er, frank. When I went back to her house this afternoon and asked her permission to take Billy for a run with his dirt bike, she told me a picnic was more what she had in mind—for two, neither of which was her son."

Cain's pale eyes narrowed until little was visible but a silver shimmer. At that moment Shelley was relieved that she wasn't the object of his anger.

"I suppose I could have finessed it," continued Cain, "but I didn't feel up to a polite fencing match. So I reminded JoLynn that I was Dave's stepbrother and that if I had to, I'd get a court order appointing me Billy's guardian as long as Dave was in Europe. And I assured her that I'd do it in such a way as to cause her the maximum embarrassment, and in the process scare off whatever wealthy sugar daddy she might have in the background.''

Cain's smile was not nice at all. ''She saw the light real quick,'' he added. ''I'd just as soon not use the courts to enforce a boy's needs, but I will if I have to. With her track record, she'd lose. And she knows it.''

''Dave?'' asked Shelley, feeling off-balance, almost battered by the leashed violence she sensed just beneath Cain's smile. ''Dave Cummings? Billy's father? You really are Billy's uncle?''

''Why? Did you think he called all JoLynn's men 'uncle'?''

Shelley shrugged. ''It's not uncommon.''

''Well, I'm a certified uncle, even though I haven't seen Billy for years. And Dave's a certified fool. He believed JoLynn's heart was as soft as his head. I met her twelve years ago, took one look and told Dave that if he wanted a piece of that action, fine, take it. But for God's sake don't marry it. Cheap shoes never wear well, especially when somebody else has already rounded off the heels.''

Shelley felt the blood drain from her face at Cain's casual, brutal summation of a woman who had obviously wanted him. Was that what Cain thought of all women? If you want it, take it, but for God's sake don't marry it. Was he one of those insecure males who couldn't tolerate marrying a woman who wasn't a virgin, a woman who might compare him unfavorably with other lovers?

Cain sighed and reached for his wineglass. ''Don't look so shocked, Shelley.'' He made an impatient movement with his shoulders. ''JoLynn deserves it.''

''Because she wasn't a virgin when she married your brother?''

"Hell, no," said Cain, his voice harsh. "Because since she married him she's had more men than a public toilet."

"Cain!"

"Sorry," he muttered. He ran a hand through his thick, sun-streaked hair. "I don't like women who use children as bargaining tools." He glanced up, pinning Shelley with an icy gray look. "How would you describe a female who offered to trade a few hours of her son's time for a few hours of mine—in bed?"

Shock and revulsion warred for control of Shelley's expressive face. She remembered Billy pleading with his mother not to kill Squeeze, Billy's vividly individual room, Billy's casual expertise as he fitted the helmet on her head, Billy's open smile and warmth. What a cruel joke life had played to pair a child like that with a woman who apparently had no desire to be a mother.

"My feelings exactly," said Cain.

Then Shelley realized that she had spoken her last thought aloud. "Forgive me," she murmured. "I have no right to judge JoLynn."

"Why not? You gave Billy more kindness in an afternoon than she's given him in a year. He loves her anyway, though." Cain muttered a searing word under his breath. "I could forgive her the men, but not the boy." With a bitter laugh, Cain added, "Who am I to talk about fools? I married a bitch just like JoLynn. If she didn't have a man on top of her, *any* man, she didn't know that she was alive. Thank God we didn't have children to grind up between us."

Shelley swallowed, feeling slightly ill. "Your wife must have been very unhappy," said Shelley, her voice barely a whisper, "to give herself so often, so cheaply, simply to be reassured for a few minutes that someone cared. And JoLynn—she doesn't even see the son who loves her."

Cain's hand touched Shelley's shining brown hair. "Soft little mink," he murmured. "I shouldn't have brought up JoLynn. She's not your problem. She's mine. That's why I left God's own mess in the Yukon and came back. And in a few months, JoLynn won't be Billy's problem either. Dave has found a beautiful French woman. He's bringing her to America in time for Thanksgiving. Billy will have a home, then. A real one, full of love. Until then, I'll be here to do what I can for him."

Tears burned behind Shelley's eyes at hearing her dream expressed so clearly—a home full of love. "I'm glad," she said in a husky voice. "Otherwise I might just steal Billy for myself and end up in jail."

"I'd break you out," said Cain, smiling, but his eyes were the color of steel. "Then I'd throw you over my shoulder and show you the world."

"Thanks, but I've seen it." Shelley's voice was as light as Cain's had been, and her eyes were almost as hard.

"All of it?"

"Everywhere they had a snake," she amended wryly.

"You didn't like it?"

"The snakes? They were fine."

"What didn't you like, then?"

"Never having a home." The words were all the more forceful for the very softness of Shelley's voice.

Cain's chestnut eyebrows dipped into a frown. "The world was your home. All of it."

"And none of it."

For a moment, Cain hesitated. Then he picked up his glass and swirled the golden wine until its heady fragrance caressed his nostrils. "Did your parents have a good marriage?"

The question was so quiet, so unexpected, that Shelley almost didn't hear it.

"Yes," she said. "Very good. It wouldn't have survived otherwise. Mom worked so hard making every place we were in a home. When I was old enough to understand that no place was home, I used to watch her fixing up our rented houses and I'd feel like crying."

"Did she?"

"Cry?" asked Shelley.

"Yes."

Shelley blinked, trying to remember whether her mother had ever cried when they had to pack up and leave. Slowly, Shelley shook her head. "I don't know. I cried, though. For a while. And then I learned that we'd always leave, so I stopped putting down roots. Or I tried to." She shrugged. "It took me a long time to get the knack of existing in a place without *living* there. I was never very good at it. That was the reason I left when I was eighteen. I decided that if I was ever going to have a home, I'd have to make it for myself."

"Did you?"

"You were in it today."

Cain's smile was wry. "That's not quite what I meant. What did you do for a home in the years between eighteen and . . . what . . . twenty-three?"

"Twenty-seven," corrected Shelley. "Well into spinsterhood."

He winced. "I'm going to be a long time living down that crack, aren't I?"

"It's the truth. Not very flattering, perhaps, but true just the same."

"You prefer 'bachelorette'?" he asked innocently.

Shelley made a face. "God, no. Awful word. Conjures up visions of a shiny-faced swinger who's still paying off the orthodontist. I'd rather be a grim-lipped spinster any day."

Cain grinned. Before he could pursue any more questions about Shelley's past, the waiter brought plates of stuffed mushrooms and oysters on the half shell. For a few moments the only sounds were the slight crunch of cracked ice shifting beneath oyster shells as Shelley and Cain forked out the succulent morsels.

"What about your childhood, Cain?" asked Shelley, her tiny fork poised between two equally tempting oysters. "Settled? Unsettled? Happy? Sad?"

"Yes."

Shelley looked up sharply. "If you persist in one-word answers, I'll gild your home with chrome mannikins and vintage punk rock album covers."

Cain shuddered. "You wouldn't."

She smiled, showing more teeth than mercy.

"You would." Cain's mouth turned up in a reluctant smile. "I just wanted to keep my answers short enough that you wouldn't have to take notes."

Shelley's fork stabbed into an oyster with enough force to grate against the shell. The notebook was her shield against taking Cain too personally, and somehow he knew it. Silently she ate her oyster and cursed his uncanny perceptivity. Even her parents hadn't understood her that well. She had always been an enigma to them with her longing for settled places, predictable days, lifetime friends.

"I'll try to refrain from taking notes," said Shelley coolly, distancing herself from Cain with her voice instead of her notebook.

Cain heard the tone, understood it and bit back any comment. Instead, he did something that he almost never did. He talked about himself. And he did it as a way to touch Shelley, the only kind of touch that she would allow.

"I lived in one place, in New Mexico. My days were as ordered and predictable as the course of the planets."

Shelley muffled a startled sound at the unsettling parallels between Cain's thoughts and her own.

"The same friends going through the same schools and the same experiences," he continued. "Until I was twelve."

"What happened?" asked Shelley when Cain stopped.

"The usual. Divorce."

Shelley's hazel eyes darkened as her pupils expanded. She made a soft sound of sympathy. Cain smiled rather ironically.

"It was a relief," he said. "Mom and Dad fought like a house afire. No time-outs and no rules. You see," Cain went on, his steel gray eyes pinning Shelley, "staying in one place with the same people, the same house, the same schools—none of that means one damn thing about having a *home*. Two people in love are a home wherever they are, however often they move. Two people without love aren't a home even if they stay in the same house until hell freezes solid."

With great attention Shelley selected a stuffed mushroom, avoiding Cain's too-perceptive, too-knowing eyes.

"You don't believe me," continued Cain, "but I'm right. I learned that when mother married again. Seth, my stepfather, taught me what a difference the right man can make in a woman's life. Mom laughed instead of crying, loved instead of withdrawing, smiled even when she thought she was alone in a room. Later, from remarks made by people who knew Seth with his first wife, I learned that a woman can make a hell of a difference for a man, too. They brought out the best in each other, not the worst."

Shelley looked up, caught by the intensity of Cain's voice. His eyes were fixed on her, their cold gray color warmed by the flare of candlelight. For a moment she was lost in their clear depths, hearing nothing, tasting nothing,

knowing only the hunger and yearning of the man who sat
so close to her. Then Cain's deep, rough-edged voice
surrounded her again, claiming her whole attention.

"Seth was an engineer," said Cain, setting aside the
wineglass he had sipped from. "He worked on projects all
over the world, and he took us with him. Dave was four
years younger than I was, Seth's son from an earlier
marriage. Mom and Seth had two more kids. Girls. Pretty
and bright and sassy as they come. They're married now,
both of them. I'm looking forward to some sassy little
nieces."

Cain's smile was something Shelley had never seen from
him before, whimsical and indulgent and loving, like a man
watching kittens cuff and tumble over each other. The smile
did odd things to Shelley, sending shivery feelings of
warmth and pleasure chasing over her nerve endings. Then
the smile faded, leaving only haunting memories.

"Wish Dave had been half as bright," sighed Cain. "But
JoLynn was the sexiest thing he'd ever seen. He had to have
her." Cain's smile was quite different this time. "Well, he
had her, all right. And vice versa." Then he added under
his breath, "More vice than versa."

Shelley watched Cain's strong white teeth crunch into a
mushroom and sensed that he would like to have crushed
JoLynn as thoroughly. He was a man who was protective of
those he loved. He clearly loved both his stepbrother and,
by extension, Billy.

Cain made a curt gesture with his fork, dismissing
JoLynn as a subject. "My stepfather was a traveling man,"
said Cain, looking at Shelley, watching the words *traveling
man* sink into her, seeing her wince. "That traveling man
taught me more about love and family and home than
twelve years of staying in the same unhappy house did.

Coming or going, staying or leaving, Seth was a man who knew how to love. That's what makes a house a home, Shelley. Love.''

"Don't tell anyone else," she said coolly, toying with a mushroom. "I'll be out of work."

"No, you won't," said Cain, his voice deep, his eyes smoky with intensity. "Your work is an expression of your ability to love. You understand your clients' hunger for an environment that reflects their individuality. Whether or not you agree with them or even like them as people, you listen to their human needs rather than your own ego. It's their home when you're finished, not yours. Even poor, silly, sad JoLynn. You're going to leave her house as perfectly sterile as you found it, because you know that's the only way she'll feel comfortable. You'll give her as much of a home as she can accept, and your only regret will be that she's too shallow to accept more.''

Eyes wide, Shelley stared at the man who seemed to know more about her than she knew about herself. It had taken her years to fully understand why she had chosen the work she had. Cain had known her less than a day—and he had seen through to her core. Had she not also experienced his gentleness, it would have been truly frightening to be that transparent to him.

"You're unnervingly perceptive," said Shelley finally. "It must be very useful to you in business."

Cain's eyes narrowed briefly as he heard the trace of fear in her voice. "Being able to judge the amount of truth and violence in people has saved my butt a few times," he admitted. "It's also ruined what could have been relaxing interludes between business problems. Some people you don't want to know a whole lot about, like temporary bed partners.''

"Amen," murmured Shelley.

Despite the softness of her voice, there was no doubt that her agreement was emphatic. Cain smiled.

"Same problem for you, too?" he guessed.

"I was never into temporary, whether it was bed or business. But"—she shrugged—"you're right. Because I could see beneath the surface I had to disqualify a lot of otherwise attractive men."

"Like Brian Harris?" asked Cain with a casualness that was belied by the icy clarity of his eyes.

"Brian is civilized, polished, wealthy, bright, handsome as the devil."

"And?" prompted Cain.

"He's just not my kind of man," said Shelley quietly. "No one woman will ever satisfy him. A lot of men are like that."

"Boys."

"What?"

"Boys are like that. Men know enough about themselves, life and women to get beyond hormones."

Shelley's sleek, dark eyebrow cocked questioningly. "An unusual point of view," she murmured.

Cain shrugged. "It's common to all the *men* I know."

The waiter intervened, bringing baby salmon for Shelley and large Gulf shrimp for Cain. For a time the conversation was confined to food. When Cain casually offered Shelley a bite of his shrimp, she took it from his fork before she realized the unthinking intimacy of the gesture. It recalled times from her childhood, when her father and mother used to laughingly share tidbits from their separate plates. Even in desert campsites when they had had exactly the same dinner of dates, figs and bread, they still would exchange bites.

"Where are you?" asked Cain softly, accurately reading the distance in Shelley's unfocused hazel eyes.

"Tinrhert Hamada," murmured Shelley, "the Great Eastern Erg of the Sahara."

"Algeria."

"Yes." Shelley smiled slightly. "I'm used to thinking in geographical rather than geopolitical terms. Comes of being raised by a scientist, I guess."

"What made you think of the Sea of Sand?"

"Eating from your fork. Mom and Dad used to do that all the time."

"Share their food with each other?"

Shelley nodded, her eyes still unfocused, her mind still in that incredibly vast sweep of country, the Sea of Sand, where only the hardiest and most careful survived. There was an austere magnificence to that land which still haunted her memory at odd moments. The Sea of Sand rolling golden to the horizon, wind-rippled dunes tiger-striped with velvet shadows. Silence as vast as the desert itself, an unearthly stillness where only the wind spoke in a husky whisper of sand sliding down the slipface of a dune.

In the long silence, Cain studied Shelley, watching memories like elusive cloud shadows change the appearance of her expressive face. He sensed a buried yearning in her, a longing for the wild places of the earth. It was a feeling he was familiar with. It had drawn him into some remote, dangerous and haunting places.

"Did you like the Sahara?" he asked.

"Yes," said Shelley simply. "There is a beauty there that is . . ." Her voice died. She spread one hand in a gesture of helplessness. She had no words to explain her response to the Sahara.

"I know," said Cain softly. "Landscapes of the soul."

Stunned by the accuracy of his perception, Shelley simply stared at Cain, caught in the clear depths of his eyes. Then she realized that her fingertips were resting on his palm, that even when she had been lost in her memories she had reached out to him as though she had a right to share his warmth, his life.

Landscapes of the soul.

She withdrew her hand, frightened by the depth of her sharing with Cain. He was a traveling man. He would take what she had and then he would leave. He would destroy everything that she had worked so long to build. Traveling men and homes didn't mix.

And a home was all she had.

"How old were you when you began to travel alone?" said Shelley, picking up her fork, her voice businesslike again.

Cain looked at the hand Shelley had touched. Slowly, his fingers curled over as though to shelter the warmth they had known. But his voice when he spoke was like hers, matter-of-fact and unemotional, despite the soul-deep hunger prowling through him with unsheathed claws.

"I hit the road right after college," he said. "I worked for a mineral survey outfit until I was married. She didn't want to travel, so I decided to stay home." Cain smiled sardonically. "I learned that being away doesn't make a wife cheat any more than staying at home ensures that she will be faithful. The time wasn't a total loss, though. I started my own business."

Shelley opened her mouth to ask about the business. What came out was, "Did you love her?"

"I was too young to know the difference between hormones and love." His mouth thinned. "Did you love him?"

"Who?"

"The one who taught you to hate traveling men."

Carefully, Shelley chewed a bit of salmon, wishing she had never brought up the subject of love and marriage and traveling men. Her innate sense of fairness told her that she had to answer, no matter how humiliating it might be to her.

"I thought I loved him," she said finally.

"And now?"

"Now I realize that it takes two people to make a home. He thought I'd be happy with a house to play in and meals to make and babies to dress up."

"You had children?"

"No." Shelley set aside her fork and took a sip of wine. "At the time, I told myself that it was because I wanted to finish college. That wasn't the whole truth, though."

"You didn't trust him," said Cain flatly.

"I didn't trust him," Shelley agreed.

"Then you didn't love him. Without trust, love just isn't possible." Cain hesitated. "How old were you?"

"Twenty."

"How old was he?"

"Twenty-nine." Then, before Cain could ask, Shelley said, "He was a sales rep for a large company."

What she didn't say, what she didn't need to say, was that her ex-husband had traveled a lot.

"How long had you been away from your parents when you got married?" asked Cain softly.

"Two years."

"Lonely?"

"As hell," said Shelley, her voice tight.

"Living in rented rooms, wanting a home of your own."

Shelley's fork struck the china with a clear, ringing sound. "Why ask questions when you already know all the answers?" she said fiercely.

Cain's long, hard fingers stroked lightly over her

clenched hand. "I was lonely when I got married, too. I wanted a home, too. Like you, I mistook one thing for another. Whatever either one of us had, it wasn't the kind of love you build a life on." Then, in the same quiet voice, he asked, "May I have a bite of that salmon?"

Automatically, Shelley offered Cain the piece of salmon that she had just slipped her fork under. His mouth opened, then his lips closed neatly over the tines. She felt the slight, sensual tug of resistance as she removed the fork from his mouth. The silver was gleaming, clean, and his eyes were watching her.

"Your dad was right," said Cain, his voice husky.

"What?" she asked, her attention still held by the chiseled male lines of Cain's mouth.

"Food tastes better from a woman's fork."

"Cain—"

"That's a very businesslike observation," he said smoothly. "It tells you that your dad and I have something in common. Do you want to write that down in your notebook?"

"I haven't agreed to work on your house," said Shelley, feeling trapped suddenly, frightened, angry. "I have more than enough work as it is."

Something in Cain's eyes changed, pupils dilating until his eyes were more steel than gray, more dark than light. "But you have to do my house," he said, his voice hard with conviction.

"Why?" she demanded.

"Because I'm a man who needs a home, and you're a woman who needs to make a home for me."

Shelley looked into Cain's changing gray eyes, now clear, now smoky, now silver, now almost black. Slowly, she realized just how much she wanted to work on Cain's home. He was too complex, too unique to summarize in a few standard *objets* and a framed oil. He offered a professional challenge that excited her. She knew that he was bent on seduction rather than homemaking, but that was hardly a new problem in her business. She had been chased by experts, and had concluded that while sex made the world go round for people like Brian and her ex-husband, she would rather curl up with a Sotheby catalog than a sweaty man. She was confident that she could keep Cain at bay long enough to answer the most interesting challenge anyone had ever offered her—to make a civilized, emotionally satisfying home for what she was quite certain was a largely uncivilized man who had found satisfaction only in seeing what was beyond the curve of the earth.

Silently, Shelley nodded her head.

Cain's answering smile contained such savage satisfaction that for a moment she almost regretted her decision. Then she reminded herself that she was safe. Cain was a traveling man. He wouldn't be around long enough to break her heart.

And then she wondered why the thought didn't comfort her.

Chapter 5

THE NEXT DAY SHELLEY INSPECTED CAIN'S RESIDENCE, A large penthouse atop a Century City highrise condominium. The view was limited only by the curve of the horizon or smog, whichever came sooner. Today the Santa Ana winds were blowing, bringing a desert clarity to Los Angeles Basin's sometimes murky air. The city surrounding the building was like a gently rumpled green and white tapestry thrown between the pale blue shimmer of the ocean and the cinnamon thrust of the San Gabriel mountains. The view was the only thing compelling about Cain's residence. The rest was expensive but not individual, done by a decorator who was both competent and unoriginal.

"Did you choose the colors?" asked Shelley, glancing at the stark white, black and oddly flat red color that dominated the living room.

"No. I just told the decorator that if there were any pastels I'd cut his fee in half."

"Yet you liked my house."

"You didn't have any pastels," said Cain, his voice slow and patient.

"Cream, buff, wheat, toast, sand, eggshell," Shelley said, ticking off colors quickly. "I have all of them in one room or another."

"Those are pastels?"

She turned quickly. Cain was watching her, a questioning look on his face. "When you say pastel, what do you mean?" asked Shelley.

"Pink, baby blue, lavender, that sort of thing."

"Easter egg colors."

"Yeah."

Shelley smiled. "You're right. They wouldn't suit you at all. Do you like this?" she asked, waving her hand at the living room.

"What do you think?"

"I think that if you were ever here for more than a few days at a time, you'd have the whole thing redone."

Cain smiled crookedly. "Know any good decorators? I can't stand the place after jet lag wears off," he admitted.

Frowning, Shelley thought of all the decorators she knew. Every one of them was excellent and not one of them would be right for Cain. "Me," she said finally, breaking her invariable rule about never becoming involved in paint chips and carpet samples. "That is, if you'd trust me," she added quickly. "I don't have any formal training."

"I'd trust you with anything I have."

The quiet statement startled Shelley. She looked up and found herself fascinated by Cain's changeable gray eyes. Against the bleak blacks and whites of the room, his eyes were alive with light, like fog just before the sun breaks through. He smiled gently, as though sensing her sudden uneasiness.

"Want to see the rest?" he asked.

Shelley accepted the change of subject gratefully. As she followed him through the penthouse, she mentally tried out different color schemes. By the time Cain led her back to the living room, she had decided upon subdued colors in a variety of textures, a natural background for the objets d'art she would add as finishing touches.

"You're frowning," said Cain. "Is it that bad?"

"I was just thinking of the turquoise tiles in the bathroom. The Jacuzzi is beautiful, and the sunken tub is big enough to swim in. I'd hate for you to go through the inconvenience and expense of replacing them just for the sake of color, but—"

"Do it. That particular shade of turquoise isn't one of my favorites. All I ask is that you get the contractor to do the work while I'm gone."

Shelley looked away before Cain could see the sudden downward turn of her mouth. "When will you be leaving?" she asked, her voice even.

"I'm not sure. I left a real mess up in the Yukon. Two of my mining engineers are arguing over Landsat interpretations, maps and ore samples. Both of them drink too much, and there's a woman, too," he added, raking his fingers through his hair.

"A woman who drinks too much?"

"No. A woman they're fighting over. Hell, she drinks, too." Cain sighed and raked his fingers through his sun-streaked hair again. "Compared to her, JoLynn looked like a piece of cake. Besides, Billy needed someone to look after him. Dave always took the brunt of JoLynn's behavior, protecting Billy. I'll stay here as long as I can."

"And then?" asked Shelley, walking over to the magnificent view.

"I'll come back as fast as I can."

Shelley said nothing.

"Seen enough?" asked Cain.

"Yes." Her voice was clipped.

He had the distinct feeling that she wasn't referring to the view, but to his lifestyle. "Shelley—"

"Call me before you fly out," she said professionally, cutting across his words. "If you leave me a key, I'll oversee the work here while you're gone."

"What if I don't leave? May I call you anyway?" Though the words were polite, Cain's tone was sardonic.

"Of course," she said, pulling her notebook out of her purse and making cryptic entries. "I'll want you to approve the paint and carpet samples. Then there's the question of furniture."

Cain's hand moved in a savage, cutting gesture. "Whatever works is fine with me. Just so it's big enough for me to be comfortable in."

When Shelley looked up from her notebook, her face was politely attentive and her eyes were very dark beneath the dense shadow of her lashes. "'Whatever works'?" she repeated. Then she shrugged elegantly. "Whatever you say, Cain. It's your home, after all."

"It's my *house*. A home is built with love, not paint and carpet samples."

"A home is also lived in. This"—the slender gold pen gleamed as Shelley waved her hand in a vague circle to indicate the penthouse—"is not."

In the silence, the click of Shelley's ballpoint pen was very loud. She returned pen and notebook to her purse and walked to the door.

"I'll call you when I have a selection of samples for you to choose from," she said, looking over her shoulder briefly.

"Not so fast, Miss Wilde."

Shelley hesitated. Then she turned fully around and waited. One mink brown eyebrow formed a questioning arch. "Yes, Mr. Remington?"

"I'm going to be with you every step of the way. Paint chips, carpet samples, panels of wallpaper, pieces of tile, the whole thing."

"I thought you trusted me," she said coolly.

"Oh, I do," he retorted, gliding toward her with his soundless stride. "I trust you to show me all the things this penthouse has been missing. Starting now."

For an instant, Shelley was sure that Cain was going to fold his arms around her and teach her again how unnerving a man's kiss could be. But he did not. He simply smiled and held out his arm. The extent of her disappointment dismayed her.

"Shall we?" he murmured.

"This," said Shelley, putting her arm through his and thinking of an endless row of color wheels and cloth swatches, "will bore the pants off you."

Cain's laugh ruffled her nerves. "I can't imagine that having my pants off around you would be boring."

A pale wash of rose heightened Shelley's color. She knew that she had to do something to diminish Cain's sensual heat, and her response to it. "Oh, but it would be," she said, her voice utterly neutral despite the heat staining her cheeks. "Ask my ex-husband."

Cain's arm tightened beneath Shelley's hand until his flesh felt as though it had been carved from wood.

"Are you trying to tell me something?" asked Cain.

"Think of it as a warning, Mr. Remington. I'll gild your house, but if you're expecting fireworks in the bedroom, you came to the wrong woman. Is that clear enough or should I set it in tile and put it in your hall entrance?"

"Did your ex-husband bore you with his pants off?" asked Cain politely.

Shelley said nothing.

"Can't remember?" offered Cain.

"What I do or do not remember about my marriage is none of your damn business," she said, remembering too much, too quickly, none of her usual defenses working.

"In short, you were bored," summed up Cain.

Shelley closed her eyes and tried to think of another description of how she had felt about her former husband's infrequent attempts to make love to her. From the start, his cutting comments about her small breasts and femininity in general had made her so self-conscious that passion had been all but impossible. The marriage counselor had told her that her husband's disparagement of her body was simply his way of dealing with his own feelings of inadequacy as a man.

Perhaps. And perhaps her husband had been right. Perhaps she simply wasn't much of a woman. After the divorce, she hadn't wanted to test the counselor's theory or her former husband's assertion. She had stayed well away from men in any but a business capacity. Until Cain came along, tempting her. And then frightening her with his temptations. What if her husband had been correct? What if she gave herself to Cain and he was disappointed? Or worse. Contemptuous. As her husband had been.

"Did I bore you, Shelley?"

Her eyes flew open. Cain was only inches away. The heat of his body radiated out to her in a tantalizing, immaterial caress. His eyes were heavy-lidded, intent, almost silver with suppressed emotion. The immense male vitality of him made her hunger for things she could not name.

"It would be impossible for you to ever bore a woman," whispered Shelley, her voice husky and almost sad.

"Tell that to my ex-wife." Shadows of emotion colored Cain's voice, fading echoes from a bitter past.

"At least," Shelley said tightly, looking from Cain's thick chestnut hair down the hard length of his body, "she couldn't complain about the basic equipment. Unless she was as blind as she was neurotic."

Cain looked startled, then speculative. "Was your husband?"

"Neurotic? In a man it's called something else. A need for variety."

"Was he blind, too?" asked Cain softly, his voice deep.

Shelley didn't bother to evade or to ask if Cain meant what she thought he did. She knew. And she knew that she was going to tell the truth. As her husband had taught her, there was nothing quite like a cold splash of truth to drain the heat from passion.

"He complained about the basic equipment." With an immense effort, Shelley shrugged lightly. "He had cause. I'm not Playmate of this or any other month."

"Is that what it took to turn him on? Measurements?"

The blunt question made Shelley wince. It sounded so much worse spoken aloud, even more harsh than her memories. Truth like ice water, chilling her. "Yes."

"Did *he* measure up?"

"Cain—" Shelley made a helpless gesture, regretting her idea of using truth like a weapon to defeat sensuality.

"Did he?" demanded Cain, but the fingertips tracing the line of her cheekbone were very gentle.

"Not with me," she said tightly. There was no color left in her face now, only memories, white and bloodless. "I'm told he was an upstanding regular on the singles bars circuit, though."

Cain's smile was almost cruel. "I wonder if he ever met my wife. God, I hope so. They were meant for each other.

Makes me wonder if Fate didn't mix up the cards a bit, dealing us exactly the wrong partners at the wrong time. We were both vulnerable as hell when we married, weren't we?''

''And dumber than a roomful of clams,'' added Shelley savagely, remembering her own naive dreams.

There was an instant of silence and then Cain exploded into laughter. He gathered Shelley against his chest and rocked slowly, laughing. She could no more resist his gentle, undemanding embrace than she could his deep laughter. Both surrounded her, sinking through protective layers that had been built over the lonely years. Laughter and gentleness and the sheer heat of Cain's body reached into Shelley, finding the woman buried beneath the shame and disappointment and fear. She hung onto him and laughed until she cried.

Then she simply hung onto him and cried.

''Even your tears are sweet,'' whispered Cain finally. His lips and the tip of his tongue took silver drops from her cheeks with feline neatness.

''Oh, Cain—what am I going—to do with you?'' asked Shelley between broken breaths, defenseless against the man who rocked her in his arms, a stranger no more.

''I have a few suggestions that would shock you.''

He looked down at her with an utterly male smile that made her want to cry again. Her laugh was as soft and broken as her crying had been.

''Cain, Cain,'' she whispered, holding him tightly, rocking him as he had rocked her, ''I'll only disappoint you.'' *And then,* she added silently, *you'll disappoint me. Traveling man, we're all wrong for each other*.

''Kissing you was the first thing in years that hasn't disappointed me,'' he murmured, rubbing his lips lightly, slowly, across hers. His tongue flicked out, tasting and adding to the moisture of her tears. "If I make you mad, will you stick out your tongue at me?" he asked hopefully.

The last of Shelley's tears vanished in quiet laughter. "You're a renegade," she accused, rubbing her cheek against the resilient muscles of his chest. "But a very gentle, very intelligent one," she added in a whisper.

Cain's hand fitted around her throat with exquisite care. Slowly, he tilted her face toward his lips. "I've never been accused of being gentle before. I like it." His lips moved softly over her mouth, the hollow beneath her cheeks, the gleaming darkness of her eyelashes still infused with tears. "I love the taste of you, Shelley," he whispered.

His arms slid down and tightened around her, holding her hips against his. There was no mistaking his intent or the extent of his arousal.

"I want to take off your clothes and taste all of you. I've never wanted to do that to a woman before." He looked down into the wide, dazed hazel eyes watching him with a combination of wariness and nascent desire. "I know," he said simply. "I know that it's too soon. But I want you to know what you do to me. I want you to think about it. I want you to know beyond any doubt how hungry you make me. You're the most exciting woman I've ever touched. Whatever lies that bastard husband of yours told you are in the past. We live in the present. And this isn't a lie."

Cain's mouth fastened over Shelley's parted lips. Slowly, inevitably, he took her mouth with slow strokes of his tongue. The sensual rhythm was reinforced by the equally slow movement of his hips against hers. After the first instant of shock, Shelley returned the kiss hesitantly, almost shyly. She felt the tiny tremor that ripped through Cain's strong body when her tongue moved against his. Knowing she had an effect on him was more heady than breathing heated cognac. Her arms crept around his neck as she stood on tiptoe, instinctively straining to match the soft fulfillment of her body to the hard hunger of his. He felt the change in her, felt the womanly promise of her caressing mouth and body. With a thick sound, he lifted one hand from her hip to her breast. Instantly she froze.

"No," she said, her voice raw as she tried to twist away.

"I'm not going to drag you into the bedroom," said Cain, moving his hand soothingly down Shelley's ribs to her waist, then slowly back up again. "I just want to touch you."

Her hand intercepted his. "No!"

"Why?" asked Cain softly, caught by the desperation in her voice.

"What I have in that department isn't worth fighting over. Take my word for it." Shelley's voice was as flat as the line of her mouth.

"I think," said Cain grimly, "that I'm hearing echoes of the past."

"Think what you like," snapped Shelley, stepping back and freeing herself with surprising strength. "The answer is still no."

Cain opened his mouth as though to argue, then thought better of it. His teeth clicked shut. He looked at her tight expression, saw her uneven breathing and remembered the exciting softness of her breast against his palm before she had twisted away from his touch.

"Am I likely to meet your former husband anytime soon?" asked Cain almost absently.

"Not unless you have business in Florida."

Cain flexed his hands. "It's just as well," he said. "I would probably lose my temper and cripple him."

The matter-of-fact statement shook Shelley as deeply as

Cain's kiss had. His predatory smile as he looked at his strong hands did nothing to make her feel more at ease.

"Cain?" she asked hesitantly, almost afraid.

Silence, then a long sigh. "It's all right. Wanton cruelty makes me angry, that's all."

"I didn't mean to be cruel," she whispered.

Cain's gray eyes widened in surprise. His expression changed, as gentle now as it had been savage a moment before. His fingertip traced the line of her mouth, and he smiled as he felt her lips soften beneath the caress. "Not you, little mink. That bastard you were married to. He did his best to ruin you, didn't he? And you know why?"

Numbly, Shelley shook her head, listening to Cain ask the question that had tormented her for a long, long time.

"Because you're all woman," said Cain quietly, "and your husband wasn't even half a man."

Tears magnified Shelley's luminous eyes. She knew that she was on the edge of crying again, and before today she had not cried since her husband's last, humiliating attempt to have sex with her.

"I think," said Cain, his voice husky, "it's time we look at paint chips. Either that, or I'll forget my good intentions."

Shelley blinked back tears and tried to smile. "You mean if I don't take you up on it right now, you'll wiggle out of having to look at all the boring samples?"

Slowly, he shook his head. "I mean that if I don't get you out of here right now, I'm going to take you down on this soft red carpet and teach you things about yourself and me that you just aren't ready to accept."

Shelley started to say again that Cain would be disappointed, then realized that her words would sound like a challenge or an invitation or both at once.

And he was right. She wasn't ready for anything more right then. And then she remembered that he was a traveling man and amended her thoughts. She wasn't ready for anything more from Cain, ever. Silently she opened the door and walked out of the penthouse she was going to transform into a home.

They took Shelley's car after she pointed out the hazards of parking the Jaguar on city streets and the impossibility of carrying samples on the motorcycle.

"Do you want to rent furniture?" asked Shelley as she pulled out into traffic.

"No. Rented things are for houses. This will be a home for me."

"Whenever you're here," she added, trying to keep the edge out of her voice.

"Whenever I'm here," agreed Cain, watching her intently. Then, "I own the company, Shelley. I can be wherever I please a lot of the time."

"And you please to roam," she said, her voice determinedly light, her eyes on the traffic. "I understand that. There are some beautiful places out there."

Cain listened to the unconscious softening of Shelley's voice and smiled with satisfaction. "You love them, too, don't you?"

"What?" asked Shelley, throwing a quick glance in his direction.

"The wild places of the earth. The Sea of Sand and the Pampas, the Outback and the Tibetan plateau, mountain ranges as tall as God and cities as old as time."

Shelley heard the resonance in Cain's voice, memories thickly layered, beauty haunting him, calling to him, making him roam.

Traveling man.

"I love my home more," she said. Her voice held a complex mixture of despair and fear, longing and desire, loneliness and hunger; and more, emotions as thickly layered in her voice as memories had been in his. "It's the only place I've ever really belonged."

He heard the accusation in her words, and the defiance. "Who told you that you can't have both a home and the world?" he asked, his voice mild.

"Life," she said succinctly.

Shelley downshifted and came to a smooth stop at a red light.

"Not everything you learn is true," pointed out Cain. "Look at what your husband taught you—a pile of crap if there ever was one."

"You can't be sure of that," she said, feeling cornered again, not wanting to talk about it.

"My wife tried to teach me the same thing."

"What?"

"That I was worthless as a lover," explained Cain matter-of-factly.

Shelley stared at him, her mouth half-open, disbelief clear in her expression. "It's a miracle you stopped laughing long enough to sign the divorce papers."

It was Cain's turn to be startled. Then he smiled slowly. "I take that as one hell of a compliment."

Shelley flushed and looked away. "It's the truth and you know it," she said grimly, sticking to her point.

"I didn't know it then. I went through a lot of women finding out what was true and what wasn't. You didn't do that, though."

"Go through women?" said Shelley flippantly. "No. I'm hopelessly old-fashioned in some ways."

Cain smiled but refused to be distracted from his pursuit

of Shelley's past. "You didn't go through men looking for your own truth."

It was a statement rather than a question, but Shelley answered anyway. "No."

"Old-fashioned or afraid?"

"Try finicky," she retorted.

"And just a bit afraid?" pressed Cain.

"Yes, damn you!" she said tightly, angry again. Then, savagely: "Are you satisfied now?"

"Far from it," he said, smiling slightly.

Shelley remembered the deep, rhythmic kiss they had shared and the hardness of his body moving against her. She bit her lip and looked away. "That's the problem with me and sex. No satisfaction for anyone involved." Her voice was bleak.

"Wrong. Your husband didn't have the first idea of what to do with a real woman. And," added Cain, his voice softening as he ran his fingertip down the tight line of her jaw, "I'm glad you're finicky, mink. Very glad."

A horn honked, telling Shelley that the light had turned green. She went through the intersection with unusual speed and a high flush on her cheeks. Determined to give Cain no more openings for too-personal conversation, she drove quickly to the Design Center, talking about colors and textures and light. Cain listened politely, commenting from time to time. As long as Shelley didn't look at him, she could maintain the illusion of having a businesslike exchange of views with a client. When she looked at him, though, his eyes and his mouth reminded her of all the feelings she was trying to forget.

It was with a sense of relief that Shelley pulled into the acres of parking surrounding the Trade Center. The Center itself was a huge, long, glass-walled building that held a

staggering variety of elegant, esthetically sophisticated
furniture. Every furniture designer who had aspirations to
national and international renown had a showroom in the
Center. A few of the designers did retail business out of the
Center. Most did not. That wasn't a problem for Shelley,
though. She had a wholesale license.

Two hours later, Cain dug in his heels and refused to look
at one more piece of furniture. He had seen hundreds of
things, each distinctive, each demanding attention, each
asserting a complex set of esthetic values.

"I feel like I've been on one of those European economy
tours of the great churches," he said flatly. "If you show
me one more chair, I'm going to turn into a babbling idiot."

Shelley smiled. "Good. Now you're ready to do some
serious shopping."

Cain stared. "Didn't you hear me? I'm burned out."

"Oh, I heard you. Did you hear me?"

"Is this some unsubtle form of torture?"

"Nope. It's some unsubtle way to get past the surface
and down to what really suits you. The way you feel now, if
anything catches your eye, it will be because it really speaks
to you."

Cain muttered something Shelley chose not to hear. Then
he sighed and followed her into the next showroom. By
5:00, they had been through every showroom at least once;
some they had gone through several times. Shelley's
notebook and pen had been in constant evidence, but Cain
hadn't objected. He knew that there had to be some way to
keep track of designers and colors and delivery dates.

And he had to admit that her technique was effective, if a
bit ruthless. After hours and hours of looking, he knew
instantly whether a piece of furniture could hold his
interest. He also knew which decorating effects were

merely spectacular and which had staying power for him. It was the same for colors and textures. Some combinations which at first appealed to him tended to pall on the third or fourth or fifth look. Others became more attractive each time he saw them. Cain's responses became reflexive, a visceral yes or no that had nothing to do with anything except his unique, personal taste.

"Mercy," groaned Cain at last.

"You're in luck," said Shelley. "They're closing up the building." She frowned. "I wish I'd taken time to measure the rooms in your penthouse."

"Do you need it to the inch?"

"No. But I can't decide between two or three groupings for your living room, and the bedroom might be too big for—"

"Twenty by thirty-five feet," yawned Cain.

"What?"

"The living room. The bedroom is fifteen by—"

Shelley got out her notebook and began writing hurriedly. When he was finished, she said, "You're sure?"

He smiled. "I'm an engineer. I've got an eye for measurements."

Shelley's pen paused, remembering how many kinds of "measurements" there were.

"You'd wear a size ten dress," said Cain, "except in the most expensive lines. Then it would be an eight. Same for your shoe size. Eight, that is." He assessed her figure with a sweeping glance. "You're about thirty-four twenty-four thirty-five. And," he continued, holding his hand out, looking at it, remembering, "you fit very sweetly in my palm. That means a nicely filled B-cup."

Shelley's head snapped up. "Stop it."

"Why? You're learning something, aren't you?"

"I know my own measurements."

"And now you know that you can trust my room measurements." Cain's smile was challenging. "Right?"

Shelley closed her notebook so hard that the pages slapped distinctly as they met. "I have some furniture to order. Why don't you settle in over there and wait for me?" she suggested, gesturing toward an unusual display.

Cain looked over his shoulder and saw a rack, a stock, an Iron Maiden and a bed of nails that a whimsical furniture designer had used to show what should be avoided in the name of human comfort. He chuckled and threw up his hands.

"I confess. Whatever it is, I'll confess to anything. Except"—he grabbed her—"lying. I never lie. You fit perfectly in my palm."

Cain's kiss was both gentle and hot, as were the hands sliding down Shelley's back to her waist. He released her so quickly that she didn't have time to object.

"Don't be long," he said. "We have reservations for dinner."

"Dinner?" she asked, feeling off-balance, caught between objection and response, able to express neither.

"At the beach. With Billy. Don't worry," Cain added, yawning unselfconsciously. "JoLynn won't be around."

"I can hold my own with her," retorted Shelley, remembering JoLynn's face when Shelley had described touching Cain as very much like touching Squeeze.

"I know." Cain waited until Shelley had turned and walked several steps before he said, "I'm glad you think I feel like Squeeze—strong and warm and hard."

Shelley's steps hesitated for an instant as she realized that JoLynn must have told Cain what had happened. She glanced quickly at him, just long enough to see the male smile on his beautiful mouth. She turned away with a rush. Her heels made a distinct, determined clicking sound in the hallway. Like her heartbeat, her steps accelerated without her conscious awareness.

Though only silence and the memory of Cain's smile followed Shelley, she felt pursued.

Chapter 6

THE SEA ROLLED TOWARD SAND THAT HAD BEEN TURNED A deep gold by the descending sun. Though sunset was hours away, the light was dense, almost tangible, touching even the most mundane things with magic and myth. A child's abandoned, half-buried plastic bucket became a wide crescent of lapis lazuli set in rough gold. Tiny stranded jellyfish became moonstones cut *en cabochon*, gleaming with mystery and riches. Rocks became ebony sculptures, enigmatic faces appearing and disappearing with each wave, each shift of light.

There were few people on the beach at the moment, though the sand had been churned by the passage of countless feet during the day, causing miniature dunes and velvet shadow creases that recalled the epic dunes of the Sahara. The sea itself was an iridescent blue that was almost tropical in its intensity.

Shelley looked over the tips of her sandy toes and
watched Billy and Cain body-surf. Despite Cain's protesta-
tions that it had been years since he had played with Pacific
waves, it was obvious that he was more than holding his
own. He caught wave after wave, riding them with little
more than his powerful shoulders showing above the
heaped foam of the breaking water. Billy stayed right beside
him, his slender body making up in determination what it
lacked in power or skill.

Nearby Shelley a fire crackled within a ring of stones.
Hot dog time was at hand. She stretched and listened to her
stomach rumble, but felt too lazy to do anything about it.
The low, rhythmic voice of the surf had unraveled her,
leaving behind only a desire to burrow into the warm sand
and watch the magnificent light flow over land and water
and Cain, transforming them.

As Cain rose from the white remains of a wave, he
looked like a god cast in pure gold. Muscles in his calves
and thighs flexed rhythmically, carrying his hard body with
a grace that made Shelley stare without realizing it. He
radiated vitality as surely as the sun radiated heat. Water
like golden tears ran down his body, burnishing every line
of muscle and sinew, limning him with liquid fire.

Shelley wondered how it would feel to flow like water
over his body, to know him as intimately as the sea did,
touching all of him. The thought made her breath hesitate,
then quicken in time with her own heartbeat. She had never
wanted to know a man's body like that, completely,
curiosity and passion rising equally within her. Would he
like to be touched that intimately? Would he allow her
fingertips and palms and lips, her teeth and tongue to learn
all of him? Would his inner thighs be as sensitive as hers?
Would his nipples harden beneath her caress? Would he

enjoy being stroked, arching into her touch like a great cat? Would she be able to bring him to the height of need— and then would she be woman enough to answer that need?

Fear and sensual hunger warred within Shelley. She closed her eyes, but still she saw Cain walking toward her, each movement of his body a separate seduction. Other men she had known had been more conventionally handsome or more socially polished, bigger or smaller or more physically perfect. None had been more intelligent, more perceptive, quicker. No man had ever called to her mind and body as Cain did. No man had made her want to abandon fear and memories of humiliation and give herself to him. No man had made a satin flower begin to bloom inside her body, petal after soft, hot petal unfolding, heat deepening until— what? What would happen if she gave in to the liquid sensations that both frightened and compelled her, whispering to her that she knew little about the incandescent possibilities of her own body.

"Wake up, mink. It's dinner time, and you promised to be the cook."

Shelley opened her eyes and then wished that she hadn't. Cain was standing next to her, so close that she could have turned her head and licked golden drops of water from his leg. The temptation to do just that shocked her. She tried to look away from the water-darkened hair and well-defined muscles of his calf, but her glance simply went higher. She remembered the hardness of his thighs as he had pressed against her; and another, more urgent hardness. Almost desperately she looked away from the dripping navy swim trunks that barely concealed Cain's masculine power. The curling line of dark hair that appeared above the waistline of his swimsuit and then fanned into a wedge-shaped mat across his chest did nothing to cool her thoughts. She wanted to rub her cheek against his chest, to seek the skin beneath the male pelt with nails and tongue, touching him.

Shelley realized that she had been staring at Cain's body far too long. She looked up and saw the sensuality darkening his eyes.

"Do you know what I'd like to do?" Cain asked softly.

Shelley shook her head, incapable of speech, for her heart was crowding against her throat, blocking it.

He sank slowly to his knees in the sand, but he did not touch her. He didn't trust himself to. He had seen her hunger and approval as she had looked at him, and he wanted nothing more than to run his fingers beneath the maddening French cut of her bathing suit and caress her deeply, discovering if her body was half as ready as her eyes had been.

"I'd like to show you how beautiful you are to me," said Cain, his voice both soft and rough.

One long-fingered hand wrapped around both Shelley's wrists. Slowly he raised her arms over her head.

"Billy will—" Shelley said desperately.

"He's playing in the waves. Even if he looked this way, he couldn't see through me." Cain's eyes moved from Shelley's face to her slender neck to the gentle swell of her breasts. Slowly, his free hand followed the line of his gaze, approaching her breasts with gentle inevitability.

"Cain—you can't!" said Shelley, realizing that he was going to touch her and this time she wouldn't be able to prevent it.

"Oh, but I can," he countered. "Scream if you like," he offered, running his fingernails lightly over the smooth garnet fabric that was drawn taut over her ribs. "I'll explain to Billy how ticklish you are." His hand hesitated just short of intimacy. "Unless you'd rather explain to me why you don't like having your breasts touched."

"You know why," she said, seething with a combination of embarrassment and anger.

"All men aren't like your ex-husband, Shelley." Cain's fingers moved in a light, maddening circle around her breast, just avoiding the soft flesh. But as he spoke, the circle became smaller, and then smaller. "Some of us prefer quality to quantity. And," he added, smiling at her gently, "if you don't believe me, ask a baby. Any more than a mouthful is wasted." Cain's hand closed around Shelley, caressing her. "Definitely more than a mouthful," he said. Then, groaning, "God, how I would love to prove it!"

Shelley felt the desire that went through Cain like an electric current, shaking him. He closed his eyes and turned away for a moment, but his hand still caressed her. An involuntary shiver took her, arching her into his touch. He made a deep sound of pleasure as he felt her nipple tighten. He slipped his fingers beneath the suit.

"Hush, little mink," he murmured when she would have objected. He captured the tip of her breast with caressing fingertips. "Billy is out there waiting for a wave and nobody else is around. Let me show you how little size counts between a man and a woman. Just for a few moments—"

Shelley gasped as she felt her breast released from the garnet cloth. She felt helpless, wholly vulnerable, afraid.

"Don't," she pleaded.

"You little fool," Cain breathed, admiring the pale, smooth breast and its dark rose peak. "Don't you know how perfect you are?"

She shivered at the brush of his mustache against her nipple. Then she heard Cain whispering against her skin, felt the heat of his breath caressing her, but most of all she felt the desire that had tightened his body like a bow. He had meant every word he said, and his body was proving it in the most unmistakable way. A hot flower began unfolding deep inside her, melting her inhibitions.

"I shouldn't," Cain said, lifting his head slightly, his eyes fastened on the ruby-tinted nipple, "but I have to. Forgive me, Shelley. Just one taste. Please."

His hand closed more tightly around her wrists, though she hadn't struggled since she had felt the exciting caress of his mustache. His head bent again. She felt his breath wash over her sensitive flesh, then the tip of his tongue traced a circle where the silk of her breast became the textured darkness of her nipple. She shivered beneath the hot touch of his tongue. Unknowingly she made a small, pleading sound, but it was not for freedom. It was for greater intimacy, a deeper holding. He answered by imprisoning her within the changing pressures of tongue and teeth, drawing her deeply into the caressing heat of his mouth until she arched beneath him and cried out her pleasure.

With a feeling like he was tearing off his own skin, Cain forced himself to release her breast. The peak glistened with moisture, a ruby hardness that flaunted her arousal. His teeth closed over her erect nipple with a fiercely restrained sensuality that made Shelley twist against him, increasing the pressure of his touch. Cain groaned and turned his head aside. He pulled her bathing suit back into place with fingers that shook. He released her wrists and gathered her against his body, letting her feel the evidence of his own arousal.

"Any more questions about what it takes to turn this man on?" asked Cain, his voice ragged.

"N-no." Like Shelley's body, her voice trembled.

"Good, because I'm about an inch from taking you right here, right now, and answering a few questions of my own."

Cain rolled aside and to his feet in a single motion. He ran down to the water, throwing himself into the waves in a long, low dive. Shelley lay motionless, too weak to move, passion like a drug in her body, outlining her nerves with fire. The breast that Cain had kissed ached sweetly, still hungry for his knowing mouth.

With a small sound she rolled over, fighting for control of her own body. She had had so little experience with passion that she felt like a stranger caught inside a network of fire, her own nerves burning her alive. After a few minutes the trembling finally stopped and the hot flower inside her folded in upon itself, hiding its satin heat deep within her. Taking a long, ragged breath, she went to work on dinner.

By the time Billy and Cain came in from the water, Shelley had set out relishes, soft drinks and potato chips and was turning a long-handled fork loaded with hot dogs over the dancing yellow flames. Except for an occasional tremor whenever she remembered Cain's touch, she was in control of herself again. The fire was cooler than her memories, though, and much cooler than Cain's eyes as he watched her bend over the flames.

"You should have come in," said Billy, scattering sand and cold drops of water with equal enthusiasm. "The waves were perfect and the water was really warm. At least seventy, I'll bet."

"Not as warm as my pool," said Shelley, putting a hotdog into a toasted bun.

"You have a pool?"

"Complete with its own waterfall."

Billy slathered mustard and catsup over the innocent hot dog. "Waves?" he asked slyly.

"Only when I do a cannonball."

Billy looked at Shelley's slender body and shook his

head. "You need more weight to do a good cannonball. You're too—"

"Skinny?" suggested Shelley with a wry twist to her mouth.

"You're just right for you," said Billy, biting into his hot dog with enthusiasm. "Any more and you'd droop at the edges, like Mother between diets."

Cain made a heroic effort not to laugh. It didn't work. He concentrated on rummaging in the ice chest for beer while his shoulders shook with suppressed laughter. When he glanced up, Shelley couldn't evade his brilliant gray eyes and the silent message: *I told you so.* She felt color climbing hotly in her cheeks and then she started laughing, too.

Billy looked up from his incredibly messy hot dog, smiled, and attacked the oozing remains. Then, with perfect nonchalance, he proceeded to eat three more, plus a whole bag of chips and three soft drinks. Shelley watched the lanky boy in stunned surprise. She looked away only long enough to refuse Cain's offer of a third hot dog.

"No, thanks," she said, smiling. "I wouldn't want to, er, droop."

After dinner, Cain pulled a Frisbee out from under his beach towel and faced his companions with a challenging smile. Billy jumped up immediately, his face alight with anticipation. Shelley was slower, but still game. The three of them fanned out in an unequal triangle, giving Cain the longest throw. Cain brought his bent arm across his body at waist level, then quickly straightened his arm and snapped his hand forward. The white Frisbee sailed straight and clean to Billy, who scooped it up and sent it flying toward Shelley. She surprised them by snatching it out of the air and sending it in a flat, sizzling curve to Cain. Billy gave a whoop of admiration and a thumbs-up signal.

The three of them settled in and ran one another ragged. Shelley laughed and jumped and sprinted, feeling like a child herself until Cain leaped high to catch the elusive Frisbee. For an instant his sun-burnished body defied gravity. When the instant passed, he landed lightly on the sand. His body coiled around the Frisbee and then suddenly released it in a powerful male surge that made her mouth go dry.

The Frisbee flew like an eccentric moon orbiting among three planets. Around them, surrounding them with light and color, southern California's huge summer sun settled slowly toward the water. Finally it was too dark to judge the Frisbee's flight with any accuracy. Cain leaped high into the air, rescuing the Frisbee from certain drowning in the rushing indigo sea. Shelley knew she would remember that moment the rest of her life—Cain's coordination, his strength and grace suspended against the subtly radiant twilight like a wave before the instant of breaking, and then the inevitable descent, as smooth and powerful as the ocean itself.

"Great catch, Uncle Cain!" shouted Billy.

Cain waved the Frisbee, but did not release it again. Instead, he walked toward Shelley, watching her with eyes the color of twilight. He held out his hand and she took it without hesitation. The warmth of his fingers threading through hers made her whole body tighten with pleasure.

"Graceful as a mink, too," murmured Cain, giving Shelley a look of approval that was a caress in itself.

"Uncle Cain?" called Billy. "Just a few more?"

"Marshmallow time," said Cain.

His voice carried clearly across the twilight, but his look told Shelley that he wanted her more than any dessert. They designated Billy the official toaster and ate the charred results without a whimper. Shelley knew that she wouldn't have cared if she were eating sand. All she could taste was the memory of Cain's tongue moving over hers. All she could feel was the memory of his mouth on her naked breast. The heat radiating from his body next to hers was a revelation, like touching a gently burning sun.

"Cold?" asked Cain, seeing Shelley shiver.

"With you so close?" she said softly. "Impossible."

His hand touched her cheek in a brief caress. She knew as clearly as if he had shouted it that he wanted to wrap his warmth around her, hold her. Just hold her. When he put his arm across her shoulders and cradled her against his body, Shelley knew an irresistible sense of homecoming. She put her cheek on his shoulder and relaxed against his strength.

"More?" asked Billy, looking up from his most recent incendiary efforts.

"No, thanks," said Shelley.

"Uncle Cain?"

"No way," he said, laughing quietly. "My mustache will never come unstuck as it is."

"Try lighter fluid," offered Billy. "It works on bubble gum, anyway." He hesitated, looking at the half-filled bag of marshmallows. "You guys sure you don't want any more?"

"We're sure," said Cain and Shelley together.

"OK."

Calmly, Billy began stuffing marshmallows onto the fork, eating one raw for every one he planned to cook. It became obvious that he didn't intend to stop until he reached the bottom of the bag. Shelley made an involuntary sound of dismay.

"Don't worry," said Cain. "I used to do the same thing when I was his age. I survived."

"Who held your head?" asked Shelley dryly.

She felt the vibration of his silent laughter beneath her cheek. "No one. Seth always made it clear that damn fools cleaned up after themselves."

"Have you told Billy?"

Though Shelley's voice was deliberately soft, Billy heard. He looked up from the fire and grinned. "The first thing Uncle Cain said when he asked me on the picnic was that he wouldn't tell me what to eat if I wouldn't expect him to play nurse afterward."

"Was your mother in on the bargain?"

Instantly, Shelley wished that she had bitten her tongue. The relaxation and pleasure vanished from Billy's face, replaced by a mask that was too emotionless to belong to a child.

"Mother has a party in San Francisco. She won't be back tonight."

"Billy agreed to babysit me," said Cain easily. "He knows that I'm not used to big city life. In exchange, I'm going to take him out on his dirt bike as soon as I find a good place."

"There are some rough dirt roads near my home," said Shelley. "Old fuel breaks and such. I've seen trail bikes out there before. Is that the kind of thing you want?"

The mask fell away as Billy looked eagerly toward Cain. He smiled. Shelley felt Cain's approval in the subtle caress of his fingers along the inside of her arm.

"Sounds perfect," Cain said.

"Oh, boy! Tomorrow?"

"Sure," said Cain, smiling.

"Just be sure you have spark guards on," said Shelley, "or whatever they call them. You know—the gizmo that keeps exhaust sparks from setting fires. The brush is dry at this time of year."

"Billy?" asked Cain.

"Dad wouldn't let me out of the garage without a spark arrester. And a regulation muffler," grumbled Billy, "even though it cuts down on the power."

"Then all we need is another bike for Shelley," said Cain.

"Wrong," she said quickly. "I'm strictly passenger material, and on city streets at that. You'll be better off without me."

Cain's fingers tightened on Shelley's arm. His head bent until his lips brushed her ear. "There's no way I'd be better off without you," he murmured too softly for Billy to hear above the crackle of flames.

"Billy needs a little undivided 'man' time," whispered Shelley, rubbing her cheek lightly against Cain. "But," she said in a normal tone, "I'll be glad to feed the conquering heroes. What's your favorite dinner, Billy?"

"Fried chicken, mashed potatoes, gravy and chocolate cake," said Billy quickly, then added, "If it isn't too much trouble."

Shelley tried not to smile at his hopeful expression. "Not at all. How about you, Cain? Any additions?"

"Fresh lemonade."

She gave him a startled look.

"There aren't many lemon trees in the Yukon," explained Cain.

There was a sudden flare of light as Billy's forgotten marshmallows burned like a cascade of falling stars. After a few futile attempts to blow out the fire, Billy jumped up and ran down to the water, waving the marshmallow fork around like a sword. The impromptu torch burned brightly against the black sea. Sounds of a fierce battle floated back as Billy slew dragon after dragon.

"That's quite a nephew you have," said Shelley, laughing softly at Billy's fiery antics.

"Yes," Cain said simply, bending to brush his lips over Shelley's hair. "And you're quite a woman. Can you ride a dirt bike?"

"It's been a long time. When I first came here, I couldn't afford a car, so I bought a motorcycle. Sometimes I kind of miss it. Especially when it isn't raining and I don't have to show up looking like a fashion plate for an appointment."

"Billy wouldn't mind if you came along tomorrow."

Shelley shook her head, sending a fall of silky hair over Cain's arm. "I don't know anything about off-road biking except that it takes more skill and strength than city streets. Besides, he's really enjoying a chance to get to know his uncle. You're a hero to him. You can see it in his eyes when he watches you."

A long finger caressed Shelley's jawline before settling under her chin, tilting her face toward Cain's lips. The kiss was gentle, a butterfly touch of warmth and sweetness.

"Normally," said Cain in a husky voice, "I'd be delighted to have Billy around. He's good company. But I was hoping to take you home tonight. And keep you. Then JoLynn told me it didn't matter what time I brought Billy back after the picnic. She'd be gone, and the maid would let him in." Cain's mouth hovered just above Shelley's. His lips touched hers lightly between words. "I keep telling myself that it's just as well, too soon for you to accept me as a lover, but I feel like I've always known you, always laughed with you, always missed you, always cared for you, always wanted you."

Shelley kissed Cain as gently as he had kissed her, moving her lips lightly around the edges of his beautifully shaped mouth, feeling a need to give warmth to him that had nothing to do with passion or desire. She wanted to touch him with her mind, but could not, so she gave him back the exquisitely tender caresses he had given to her. She had never kissed a man like that before, a sweet sharing of self that was as deeply moving in its own way as passion had been earlier.

It was the same when Cain walked Shelley to her front door. He held her as though she were more fragile than a butterfly's wing, and his lips were very gentle over hers.

"Tomorrow," he said, his deep voice husky.

"Come early," she said, running a fingertip over his soft mustache. "You can go swimming before dinner."

"I feel as though I'm drowning now," he whispered. "Will you save me?"

"Cain . . ."

"Thank you," he murmured, taking Shelley's mouth as gently as he had taken her lips.

He touched the tip of his tongue to hers, felt her shiver at the caress, tasted her sweetness as she touched him in return. Warm and soft, trembling in his arms, she made him want to worship and ravish her at the same time, to protect her from any harm and to crush her body to his with every bit of strength he had. There was paradox in his feelings, but no conflict; he wanted her in every way it was possible for a man to want a woman.

And he knew that she did not want him in the same way. Not yet. At some level she was still afraid of herself and of him. Traveling man.

"Tomorrow," said Cain, slowly releasing her.

Shelley watched him walk back to the car where Billy waited. Tomorrow had never seemed farther away.

Normally, Shelley spent Saturdays attending auctions or rummaging among the new catalogs that poured into the Gilded Lily during the week. There were no auctions this week, however. The business was entering its fall decline.

The nadir would be reached in December. Then, about the second week in January, everyone realized that the holidays were over and it was time to get back to work.

Shelley went restlessly through the house Saturday morning, wondering how to fill the hours until Cain came back into her life. There was no point in vacuuming, for the cleaners had come not two days ago. There was nothing new to add to her home; it was finished, perfect, complete unto itself. It was too soon to go swimming and too late to putter in the garden. The art catalogs that she had been itching to go through a few days ago now seemed uninteresting. She flipped through one of the glossy books with the distinct feeling that she had seen all of its treasures many times before.

When the phone rang, Shelley reached for it with a sense of relief.

"Hello?"

"Shelley? Cain. Look, I've got to talk fast before Billy comes back. Dave called this morning. It's Billy's birthday. Could you surprise him and add ice cream and candles to tonight's menu?"

"Sure," said Shelley, delighted. "Does he need anything else? What time will you be here? Does he have any friends he'd like to invite?"

"We'll keep it simple this time. Oops, here he comes. I miss you, mink."

Cain hung up before Shelley could answer. She stared at the phone for a moment, hearing the echoes of his deep voice. *Mink*. Did she really seem like that to him, soft and wild?

Smiling, Shelley started making a shopping list in her head. Her first stop was Billy's house. Lupe, the maid, recognized Shelley's business card, let her in and went back to cleaning silverware. For the sake of appearances Shelley made a lightning tour of the house, but she concentrated on Billy's room.

A quick look at his overflowing closet told her that clothes wouldn't be on Billy's birthday list. His record collection was equally intimidating. If quantity alone hadn't warned off Shelley, the boggling album covers would have. After reading the names and looking at the photos, she couldn't imagine what the music would sound like. Elephants mating, perhaps. During a volcanic eruption.

Feeling well out of her depth, Shelley turned toward the software stacked on top of the computer. She felt more comfortable with the computer. She had just finished gilding the home of an electronics freak, using everything from framed "first editions" of software to framed promotional posters from computer conventions. Notebook in hand, Shelley flipped through the contents of Billy's software pile, writing down the titles of games. Then she turned toward the bookcase that was supporting the languid turtle's home. She had read enough science fiction herself to recognize authors' names. Not surprisingly, Billy showed a distinct preference for sword and sorcery epics. He also had gravitated toward the better writers within that specialty. She noted the gaps in his collection of favorite authors.

With a feeling of triumph, Shelley discovered that Billy had only one of the many surprisingly good science fiction art books that were available. The fact that Billy's art book had been given a place of prominence and showed every appearance of being well thumbed told her that Billy enjoyed it.

Humming "Happy Birthday," Shelley let herself out of JoLynn's perfect house and drove to a bookstore that specialized in science fiction and fantasy. Next to it was a store that concentrated on role-playing games such as

Dungeons and Dragons. The game store caught her interest because it had a cunning window display of gleaming lead miniatures. Dragons, knights, trolls and assorted monsters guaranteed to delight a genially bloodthirsty imagination were all locked in death battles beneath the clear southern California sun.

The centerpiece was eighteen inches of shining silver dragon that looked both graceful and deadly. Unlike the miniatures, the dragon had been cast with a loving attention to detail that showed in the intricate patterns of each scale and the polished, deadly curve of tooth and claw. Whoever had created the dragon had a working knowledge of art as well as anatomy and myth. Light shimmered over the creature in rhythmic patterns, as though the dragon were slowly breathing.

A few minutes later, Shelley had the name and number of the artist as well as the dragon itself. The name and number were for future Gilded Lily customers. The dragon was for Billy.

The bookstore had everything Shelley thought Billy might want, and more. In the end, she bought several of the irresistible art books, an illustrated collection of Billy's favorite author's work, and a few other paperbacks. Just as she was getting ready to leave, she spotted an unusual painting tucked away in the corner. Vivid, almost surreal in its clarity, the painting depicted the universe as seen from the center of the Milky Way Galaxy. An ocean of stars swirled in cosmic currents across the sky, pulled by tides undreamed of by man. Vague faces and alien places seemed to coalesce out of the primordial star sea, possibilities turning and then returning with each shift of attention, each blink of the eye.

Transfixed, Shelley stood in front of the painting. When she finally could force her attention away, she went back to the store owner, determined to buy the painting despite the fact that it bore no superficial resemblance to anything in her home. The painting was like a window looking into a limitless, extraordinary future, challenging and seducing her at the same time, demanding that she look up from her comfortable life and acknowledge an expanding universe of possibilities.

Dragon under one arm, fantasy books under the other and a universe clutched in both hands, Shelley walked back to the parking lot, bemused to find herself in a world that looked the same as when she had left it less than an hour ago.

Chapter 7

SHELLEY WAS STRETCHED OUT ON THE CHAISE LOUNGE BY the pool, a bowl of fresh greenbeans resting on her stomach. Lazily, she snapped off the top and bottom of each bean, tossed the rejected bits back into the metal bowl, and then broke the remainder of the bean into bite-size pieces which went into a second bowl on the ground beside her. She was half asleep, wholly under the spell of the waterfall at the end of the pool. The waterfall spoke in husky, tumbling syllables, promising relief from the heat that welled up from the wild ravine below her house, a summer's worth of hot sunlight radiating back through pungent chaparral.

Cain and Billy chased each other through the clear depths of the pool, leaving silver trails of bubbles behind. When Billy surfaced, his cupped hand sent a fountain of water flying to the point where he thought Cain would come up. Then, laughing aloud with glee, Billy dove again, eluding the quick, powerful man who somehow never managed to catch him.

Smiling, eyes closed, Shelley fished among the bowl of unsnapped beans. With languid motions she selected a bean by touch, prepared it the same way and dropped the pieces in the bowl on the flagstones. She sensed as much as felt the sudden depression of the lounge cushion as something settled ever so lightly next to the bowl of unbroken beans. Sighing, eyes still closed, she searched for a U-shaped bean, knowing from experience that Nudge liked the curvy ones best.

Nudge bumped her head against Shelley's hand, urging her to make her choice quickly.

"Here you are," said Shelley, holding out a curled bean on her palm.

Nudge scooped up the bean in her mouth, jumped lightly to the ground and began to bat the inoffensive vegetable around the flagstones. Without opening her eyes Shelley smiled, knowing what the cat was doing. Nudge had conceived an odd passion for greenbeans as a kitten. She hadn't outgrown it.

The cushion gave slightly again. The bowl of greenbeans on Shelley's stomach shifted under another gentle nudge.

"Back so soon?" murmured Shelley, eyes still closed. "What happened? Did you knock the poor bean into the pool and drown it?"

The bowl slid to one side. "Nudge!" gasped Shelley, eyes flying open as she grabbed for the bowl. "Watch it!"

"Not Nudge," said a deep voice. "Squeeze."

Cool, wet arms wrapped around Shelley, lifting her from the chaise. The metal bowl tipped upside down onto the flagstones with a clear, ringing sound. Cain squeezed gently, pulling Shelley against his chest. She felt the heat of him beneath the evaporating water, saw sunlight glittering in the drops caught amid the burnished golds and browns of his chest hair, and wondered if the drops would taste warm or cool, sweet or saline. Slowly, almost helplessly, Shelley turned her head and licked up a single drop of water from Cain's chest. She felt the tightening of muscles that went through his whole body.

"I wish to God," he said huskily, "that we were alone."

"I'm sorry," whispered Shelley, flushing. "I didn't stop to think."

"I know. That's what made it so damn sexy."

Startled, Shelley looked into the face that was very close to hers. The subtle tones of blue in Cain's eyes were more pronounced beneath the open sky, making his irises a pale, silvery azure that shifted color with each movement of his head. Now almost blue, now nearly transparent, now silver, now darkening to steel gray as the pupils expanded; Cain's eyes fascinated her.

"Your eyes are as beautiful as your mouth," said Shelley, thinking aloud. Then she realized that she had done it again, acted without thinking. "Sorry," she said, closing her eyes. "You have a drastic effect on my self-control."

"I think," said Cain distinctly, "that we both need a bit of cold water."

"The pool is ninety-two," she muttered.

"That's a hell of a lot colder than either one of us right now."

In three strides Cain was at the edge of the pool. The fourth stride took him into the deep end near the waterfall, still firmly holding Shelley. While the initial burst of bubbles shielded them from Billy's sight, Cain took Shelley's mouth in a hard, quick kiss. Then he pushed up from the bottom of the pool in a powerful surge that brought both of them shooting back into the air. The first thing Shelley

You know the thrill of escaping to a world of Love and Romance as it is experienced by real men and real women...

Escape again...with 4 FREE novels and

**get more great Silhouette Intimate Moments novels
—for a 15-day FREE examination—
delivered to your door every month!**

Silhouette Intimate Moments offers you romance for women...not girls. It has been created especially for the woman who wants a more intense, passionate reading experience. Every book in this exciting series promises you romantic fantasy...dynamic, contemporary characters...involving stories...intense sensuality...and stirring passion.

Silhouette Intimate Moments may not be for everyone, but if you're the kind of woman who wants more romance in her life, they will take you to a world of *real* passion, *total* involvement, and *complete* fulfillment. Now, every month you can thrill to the kind of romance that will take your breath away.

FREE BOOKS

Start today by taking advantage of this special offer—the 4 newest Silhouette Intimate Moments romances (a $10.00 Value) *absolutely FREE,* along with a Cameo Tote Bag. Just fill out and mail the attached postage paid order card.

AT-HOME PREVIEWS, FREE DELIVERY

After you receive your 4 free books and Tote Bag, every month you'll have the chance to preview 4 more Silhouette Intimate Moments novels *—before they're available in stores!* When you decide to keep them, you'll pay just $9.00, (a $10.00 Value), *with never an additional charge of any kind and with no risk!* You can cancel your subscription at any time simply by dropping us a note. In any case, the first 4 books, and Tote Bag are yours to keep.

EXTRA BONUS

When you take advantage of this offer, we'll also send you the Silhouette Books Newsletter free with each shipment. Every informative issue features news on upcoming titles, interviews with your favorite authors, and even their favorite recipes.

Get a Free Tote Bag, too!

EVERY BOOK YOU RECEIVE WILL BE A BRAND-NEW FULL-LENGTH NOVEL!

Escape with 4 Silhouette Intimate Moments novels (a $10.00 Value) and get a FREE Tote Bag, too!

saw was Billy's anxious face as he leaned toward her from the side of the pool.

"I told him not to get your hair wet! You aren't mad, are you?" Billy asked, his voice anxious and his expression telling her that he was afraid that the day had been spoiled.

Shelley knew in that instant that Billy was expecting her to be angry. Her next thought was that JoLynn would have been furious if her careful appearance were marred by a casual dunking in the pool. Shelley smiled up at Billy as she slung dripping lengths of hair out of her eyes and swam lazily to his side of the pool.

"I don't get mad," she said. "I get even."

With no more warning than that, she grabbed Billy's wrist and pulled him into the pool. He surfaced with a delighted grin. A three-cornered, wildly unstructured game of tag ensued. The shouts and laughs, splashes and thrashing limbs attracted Nudge's predatory attention. She paced around the pool, following the action avidly, ducking her head when random jets of water squirted her way.

When no one had breath left for tag, Billy suggested a few rounds of Blind Man's Bluff. He even volunteered to be It. Shelley and Cain evaded Billy for a while, until Cain winked at her and "accidentally" splashed noisily. Billy lunged, grabbed Cain's arm and pronounced his uncle It. After a decent interval, Cain caught a giggling Billy, who caught a giggling Shelley. They traded being It until Billy began to get bored. Then Cain allowed himself to be caught. He and Billy whispered for a minute before Cain closed his eyes, counted to ten very slowly, and began to search for victims.

Shelley watched through half-closed eyes, squinting against the late afternoon sun. Cain moved easily in the water, making no unnecessary noises, his arms spread wide to sweep as much of the pool as possible. Billy submerged silently, swam under water toward the deep end of the pool and then slipped out onto the flagstones under cover of the waterfall's gentle splashings. He put his fingers over his lips and tiptoed toward the house. With great stealth he opened and closed the door, leaving Shelley alone in the pool with Cain.

Shelley tried to be as quiet as Billy, but she was in the middle of the pool. As she eased over to the side, Cain turned suddenly toward her, sensing the currents that she made when she kicked her legs under water. She moved aside, letting herself drift. As though he had sonar, Cain turned as she did, pursuing her in slow motion. There was an eerie silence and a predatory grace to Cain as he herded Shelley toward a corner of the pool. Shelley's heart began to beat faster in a combination of anticipation and vague, instinctive fear. He looked unreasonably large, impossible to evade, smooth and very powerful. She slid beneath the water and fled toward the waterfall.

A large hand fastened around Shelley's ankle just as she surfaced behind the waterfall's liquid veil. Cain surfaced very close to her, shaking water out of his eyes with a toss of his head.

"Guess I'm It," said Shelley, suddenly breathless.

Gently, Cain used his chest to crowd Shelley against the edge of the pool. He braced his arms on either side of her, caging her.

"Billy will—" began Shelley, her voice a whisper.

"Billy's making lemonade for his poor, worn-out uncle," interrupted Cain. Silently, he looked at the sleek, water-polished woman in front of him, her hair smooth and dark, her eyes almost green in the pale radiance that filled the grotto behind the waterfall. Water gleamed on her skin, made black stars of her eyelashes, transformed her hair into a near-black veil floating against him, touching him. "Mink," he said thickly. "I want you."

Shelley saw Cain's lips open as his head bent to hers. She could have turned aside but she did not. She wanted his kiss with an intensity that shook her. His mouth was warm over hers, and his tongue was hot enough to burn. He thrust slowly, deeply into her mouth, silently telling her that he would be both hard and gentle as he became a part of her, that he wanted to fill her with himself and be fulfilled in return. When the kiss finally ended, Cain was trembling with a bittersweet combination of pleasure and raw hunger.

"Do you want me?" asked Cain, his voice hoarse. "Tell me you want me just a little bit, Shelley. Tell me I'm not the only one who is aching."

She moaned deep in her throat and flowed against him, wrapping her arms around his neck, opening her mouth beneath his, denying him nothing of her response. He took what she offered with a hunger that was just short of uncontrolled. His mouth bit into hers as though he were starved for the taste of her, the feel of her, the heat of her tongue sliding over his.

And he was.

Shelley returned the bruising kiss with every bit of her strength, her flame-colored nails clinging to his shoulders, her body straining against his, her teeth nipping him. The violence of her hunger should have shocked her, but all she could feel was the burning of his flesh against hers. Even so, as his hand moved to her breast she stiffened in reflexive withdrawal. Yet when he tore his mouth away from hers, she whimpered in protest.

The sound went through Cain like a knife, tightening every muscle in his body. He did not want to let go of Shelley, but he knew that he must or he would forget about Billy, forget about her harsh experiences with her ex-husband, forget about everything but the raw need clawing at his own body. He didn't want to do that. He didn't want to be as selfish as the man who had humiliated Shelley years ago, making her bury her sensuality beneath layers of fear.

Cain kissed her very gently, brushing his lips over her flushed face, murmuring reassurances. As he felt the tension begin to leave her, he hugged her gently.

"I—I'm sorry," said Shelley, her voice ragged. "I don't know what got into me."

Cain realized that she was telling the exact truth. The level of arousal she had just experienced was new to her. "I'm not sorry," he said distinctly.

Shelley said nothing, refusing to meet his eyes.

"Look at me, mink."

Slowly, she raised her head. Her eyes were still darkened by the storm of passion that had shaken her.

"That's the way a woman is supposed to be in the arms of a man she wants," he said. "Soft and wild."

"I all but attacked you," Shelley said in a rush, as though she couldn't hold in the words.

"I enjoyed it, Shelley. Teeth and nails and all."

She looked startled, then disbelieving. Before she could speak, Cain's head bent. His teeth closed on the taut skin where her neck curved into her shoulder. Gently, firmly, he caressed her smooth flesh with his teeth. He heard her breath catch with surprise and then he felt the shudder of her response, her nails digging into his shoulders again. He laughed softly and kissed away the small marks where his teeth had been.

"Now do you believe me?" he asked, smiling. "You can touch me any way you want to, Shelley. I'm as hungry for it as you are."

The outside screen door banged, announcing Billy's return. Cain looked at Shelley for a moment longer before he released her completely. He dove beneath the surface of the water and pushed off from the side, shooting out from behind the waterfall with a speed and power that reminded Shelley of how much strength he had held in check despite his own desire and her unknowing provocation.

"Did you catch her?" called Billy, carefully balancing a tray of plastic glasses brimming with lemonade.

"Yeah, but I cheated."

"You peeked?" guessed Billy.

"Nope," said Cain. He smiled wickedly. "I used my teeth."

Prudently, Cain stayed in the pool, sipping his lemonade from the glass while he kept his head out of water by hooking his arm over the sun-warmed flagstones. Shelley, whose arousal showed only in a flush that could have come from the sun, was free to get out of the pool and enjoy her lemonade while sitting in a chair. Smiling quietly to herself, she decided that despite Cain's superior strength, the female of the species definitely had an advantage over the male in certain situations.

"It sure smelled good in the kitchen," said Billy, setting down his empty glass.

"Did you notice what time it was?" asked Shelley.

"Five-thirty. There was a timer buzzing on the stove."

"The potatoes!" said Shelley, leaping to her feet.

Cain laughed aloud, then his laughter died as he watched Shelley's graceful, long-legged retreat. The garnet two-piece suit she wore fit her like wet satin spray paint, showing every curve, every swell, the taut rise of nipples hardened by evaporating water and a desire that was far from evaporating.

A few minutes later Cain pulled himself out of the pool with a smooth, muscular surge that Billy envied. Cain wrapped a towel around his narrow hips, scooped up all the empty glasses and began leaving wet tracks on the rock stairs that skirted the waterfall on the way to the second-level kitchen entrance.

"Pick up the greenbeans," Cain called over his shoulder. "And then it's time you learned how to set a table. You won't always have a maid to do your work."

"Aw, Uncle Cain."

"Aw, Nephew Billy," said Cain, exactly imitating the boy's plaintive tones.

Billy grinned and squatted down beside the greenbeans. Nudge glided over, intent on more vegetable prey. Cain saw what was going to happen, started to warn Billy and then decided to let nature take its course. Just as Cain opened the kitchen door he heard Billy's startled shriek.

"What was that?" asked Shelley, looking up from the potatoes she had rescued.

"Nudge nudging."

"Sure it wasn't Squeeze squeezing?" asked Shelley wryly.

Cain wrapped his arms around Shelley from behind and pulled her against his body with a gradual force that made muscles stand out along his arms. "This," he said, "is a squeeze."

Shelley didn't have the breath left to do more than nod agreement. Cain kissed her shoulder and then released her reluctantly.

"Anything I can do?" he asked.

Shelley gave him a sidelong glance and a raised eyebrow that made him smile.

"Anything that we won't mind doing in public," Cain amended.

"How are you on squeezing potatoes?"

"Terrible. I mash the poor devils every time."

Shelley winced. "I should have drowned you when I had the chance."

"Oh? When did you have the chance?" he murmured, lifting her damp hair aside and nibbling on her neck.

The potato masher slipped out of Shelley's fingers and hit the counter with a metallic ring. Cain caught the implement before it hit the floor.

"Did anyone ever tell you that you're a distracting man?" muttered Shelley, but her question was too breathless to be a complaint.

"You. Just now. Do I really distract you, mink?"

"Yes!"

"Good," he said simply. "God knows that you play hell with my concentration."

Gently Cain lifted Shelley, pivoted and put her down out of reach. With quick, efficient motions, he reduced the steaming potatoes to a thick, smooth mass.

"Now I know what women did before electric mixers," said Shelley, standing on tiptoe to peer around Cain's broad back. She poured in hot milk and melted butter. When he flexed his arm to resume mashing, Shelley delicately bit his biceps. Cain froze.

"Shelley—" he began, his voice husky, warning.

Billy opened the kitchen door.

"Lucky for you," muttered Cain.

"Luck?" scoffed Shelley. "It was superior timing." But she wisely stepped out of his reach before she spoke.

"What's timing?" asked Billy, bringing in bowls of greenbeans in various states of disarray. Nudge slipped inside before the screen sprang shut.

"The secret of mashed potatoes," Shelley said serenely, taking the prepared beans from Billy.

"Real potatoes?" asked Billy, disbelief in his voice.

The rhythmic, heavy thump of the masher against the pot answered his question.

"Oh, wow! I was afraid we'd have mashed potatoes out of a box," said Billy.

Shelley shuddered. "Wallpaper paste."

"What?" asked Billy.

"Library glue," offered Cain.

Shelley snickered. "Papier mâché."

"Concrete."

Billy looked from side to side like a spectator at a tennis match. Then he realized what they were referring to and began giggling. "You don't like instant mashed potatoes either."

"Oh, they're not bad if you're hiking in the wilderness," said Cain.

"And you've already walked fifty miles," added Shelley.

"Without eating."

"For five days."

"And there's no other food around," said Cain.

"For a hundred miles," added Shelley.

"And your leg is broken."

"And you need to make a cast!" Shelley said triumphantly.

Billy waited, but Cain was laughing too hard to respond to Shelley's topper. Shelley went back to sorting out beans. Nudge attained the countertop in a breathtakingly graceful leap and watched the vegetables with feline intensity.

"She likes beans," offered Billy.

"Really?" asked Shelley, smiling. "What was your first clue?"

"Her cold nose in my—"

"Billy," interrupted Cain warningly.

"Er, leg."

"Set the table, Billy," said Cain.

"Yes, sir."

While Billy worked on the table, Cain called his answering service. Shelley heard him curse, then punch out a long series of numbers on the phone. Cain talked on and off for several minutes, but Shelley could make out only the tone, not the words. Cain was angry. When he came back into the kitchen a few minutes later he was preoccupied. Then he made a visible effort to throw off whatever was bothering him. Shelley started to ask what had happened, then decided against it. If he wanted her to know, he would tell her.

Quietly, Shelley washed the beans and dropped them into boiling water. When everything else was ready, she brought out a platter heaped with fried chicken that had been kept crisp in the oven. She had cooked twice what she thought would be needed, and then had added another whole chicken for good measure. As she watched the pieces disappear, she began to wonder if she had cooked enough. Between bites Cain quietly, efficiently began to pry information out of his nephew.

"How's it going in math this summer?" asked Cain.

Billy grimaced. "OK."

"Is that A-OK, B-OK—"

"C-minus," said Billy glumly.

"Fractions?" asked Shelley, trying to remember what she had studied when she was Billy's age.

"And decimals and algebra. Algebra," he repeated in an outraged voice, "and I'm only in seventh grade!"

"What about English?" Cain asked, pouring gravy over his second helping of mashed potatoes.

"Don't ask," groaned Billy. He looked at the drumstick on his plate. "Can I eat with my fingers?"

"I don't know," said Cain, looking up with interest, *"can* you?"

"Of course I—oh. *May* I eat with my fingers, Shelley?"

"Miss Wilde," corrected Cain.

"Shelley," she said firmly. "And yes, you may. It's not fried chicken if you have to use a knife and fork."

"Do you have homework to do this weekend?" persisted Cain.

"You've been talking to Dad," accused Billy. He gave his uncle a jaundiced glance. Cain gave it right back. Billy sighed. "Yeah. Lots," he said in a disgusted voice.

"Do you know how to do it?" persisted Cain.

Billy shrugged. "I'll find out tomorrow."

Cain frowned. "Maybe you'd better find out tonight. I won't be here tomorrow."

Shelley looked up sharply from her plate. Cain caught the motion out of the corner of his eye, but he kept his attention on his nephew.

"I thought you were going to be here until Dad gets back," said Billy.

"I wanted to. But"—Cain made a cutting gesture with his hand—"I've got to go back to the Yukon for a few days. There was an accident."

"Serious?" said Shelley, remembering his anger.

"Someone bent a hammer over my site engineer's thick skull," said Cain, his voice rich with disgust.

Billy looked startled, then whooped with excitement. "Did he really, Uncle Cain? Did they fight?"

Cain slanted his nephew a look that made Billy lower his voice very quickly. "Yeah," said Cain. "They fought. Like two bloody kids in a kindergarten sandbox."

"School children don't use weapons," said Shelley.

"You haven't been to school lately," muttered Billy.

"Did they arrest the man?" asked Shelley.

Cain shrugged. "It's the Yukon. Besides, it was his wife."

Shelley's lips struggled not to smile, then she gave in and laughed silently. "Some things are pretty much the same the world over. My dad used to say he spent more time sorting out people than snakes."

Cain's smile flashed briefly. "Amen. Except that I spend more time sorting out fools than rock strata." He looked directly at Shelley. "I'm sorry, mink," he murmured.

She looked away very quickly, not wanting to acknowledge how unhappy she felt about Cain's leaving. "No problem," she said neutrally. "Traveling men . . . travel." She looked at Billy. "When will JoLynn be back?"

He paused, took a mouthful of potatoes and muttered, "Tomorrow."

Something about the way Billy answered made both Cain and Shelley hesitate.

"You're sure?" asked Shelley gently.

For a moment she thought that Billy wasn't going to answer. Then, with elaborate casualness, he picked up a fat drumstick. Just before his teeth sank into the juicy meat he said, "Some of her parties used to last a week. It's OK, though. Lupe does the wash and cooks for me, and Mother always gets home before Dad." Billy hesitated, obviously remembering that his dad wasn't coming home to his mother anymore. "Anyway," he said fiercely, tearing into the drumstick, "it all works out."

Cain said something soft and vicious that only Shelley heard. She put her hand over his forearm, as though holding him back. The tension in his body was almost frightening.

"Cain will bring over your clothes and school books," said Shelley. "You'll stay with me until JoLynn gets back." Cain and Billy started to talk at once. "No arguments,'' she said firmly. "I've spent hours trying to figure a way to trap Billy into being around when Squeeze gets hungry. This,'' she added triumphantly, "is a definite gotcha.''

Billy looked hopefully at Cain.

"If you give Shelley one bit of trouble, I'll peel you like a grape," promised Cain in a soft voice.

Billy believed him. So did Shelley.

"Speaking of Squeeze," Shelley said into the silence, "I'd better check the aquarium lid."

"Nudge?" guessed Cain.

"Nudge," confirmed Shelley. "She just ghosted down the stairs toward my room."

Shelley got up and walked quickly down the stairs. She wasn't worried about Squeeze, but she had a few things to set up. Billy's presents, to be exact. She pulled the presents out of her closet and set them on the bed. They looked rather odd. She hadn't realized until she'd gotten home that she had no wrapping paper, but she had found some outdated foil wallpaper samples that worked almost as well. No ribbons, though.

An idea came to her. Smiling widely, she went to Squeeze's glass cage. The snake was definitely torpid, lying in loose coils, quite cool to her touch. She lifted Squeeze out and went to the bed. Quickly, she arranged the reptile's coils around various presents.

"Cain? Billy? Could you come down and help me with Squeeze?" she called.

Hurriedly she pulled the drapes, turned off the light and stood by the doorway, listening to conversation float down as Cain speculated on what trouble Squeeze and Nudge could have gotten into. The door opened.

"Shelley?" Cain's hand felt around for the switch and encountered Shelley's fingers.

"Happy birthday, Billy!" she said, flipping on the light.

The boy's eyes widened. He looked from the bed to Shelley in disbelief. "How did you know?"

"Squeeze told me."

Billy blinked fiercely and went toward the bed. He bent over Squeeze, hiding his face. "Boy, I'll never trust you with my secrets again. You're such a blabbermouth." Hesitantly, Billy's fingers touched a brightly wrapped package.

"Well, go on, get to it," urged Shelley. "You can't expect Squeeze to wrap *and* unwrap your presents for you."

Billy looked up for an instant. His flashing yet almost shy smile made Shelley want to cry. He draped the torpid snake around his neck and picked up the first present. Shelley watched, smiling, as Billy unwrapped the package while keeping up a running commentary on babbling boas and how in heck did Squeeze manage all the sticky tape.

Cain's hand enveloped Shelley's, lifting it from the light switch to his lips. Very gently, he kissed her palm.

"You're a special woman, Shelley Wilde," he whispered. His fingers tightened and he kissed her hand again, pulling her close, rubbing his cheek against her hair slowly, savoring the unique fragrance and feel of her. "Thank you."

"Don't thank me," she murmured, watching Billy's delight as he pulled a book out of the stiff wrapping paper. "I haven't had so much fun since I was a kid myself."

"Oh, wow! His latest book!" said Billy. "I didn't even know it was out yet!"

"How did you know what Billy liked to read?" asked Cain softly as his nephew gloated over the book for a few moments before going on to the next present.

"Snakes are very talkative creatures," said Shelley serenely, relaxing against Cain's strength.

"Bull," he said quietly, nuzzling her ear.

"Would you believe a little breaking and entering?"

"Billy's room?"

"Actually, Lupe let me in. After that," added Shelley softly, "it was just a matter of time. His room is like he is. Vivid and open."

"Look, Uncle Cain," said Billy, waving an art book triumphantly. "Now I can show you what Gorpian fighting slugs look like, and Tannax IV wierdmasters, and"—he flipped rapidly through the index—"cherfs! They even have cherfs!"

Shelley felt the silent laughter go through Cain as he pulled her even closer.

"I can hardly wait," he said. Then, very softly in Shelley's ear, "What in hell is a cherf?"

"Don't ask," she muttered. "Dreadful creatures."

They nearly lost Billy in an art book depicting alien landscapes, but finally the lure of the last, biggest package was too much. He lifted it, rattled the box cautiously, then began unwrapping with a combination of eagerness to see what was inside and reluctance to open the last present. Gradually, the glittering silver dragon emerged from the mounds of tissue paper. With a sound of disbelief, Billy lifted the dragon and turned it reverently in his young hands.

"It's—it's beautiful," said Billy. "Look at those scales and teeth. And the claws!"

"Careful," Shelley said. "The artist made everything very pointy."

"Sharp, too," Billy said admiringly, touching the curving fangs and claws. "This dragon is no wimp. Bet he eats knights for breakfast and armies for dinner and kings for dessert."

Squeeze shifted on Billy's body. The boy's warmth was

beginning to revive the reptile. A dark, forked tongue flicked rapidly over the dragon. Squeeze rested his head on the silver dragon and gave Shelley a long, unblinking look.

"Do you think he approves?" said Cain.

"I think," said Shelley, spotting Nudge stalking along the bedroom wall, "that it's time for Squeeze to go back in the box."

Cain took two steps, scooped up the snake and stuffed it gently back into its glass home. Nudge watched with normal feline curiosity but no real bloodthirsty intent as Cain replaced the heavy lid.

"Think they'd ever get along?" asked Billy.

"As long as there was a referee," said Shelley dryly, "they'd probably both survive."

Cain helped Billy carry his presents back upstairs while Shelley raced ahead, shutting off lights and listening to the two males complain about breaking legs in the darkness.

"So walk slowly," she yelled from the kitchen.

She pulled Billy's cake from its hiding place in the cupboard.

"Slower," she demanded, hearing voices approach. She lit the candles one after another, dancing with impatience as the limp wicks reluctantly caught fire. "Close your eyes!" she commanded.

"Can I sit down first?" asked Billy plaintively from the next room.

"I don't know," retorted Cain, *"can* you?"

The conversation degenerated into the kind of repartee more usual between brothers than nephew and uncle. Shelley tried not to laugh at the outrageous suggestions and countersuggestions she overheard, because laughter ruined her aim with the guttering match.

Cain came into the kitchen with an armload of dirty dishes that he hadn't had time to clear from the table before

Shelley had called for "help" with Squeeze. The picture of Shelley bent over the birthday cake in the dark kitchen, her eyes alight with reflected fire and her mouth curved in a secret smile, made Cain want to dump all the dishes in the trash and carry Shelley away into the night. But he did not. He simply stood and watched, smiling as she was smiling, his gray eyes brilliant with the tiny dance of flames.

Finally all the candles were burning in unison. Shelley picked up the cake tray and carefully began walking to the dining room.

"Are your eyes closed?" she asked, as Cain reached for the kitchen door.

"Yes," called Billy.

"Don't peek."

Billy didn't dignify Shelley's command with a reply. He sat upright, scowling fiercely to demonstrate that his eyes couldn't be closed any tighter. As she set the cake in front of him, she began to sing "Happy Birthday." The good-natured rumble of Cain's voice joined in. As soon as the last word was sung, Billy's eyes popped open. His expression as he took in the loaf cake was worth every bit of time Shelley had spent on it. Against chocolate icing hills and lemon rivers, fantastic animals cavorted, their figures lit by birthday candles. The miniature beasts glittered and ran with flame as though they were moving. For a long time Billy simply sat, staring at the fantasy in front of him.

"Make a wish," said Shelley softly.

Billy nodded, his eyes wide and bright with tears. He bent over, blew mightily, and the dining room was suddenly dark.

"Good job," said Cain, flipping on the light. "That wish is a sure thing."

While Cain dished out ice cream, Shelley wiped icing

from the miniature beasts and lined them up by Billy's
plate. He watched her almost shyly. When she was finished,
he looked up.

"Thank you," he said simply.

"My pleasure," said Shelley. Her hand rested for an
instant on Billy's fine blond hair. "I'm trying to remember," she said, looking at Cain. "Is thirteen too old for a
birthday hug?"

Billy threw his arms around Shelley's waist and buried
his face against her warmth. He was surprisingly strong,
nearly squeezing the breath out of her, but she didn't
complain. She just hugged him in return and silently asked
herself again why a child like Billy had been given a mother
like JoLynn.

Later, as Shelley helped Billy carry his presents out to
the pick-up truck Cain had used to transport the dirt bikes,
Billy asked the question that she had been afraid to.

"How long will you be gone, Uncle Cain?" asked Billy
as he swung lithely into the cab.

"I don't know."

"A week? A month?" persisted Billy.

Cain hesitated. "A week, maybe less."

And maybe a lot more, added Shelley silently, wondering
at the pain she felt. She sensed that Cain was looking at her.
She did not look at him. Instead, she handed Billy his
presents.

"See you tomorrow, Billy." She stepped away from the
cab. Her childhood had taught her to hate good-byes, and
this was definitely good-bye. The pain tightening her body
frightened her, telling her that she had ignored the harsh
lessons of her childhood and marriage. She had given too
much of herself to Cain, too quickly. Her physical hunger
for him was bad enough. Her mental hunger could destroy

her. She had to end it now, right now, cutting her losses and
moving on, repeating the rituals of her childhood all over
again.

"So long, traveling man," Shelley said quietly, turning
away and not looking back, walking quickly up the dark
walkway to her home. "Hope everything works out for you
in the Yukon."

Cain froze, hearing the finality beneath the politeness of
Shelley's voice. He slammed the truck door shut without
getting in. "Stay put," he told Billy. "I'll be right back."

Shelley closed the front door behind her. She saw her
shaking hands, felt the tears closing her throat and wanted
to scream at her own stupidity. She had known Cain only a
few days and already the thought of a week without him
made the world seem empty. That was insane. She had the
life she had always wanted, a satisfying career and the home
she had dreamed of during all the rootless years of her
childhood. She had achieved every goal she had set for
herself after her divorce. She had everything.

Except Cain.

The front door opened and Cain glided inside with the
silence and grace of a cat. He kicked the door shut behind
him.

"You forgot something," Cain said, his voice almost
rough. Long arms wrapped around Shelley, dragging her
close with stunning ease. "Fight if it will make you feel
better," he said, his mouth descending, "but it won't do
you one damn bit of good."

Shelley had no chance to fight. Cain's strength simply
overpowered her, pinning her to the hard length of his body
while his mouth broke open hers so that he could find all the
softness and heat she had been trying to deny him. He
thrust into her, taking all he could with a force that shocked
him. He tried to slow down, to temper the rage that had

exploded in him when he had seen her turn her back and walk away as though he were no more than Billy's chauffeur. Only when he tasted her tears running hotly over his lips did he succeed in controlling himself.

"Shelley," he said urgently, murmuring her name again and again as he kissed her with ravishing tenderness. "Shelley, don't ever turn your back on me like that again," he said, his voice harsh. "I need you too much."

"But we've only known each other—"

"I know myself," said Cain, cutting across Shelley's words. "I've needed you forever. And you," he said, kissing her deeply, gently, feeling her tremble and soften against him, accepting him once again, "you've needed me." His arms tightened, then released her. "I'll be back, Shelley. And you will be here for me."

The front door opened and closed softly, leaving Shelley alone with silence and tears, the bittersweet taste of a traveling man on her lips.

Chapter 8

THE MATH BOOK HAD THE SAME FRAYED LOOK ABOUT IT that Billy had had before Shelley began helping him.

"But if they don't tell me the length or the width of the room," said Billy, "how can I—Nudge, back off!—know the area?"

Nudge gave Billy a hurt look and stopped pawing at Squeeze, who was slowly uncoiling from Billy's waist.

"You do know the dimensions of the room," said Shelley. "Think about it. How long is the room? Not in feet or inches, but as though you were describing it to a friend."

Billy frowned and pushed aside a reptilian coil that was covering the diagram in the math book. "Twice as long as it is wide?"

"Good," said Shelley, casually snagging Nudge by the scruff as the cat batted with sheathed claws at a firm section of boa slithering by. "Now, if you call the width X— enough, Nudge!—what would you call the length?"

"2X?"

"Right!"

"Then the area is X times 2X," said Billy, excitement lighting his lean features.

"Right again."

Shelley watched as Billy attacked the assignment in deep silence, writing quickly. Once he had accepted the theory that X could stand for anything, anytime, anywhere, he had soon learned to put X to use. He had a quick, inquiring mind—though at first it had been a test of wills to get him to use his mind for anything other than stubbornness and evasion. To Billy's surprise, Shelley had proved to be more stubborn than he was and every bit as quick.

The intercom buzzed.

"That's probably your mother," said Shelley. "Go and let her in."

Billy bounced to his feet, pressed down the intercom button, and said quickly, "Door's open, Mother, c'mon in. We'll be up as soon as Shelley helps me with my last math problem and we put Squeeze away."

He flipped off the intercom and flopped on Shelley's bedroom floor with the kind of coltish grace that only teenagers are capable of. Squeeze, who had been dislodged when Billy got up, started coiling across the room in search of new mountains to conquer.

"This can wait while you say hi," said Shelley, rather nonplussed that Billy hadn't run upstairs to say hello to his mother, who had been gone for six days.

"She won't care," said Billy absently.

Lying down, head propped on his hand, he leaned over the math book, frowning, trying to order the elements of the algebra problem he was having difficulty with. Nudge, who had as fine an appreciation of warmth as any snake, immediately took up residence along the boyish midsection that Squeeze had abandoned. That made it awkward for Billy to write, but he didn't complain. He and Nudge had been bunkmates for the last six nights.

Out of the corner of her eye, Shelley saw Squeeze begin to climb her dresser. She reached out, captured the snake's tapering tail, and began gently dragging the adventurous boa back across the carpet. Squeeze turned and looked over his nonexistent shoulder, but made no attempt to escape. The instant that Shelley let go, Squeeze flipped a coil over her wrist and tried to drag her over to the dresser.

"Won't work, snake," said Billy without looking up. "She's got a lot more X's on her side than you do." Nudge batted at the pencil that was wig-wagging so enticingly across the paper in front of her black nose. "Cat, you're getting to be a pest," Billy said, but his tone was more absent than threatening. "Shelley?"

"Hmm?" she said, peeling the snake off her neck before Squeeze could settle in.

"They left something out of this one."

Shelley leaned over. Billy turned the book so that she could read it at the same time he did. Squeeze and Nudge found themselves nose to nose across a prostrate math book. The snake's tongue flickered like a slender black flame. Nudge's whiskers quivered with reciprocal interest.

"They say that B equals ten," summarized Billy, "And C equals A, and 2A equals B. Then they ask what C equals. How the heck should I know, when I don't know what A equals?"

"How many B's does it take to equal A?" asked Shelley, sweeping aside a rosy coil just as it snaked toward Nudge.

Billy frowned and began talking through the problem under his breath. After a minute he said, "It only takes half of a B to equal an A."

Shelley waited expectantly.

"Oh, I get it now," breathed Billy, bending over the book, a triumphant smile settling onto his mouth.

With an expert swipe, Billy fended off both Nudge and one of Squeeze's coils. Shelley looped the acquisitive coil around her own arm while Billy went to work.

"B is ten and A is one-half of B," continued Billy, his voice filled with the excitement of discovery once again, "which means one-half of ten which equals five which equals A which equals C. Simple!"

"But not always easy," said Cain's deep voice from the doorway. "A lot of life is like that."

Shelley turned over with the quickness of a startled cat. Cain looked at the woman lying gracefully at his feet, a rosy boa peeking out from her shining unbound hair and a huge Coon Cat's paw patting her other shoulder in search of the snake's elusive head.

"Hi, Uncle Cain," said Billy, writing quickly. "I'll be with you in a minute."

"No hurry," said Cain, sinking to the floor Indian-fashion. "It's been years since I've been to the circus. You must be the snake lady," he murmured, smiling down into Shelley's wide, gold-flecked eyes.

"Actually," Shelley said in a voice that was husky with surprise and racing pleasure at seeing Cain again, "I'm the lion tamer."

Cain reached over Shelley's shoulder, grasped Nudge firmly by her scruff and lifted her. "This must be the lion."

Nudge dangled from Cain's large hand with a complete lack of concern. The only movement the cat made was to twist her head, following Squeeze's movements with unflagging interest.

"You've done a hell of a job taming this one," said Cain, lowering Nudge to the floor well away from both snake and lady. "Billy?"

"Yes, sir?"

"Concentrate on your math for a few moments, OK? I've got an X factor of my own that's been missing for six days."

Billy glanced up in time to see Shelley being pulled onto Cain's lap. For an instant Billy looked startled. Then, smiling, he took Cain at his word and concentrated on math.

"Hello, mink," whispered Cain.

The kiss was utterly discreet, almost chaste, but Shelley felt the tremor that rippled through Cain when their lips briefly touched. The pulse accelerated visibly beneath his tan neck as she came willingly to him, nestling against his chest without a murmur. Her slender fingers threaded through his sun-streaked hair, stroked his stubble-roughened cheek, delicately traced his beautiful mouth, then snuggled warmly against his chest just above the opening of his khaki shirt. Whatever defenses she had tried to build against him in his absence had crumbled beneath his unexpected appearance.

"I must feel like a cactus," he said, rubbing his unshaved cheek against her hair, "and look worse."

Shelley looked up at him with green and gold eyes. Mutely, she shook her head. "You look . . . wonderful," she whispered, gazing at each line on his face, the dark circles beneath his eyes and the heavy shadow of stubble blurring his hard jawline.

"Beautiful liar," he murmured, kissing her eyelids gently, closing her brilliant eyes. "I look like hell."

"Not to me," she said simply.

Cain's arms tightened around Shelley as he pulled her more closely against him and buried his face in the dark silk of her hair. For a moment the sense of homecoming she felt in his arms frightened Shelley. Then she let fear and unhappy memories slide away, holding onto the moment and the man with an intensity that was new to her. Cain felt her arms slide around his back, felt the soft woman-warmth of her resting against his body. Slowly they closed their eyes and rocked each other, saying silently what they could not say aloud.

"I hate to tell you this, Uncle Cain," Billy said after a few minutes, laughter lurking beneath the careful syllables, "but that's not Shelley's arm around your neck."

Cain opened one eye. Squeeze's polished black eyes stared back unblinkingly. Cain flicked his tongue in and out like a snake. Squeeze froze, transfixed by the odd sight. Slowly the narrow, dusky rose body gathered itself as the snake readied another coil for Cain's neck. Shelley laughed soundlessly, amused by the look on Cain's face.

"Need any help?" she asked.

"Can you talk snake?"

Shelley flicked her tongue in and out with a rapidity that equaled Squeeze's. Cain's eyes changed to a smoky gray as he looked at Shelley's delicate pink tongue.

"I accept," he whispered.

"Uncle Cain—"

"I know, I know," said Cain.

One strong hand captured Squeeze's head and the other grasped a muscular coil. As Shelley slid off Cain's lap and out of the way, he peeled the boa from his neck. There was no real danger, although Squeeze was big enough to put a painful chokehold on an unwary human. Cain held the boa constrictor at eye level.

"Feeding time at the zoo?" suggested Cain calmly.

"Uh huh," said Billy, gathering up his completed homework.

"Bon appetit," said Cain, thrusting the snake into Billy's arms.

The doorbell rang.

"I'll take the homework," said Cain to Billy. "You feed the snake. Shelley will get the door."

When Shelley opened the door, an impatient JoLynn stood on the other side. Despite the lavender smudges under her eyes, she looked good enough to serve to a king. Abruptly Shelley became aware of her own tousled hair, faded jeans and oversized cotton shirt tied in a knot at her waist.

"Lupe said that Billy's been staying with you," said JoLynn.

"Yes."

"Tell him to get ready, would you? I'm running late." JoLynn's jade green eyes widened as she saw Cain walking up behind Shelley. "Well, well, what have we here? Wouldn't the little chippy even let you out of bed long enough to shave?"

Shelley's mouth flattened with anger. All that prevented her from tearing into JoLynn was the fact that Billy might come upstairs at any moment. Cain, however, had no such compunctions.

"Jealous?" asked Cain softly, stroking Shelley's rich hair with his hand.

A flush climbed beneath JoLynn's porcelain skin. "I can have all the men I want," she retorted, "and you know it."

"Yeah. And you can't keep a one of them, can you, baby?" The contempt in Cain's voice was like a whip. Then his voice changed, became hard and merciless, utterly without emotion. "If you run your mouth at Shelley's expense again, you will regret it. Do you understand me?"

The promise of violence in Cain's voice made JoLynn step backward. She looked from Cain to Shelley and then back to Cain. For an instant Shelley saw pain in those flawless jade eyes.

"I understand," said JoLynn, her voice stretched to

breaking. She turned on her high heels and walked back to her car. "I'll wait for Billy out here."

"I'm sorry, mink," said Cain, pulling Shelley against his body while he watched JoLynn's retreat with ice-pale eyes. "She has a poisonous tongue. I don't want you or Billy hurt because I won't crawl into bed with her."

"She really wants you."

Shelley felt Cain's shrug. "She wants whatever she can't have. Dave loved her anyway, the kind of love most women would kill for. But not her. She almost killed him instead. Don't feel sorry for that one. It will give her something to use against you."

"Why did Dave leave Billy with her?" asked Shelley.

"He couldn't reach me in time. He couldn't take Billy to France, because Billy already has lost a semester of school. The divorce was rough on him. And JoLynn pleaded so nicely to have custody of her son for a few weeks."

"Why?" asked Shelley starkly, for JoLynn had made no effort to spend time with Billy.

"To keep her hooks in Dave," said Cain, his voice as cold as his eyes. "Now that she doesn't have him, she wants him. He doesn't understand that though. He never was very bright where JoLynn was concerned."

Shelley made a small sound. Cain's hands tightened on her shoulders, trying to soothe her.

"Where's Mother?" asked Billy, coming up behind Cain.

"She decided to wait in the car," said Cain, his voice carefully neutral.

Billy threw Cain a very adult, sideways glance but said nothing more on the subject of his mother. "Squeeze was good and hungry," he said to Shelley, shifting his one-armed grip on his suitcase and school books. Then, shyly, "Thanks for everything."

Shelley held out her arms. Billy let go of his suitcase to give her a hard hug and a brilliant smile. A horn honked three times, impatiently.

"Your mother said she was running a bit late," Shelley said, handing Billy his suitcase. "I'll see you soon. And if you get stuck on homework, call me. OK?"

"OK. Thanks again, Shelley."

"I enjoyed having you."

Billy searched her eyes for a moment, more adult than child, looking for truth beneath the social amenities. Then he nodded his head and grinned. When the horn called curtly, he turned and trotted down the walkway to his mother's Mercedes.

"Billy," called Cain.

"Yes, sir?" asked Billy, turning around.

"If your mother—if you need anything, anything at all, call me."

"Thanks, but I don't think mother's really mad at me," said Billy, understanding what Cain hadn't said. "And even if she is, it won't last long."

"With her, nothing does," said Cain, but he said it too softly for Billy to hear.

Cain put his arm around Shelley and led her back into her home. As the door shut behind them, she realized that she was alone with Cain, truly alone. The look she gave him was half-wary, wholly unsettled. He removed his arm from her shoulders and picked up two suitcases. She eyed them, wondering if that was what he had meant when he had told her that she would be there for him when he returned. Did he assume that he was moving in with her?

"What are you doing?" she asked.

"I'm going to take a shower," said Cain, measuring the change in Shelley, understanding it. He walked swiftly downstairs. "Seems that some damned contractor tore up my bathrooms. They won't be put back together for another week. I don't feel like waiting that long for a shower.''

A look of comprehension came over Shelley's face. "Oh, God," she muttered, remembering what Cain had said about redoing his residence: she could do whatever she wanted, so long as it was cleaned up when he got home. She raced downstairs after Cain. "It's my fault. I'm sorry."

"I didn't know you were a contractor," Cain said, dropping his bags in the spare bedroom.

In front of Shelley's somewhat dazed eyes, Cain proceeded to make himself comfortable. He yanked off his scarred work boots. Socks followed immediately. Before the socks had hit the floor, he was unbuttoning his khaki shirt. He pulled the shirttails out of his jeans with quick motions of his hands. Shelley took one look at the tempting male pelt curling down Cain's chest and closed her eyes, trying to remember what she had been going to say. All that she could recall was the instant six days ago when she had licked a drop of water from his body. Hastily she opened her eyes, only to see him unbuckling the worn leather belt that secured his jeans.

"Are you?" asked Cain, his hands never pausing as he undressed.

"What?" she asked nervously.

"A contractor."

The zipper descended with a brisk, efficient sound. Desperately, Shelley closed her eyes.

"No," she said quickly. "I can't even hang pictures."

"How are you at scrubbing backs?"

"Cain—"

The jeans slid down the muscular length of his legs and landed in a faded heap on the floor.

"Not so good, huh?" said Cain sympathetically. "That's OK. I'm a great believer in on-the-job training."

Cain's hands went to the elastic band of his briefs. Shelley retreated, slamming the door behind her and yelling through it.

"Cain Remington, what the hell do you think you're doing!"

"Taking a shower," he said laconically. "Am I to assume that you're not going to scrub my back as an apology for tearing up my house?"

"I thought you'd be gone at least two weeks," explained Shelley in a carefully controlled voice, "so I gave the contractor the go-ahead."

"I haven't had a shower for four days and I haven't eaten for eighteen hours."

"Is that a hint?"

Shelley's only answer was the sound of water being turned on full force. She sighed and pushed away from the door, deciding that discretion and a plate full of ham sandwiches might save the day. She went to the kitchen, made several oversized sandwiches and a pitcher of fresh lemonade, and tiptoed back down the stairs. The shower was still running, so she opened the door, juggling the tray precariously. As she backed into the room, she realized that the shower had stopped.

"Lunch is on the dresser," called Shelley, warning Cain that he wasn't alone.

The bathroom door opened. A freshly shaved Cain walked into the room wearing a towel around his lean hips and a mist of water shining in his hair. Shelley started to retreat again. He gave her a sidelong glance, rummaged in his suitcase and faced her with clean jeans in hand.

"I assume that if I start to dress, you'll run out on our unfinished conversation again."

Mutely, she nodded.

"Mink," he murmured, as though confirming the endearment he had chosen for her. "Soft and wild and very, very shy. Don't go away, mink."

Shelley watched the bathroom door close behind Cain. A few moments later he was back. The jeans were worn and soft, fitting him like a pale blue shadow. The waistband didn't come to his navel. Dense, curling hair defined a wedge across his chest and the median line of his body. The dark line of hair widened just beneath his navel, foreshadowing the thicker hair below. Water drops sparkled everywhere, shifting and gleaming with each breath he took. Like a sculpture by a master artist, Cain compelled Shelley's mind and her senses at the same time.

"Why did you tell the contractor two weeks?" asked Cain, his voice almost husky as he saw the admiration in Shelley's eyes. "I said I'd be gone a week."

"Yes, but"—she waved her hand vaguely—"I thought that meant at least two weeks and probably a month."

Cain watched her intently, waiting for her attention to shift back to his face. Then he said quietly, "Is that what he did?"

"Who?"

"Your husband. Did he say he'd be gone a day and stay away a week?"

Shelley shrugged. "Something like that. I'm really sorry, Cain," she said as he walked closer. "I didn't mean to—"

"When are you going to realize," interrupted Cain, drawing Shelley closer with each word, "that I'm not a damn thing like him?"

Shelley watched Cain's face come down toward hers and thought once again that he had the most beautiful mouth she had ever seen. Hard and yet sensual, cleanly curved and utterly male. It had fit exquisitely over her own lips, the pulse in her neck, the tip of her breast. His mouth had fit perfectly everywhere he had ever touched her. She was aching to feel it again, caressing her body. The pain of her wanting surprised her.

Cain's mouth hovered just above Shelley's, his lambent gray eyes watching her, wanting her with a hunger that hadn't abated in all the hours he had been away. "What are you thinking?" he asked softly.

"That I'll die if you don't kiss me," she whispered.

The husky confession drew a thick sound from Cain in the instant before his mouth closed over Shelley's trembling lips. She opened herself to him, inviting him into the soft heat of her mouth, shivering when his tongue rubbed hotly over hers. Her fingers flexed, sending her nails into the thickness of his hair even as his hands worked down her back to the firm swell of her buttocks. He caressed every part of her mouth, lingering over the special softness behind her lips and the sliding delicacy of her tongue until he groaned and thrust deeply into her, filling her with an aggressive sensuality.

Shelley trembled and softened, flowing over his hard male surfaces, trying to fit his body as perfectly as his mouth fit hers. He held her tightly, moving slowly, proving beyond doubt that he was not in the least like her ex-husband. He wanted her, and the proof of his growing desire caressed her softness with every sliding movement of his hips. By the time the kiss ended, Shelley could barely stand. A strange weakness consumed her even as it turned her body to hot satin and liquid fire. She clung to Cain, feeling helpless, almost afraid.

"Cain? . . . I feel . . . dizzy."

He heard the confusion and nascent fear in her voice. In that instant he realized that despite her response to him, despite her hunger for him, despite the fact that she had once been married, she didn't know what real passion did to a woman's body.

"It's all right, little mink," he murmured, shifting her in his arms, gentling her where he had once aroused. Then he laughed softly, triumphantly, rocking her against his chest. "It's better than all right," he said in a husky, sensual voice. "It's incredible. This is the way it should be between a man and a woman. Touching you is like putting a torch to wind-dried chaparral. Wildfire."

"Is it . . . is it the same when I touch you?" asked Shelley hesitantly, remembering all the times when she hadn't been able to arouse her ex-husband.

"Touch me and find out," whispered Cain, lifting Shelley's fingers from his chest and sliding them down his body until the hard proof of his hunger lay just beneath her hand. "Touch me, Shelley. Watch me burn."

She touched him so lightly that even her delicate fingertips barely registered the caress. His aroused flesh was far more sensitive, though. He tightened like a drawn bow. Eyes closed, he shivered when she ran delicate fingertips over the length of him again. She looked at his face. It was drawn with a pleasure so intense that it was almost pain, making his mouth a hard, sensual line. Standing on tiptoe, she traced the line with the tip of her tongue at the same moment that her hand moved warmly over him. Smiling, her own eyes half-closed, she watched him burn.

"You're not going to run away from me now, are you?" asked Cain huskily, opening his eyes.

"Run?" She laughed breathlessly. "I can barely stand."

Cain lifted her in his arms. "That's Mother Nature's way of telling you it's time to go to bed," he said, kissing Shelley's lips gently despite the hunger ripping through him.

"Then why aren't you weak, too?"

"The man gets a few extra minutes of grace," he said, walking toward the bed. "But I'll tell you," he added, placing her on the bed and coming down beside her in a controlled rush, "when you kiss me I can feel it all the way to my knees."

"We're going to be too weak to do anything," she said, half-laughing, half-serious.

Cain's smile went from gentle to very male. "That's not quite the way it works," he said, unbuttoning her blouse.

"It isn't?" Her breath caught as his fingers traced a line of fire down to her waist.

"No." The knotted tails of her blouse gave way to Cain's insistent fingers. "Once you lie down, you get strong again. Very strong."

"I'll take your word for it. I'm still at the weak stage, myself," she whispered.

Shelley trembled as Cain removed her blouse. When his hands came back to her body, her breath stopped in her throat. She hoped she wouldn't flinch when he inevitably touched her breasts. She didn't want to flinch away from him. She wanted to feel again the extraordinary fire that had swept over her at the beach when his mouth had caressed her so intimately. She wanted to forget everything a humiliating marriage had taught her. She wanted to burn in her lover's arms, consuming him, consuming herself.

Wildfire.

Yet when Cain's hands came up to Shelley's breasts, she froze. It was just an instant, but Cain felt it. His hands stilled and his mouth tightened.

"Cain, I'm sorry, don't be angry," said Shelley, tears filling her throat, strangling her. "It's not you, it's me. I told you. I'm no good at—"

His mouth stole her fearful words and replaced them with

a deep, gentle kiss. Long fingers caressed her breasts, teasing the tips until they were ruby hard and streamers of fire ran down to her loins. She arched against him, burning for him.

"Your husband didn't want you to know what this was like," said Cain, his voice thick as he watched Shelley twist against him, increasing the sensual pressure of his fingers. "He didn't want you to burn because he knew he wasn't man enough to put out the fire." Cain's hands went beneath her back, arching her toward his beautiful, hungry mouth. "But I like it when you burn."

Shelley gasped as his teeth raked lightly over her nipple. He drew her heavily into his mouth, making her forget everything but the rhythmic pull of his tongue and teeth. Waves of sensation swept over her, shaking her with their heat. Her head fell back as she gave herself to Cain's elemental lovemaking with an abandon that was more inflaming than any declaration of passion could have been. She didn't know how long she was held suspended between his powerful hands and his hard, caressing mouth. She only knew that she had never felt more beautiful, more desirable, more desired.

And then Shelley knew even that wasn't enough. She had to have more of Cain, give more to him, make him burn as she was burning. She threaded her shaking hands into his hair, letting it slide between her fingers. It was a deliciously sensual feeling, his hair damp from the shower and hot with the passionate heat that radiated through him. Her fingernails scored lightly over the bunched muscles of his shoulders and then her palms rubbed across his burning skin. Suddenly she had to feel his tongue against hers, had to taste his heat, absorb it, become part of it.

As though Cain knew her need, he lifted his head from her breast and took her mouth without restraint, crushing her back into the bed with the force of his kiss. She didn't complain about his weight. She simply wrapped her arms around him and pulled him even closer, glorying in the masculine heaviness of his body as he settled between her legs. He moved sinuously against her, reflexively seeking the waiting softness of her. Her hips moved against him, silently asking, burning.

Suddenly Cain shifted aside and peeled off their remaining clothes. Urgently his hands stroked Shelley from her ankles to her temples while he fought to control a sensual hunger that was like nothing he had ever experienced before. When his fingers found the hot, soft center of her, he groaned and took her mouth fiercely, ravishing her with thrusts of his tongue as he wanted to ravish her with thrusts of his body.

Shelley came apart beneath the sensual assault, crying out her pleasure, telling of the fire raging through her, shaking her until she could only call his name again and again. Blindly, her hands slid down his body until she touched him and knew the full measure of his need. He groaned as he moved between her soft palms in an agony of pleasure; then he captured her hands and pulled them back up his body.

"God, how I want you," he said biting her palms. His voice was harsh, his body flushed. His fingers slid down her skin and sank into her satin depths, caressing her until fire melted her. He closed his eyes for an instant, deepening the caress, savoring the tangible evidence of her passion.

With a shudder he withdrew slowly, lying back, not touching her at all. She turned restlessly toward him, wanting him. And then she saw his face.

"Cain?" Shelley asked, searching his harsh expression. His skin was tightly drawn, as though he were in pain. "What's wrong?"

"I want you too much."

"I don't understand," she whispered, touching his face, feeling the shudder that took him at even such a simple caress. She had no doubt that he wanted her as no man ever had. To be wanted like that set fire to her. Heat twisted through the core of her, bringing a wild kind of strength. She had never dreamed such wanting was possible. "Tell me what's wrong," she pleaded, knowing only that they needed each other too much for her to retreat as he had.

Hungrily, gently, Cain's fingers moved up Shelley's inner thigh until he knew once again the satin heat of her. She was ready for him, needed him, yet—"It's been so long since you've been with a man. You're as tight as a virgin," he murmured, caressing her slowly, deeply, until she melted over him again. He shuddered, fighting the urge to sheathe himself in her liquid fire. "I'm too damn hungry. Look at me. I'm afraid I'll hurt you."

Cain withdrew his touch again, visibly fighting for control. Shelley felt empty, aching. Slowly she kissed his cheek, his neck, the tangled mat of hair on his chest, the dark line leading to his navel.

"Shelley—"

But that was the only word Cain got out before he felt the butterfly softness of her lips brushing over him in a caress that tightened every muscle in his body.

"You won't hurt me," she breathed, touching him delicately with the tip of her tongue.

"Shelley—"

"I'm empty, Cain."

His control snapped. He turned swiftly, pinning her to the bed, filling her with a single powerful movement of his body. She cried out, but it was with pleasure not pain, and the sweet shivering of her body told him how great that pleasure was. It was no less for him. He moved inside her again, setting her afire, burning her, until she burned him in return. He rocked slowly against her, tightly sheathed in her liquid heat, feeling a pleasure so great that he could only groan. At each movement she cried out, her nails like flames licking over him. And then her body tightened and her eyes opened with surprise as wildfire consumed her.

Cain saw the instant of surprise, felt the heat and satin pulses within her. He wanted it to last forever, to stay joined with her endlessly, savoring the hot, wild instant when she first knew ecstasy. Another tiny convulsion swept over her, and her heat rippled around him again, tugging at him. He felt control slipping away, ecstasy claiming him as completely as it had claimed her. With a low cry he arched into her, utterly consumed by fire. For a timeless moment they burned together, giving each other a shimmering pleasure that neither one had ever known.

Chapter 9

SLOWLY, SHELLEY CAME BACK TO AWARENESS OF THE LATE afternoon sun slanting through the bedroom, turning Cain's body into a golden sculpture so perfect that she could not help touching him. Cradled in his arms, she smoothed her lips over the resilient muscles of his shoulder and chest. She smiled as memories licked over her like another kind of sunlight. She decided that it was fitting that Cain was bathed in radiance, a god cast in gold, for no simple mortal could have shown her that paradise was a place of ecstatic fire.

Cain's stomach growled beneath Shelley's cheek, disclaiming godhood in favor of a very human hunger. She laughed softly.

"Could I interest you in some ham sandwiches and fresh lemonade?" she asked.

"Who do I have to kill?" asked Cain hungrily.

"No one. I slaughtered the lemons myself while you were in the shower," she said, sliding a bit further down his body, closing her teeth gently on the skin over his stomach, savoring the musky, male taste of him.

"Mink," he said, running his hard thumb down the length of her backbone to the crease below. "Soft and wild." Then his body tightened in sensual reflex as her mouth drifted even lower. "But no longer shy."

Shelley turned her head quickly, facing toward him. The sudden movement sent her hair drifting over him, covering him like a loincloth made of silk. His breath caught in a husky groan as the cool, soft strands licked over him, sliding between his thighs caressingly.

"Should I be shy?" she asked, her eyes watching Cain, her cheek resting on his hard abdomen. She felt no shyness with him, simply a *rightness* that was like homecoming, a feeling of being wholly alive. "Is that what you want? Tell me what you want, Cain. You've given me so much. Let me give you everything you want."

Gently, Cain's fingertips caressed the dark arch of Shelley's eyebrow, her cheekbone, the soft curve of her lips. "Right now," he said, his voice husky, "you could skin me with a dull knife and I'd thank you every inch of the way." He saw the puzzlement in her hazel eyes, the frown drawing together her eyebrows, and he knew that she didn't understand. How could she? She hadn't slept with enough men to know the difference between individual biological release and the kind of mutual pleasure that he had once believed existed only in fantasy.

Now he knew different. He had made love with her, burned with her, joined himself wholly with her, and in doing so had discovered a pleasure greater than he could have imagined.

"Shelley," Cain murmured, tracing her mouth again, loving its softness and promise of heat.

Her tongue appeared, touched his fingertip briefly, then vanished again. The caress was like the moment when she had licked a water drop from his chest, a touch that was incendiary simply because it was wholly spontaneous.

"What we just shared is unbelievably rare," said Cain, sliding his fingers around to the back of Shelley's head. His breath caught as she rubbed her cheek against the musky thickness of his abdominal hair. The movement sent her own much softer hair sliding intimately over him. His body tightened again, magnifying the beat of his heart with each second. "Believe me," he said huskily, "I've never known anything that even came close. It makes me want to bury myself in you all over again, and then again, and again—"

Shelley felt the stirring beneath her hair as Cain's body changed, his passion renewing itself with startling speed. Sheer pleasure swept through her at the sweet certainty that she could both arouse and satisfy a man like Cain, a man of laughter and intelligence and strength, a man whose sensuality and hunger spoke to her own elemental feminine core. She realized suddenly that she wanted to possess him, to keep him locked within herself, to ensure that no other woman would ever take him from her.

"Shelley?" asked Cain, seeing the darkness in her hazel eyes.

She looked at him strangely, as though she were almost afraid.

"What is it? Did I hurt you after all? We don't have to make love again now, if that's worrying you," he said gently. "Just holding you is more pleasure than I ever expected to have from a woman."

Shelley shook her head slowly, and her hair was a dark

fire caressing Cain. She felt the tightening of his body and another wave of possessiveness shook her. She couldn't bear to think of Cain going from bed to bed like her ex-husband.

"Shelley?" Cain's voice was as gentle as the fingers stroking her cheek.

"You didn't hurt me," she said, her voice husky, trembling. "It's not that. I just realized—" Her voice broke. The newness of her feelings overwhelmed her, shaking her, making tact or evasion impossible. "I don't want you to be with other women," said Shelley bleakly, smoothing her cheek against Cain's warm flesh. "It was bad enough with my husband. With you, it would—" She closed her eyes, trying to bring her voice and her emotions under control.

Understanding lit Cain's gray eyes, making them burn. "You weren't listening very well a moment ago, were you?" he asked quietly. "I've never known this kind of sharing, this incredible pleasure, with another woman. I never will. It's you, mink, not me."

"But I'm not like this with other men," said Shelley, searching Cain's face and finding hot silver eyes watching her, devouring her.

Cain's smile was both gentle and fierce, like his eyes, like his fingers caressing the nape of her neck. "Then I guess we're stuck with each other," he said, his voice thick with satisfaction as he pulled her up the length of his body and kissed her deeply.

Shelley clung to him with a softness and strength that were new to her. Finally her arms loosened and she buried her face against his neck, breathing in the warm male scent of him. After a moment she began to laugh softly.

"Your stomach is growling again," she said.

"There are two parts of a man's body that he doesn't

have a hell of a lot of control over," answered Cain, his voice crackling with subdued laughter. "His stomach is the other one."

Soft lips feathered over Cain's shoulder as Shelley slid away from him. She went to the dresser and returned with the tray of sandwiches. When she saw him watching her, his glance going slowly from her tumbled hair to her painted toenails, she felt suddenly very aware of herself. It wasn't shyness, precisely. It was simply that she felt as though she were looking at her own body through a man's eyes, seeing for the first time the ripe invitation of deep rose nipples, the beckoning curve of waist and hips, the nearly black hair gleaming at the apex of her thighs, and the hot inner softness that so perfectly matched Cain's body. For the first time in her life she felt confident, every inch a woman.

Shelley set the tray on a bedside table. As she bent over, Cain's long fingers caressed the soft skin of her inner thighs and then slid upward to find even softer skin. She shivered as his thumb sought and found her most sensitive flesh. Heat and a golden weakness flowed through her, making her sway slightly. She started to say something but the word was lost in a gasp as his thumb moved again, sending lightning through her.

"Don't worry," Cain murmured, smiling as he felt the sensual tightening begin to take Shelley's slender body. "I'm not going to make a lunch out of you. Dessert, now," he added, leaning over to nibble on her thigh, "is an entirely different matter. Would you be my dessert, Shelley Wilde?"

"I've never been dessert," she said. Her voice was throaty, unrecognizable as she looked down at Cain's sun-streaked hair feathering across her thigh.

"And I've never wanted to make dessert of a woman." His mustache smoothed against her skin as he turned his head away from her too-tempting warmth. "It seems we're destined for a long list of firsts," he added, biting her thigh with measured force. When he felt her shudder and sway against him, he cursed quietly and released her. "Wildfire," he whispered, looking from the fine trembling of his hands to the sudden, heavy urgency of his body, knowing that even if he took Shelley now, he would want her again and then again. There was no end to his need of her, and no beginning. He had always needed her. He always would. "My God," he said softly, disbelief and passion resonating in his voice. "Do you know how much I want you?"

Shelley sank down onto the floor and slumped against the bed. She took a long, ragged breath. "I can see the headlines now: Man And Woman Starve To Death In Bed."

Cain lay back and laughed suddenly. Shelley took another long breath, then began to laugh with him, releasing them from the sensual tension that had begun to wrap hot, silken coils around both her and Cain. When his hand appeared over the edge of the mattress, blindly seeking her, she grabbed a sandwich and thrust it against his palm.

"Eat," she demanded. "I refuse to be a three-day wonder for the *Enquirer*."

Cain snickered, but hand and sandwich disappeared. Sounds of quiet munching drifted down to Shelley as she rested her forehead against her knees and tried to think of anything but Cain's magnificent body stretched out naked on the rumpled sheets. She looked up in time to see another sandwich disappear. Her own stomach entered a loud complaint. The hand reappeared, waving a partially eaten sandwich under her nose.

"You called?" he asked.

Shelley grabbed his hand and sank her teeth neatly into the sandwich, just missing his fingers.

"Come up and eat with me, mink."

"Can I trust you?"

"Probably not," he admitted. Then, softly, "Want to find out?"

Shelley rose to her knees and peered over the edge of the mattress. Cain was propped on his elbow, all six feet three inches of him sprawled at ease against the lemon yellow sheets as he efficiently reduced the sandwich to a memory. The color of his hair ranged from streaks of spun gold on his head to nearly black between his legs, shades and patterns blending as they spread across his body, outlining muscles and bone in velvet strokes. Beneath the surface of flesh and bone, Cain's beauty simply increased geometrically with everything he said or did, every bit of laughter he shared with her, his gentleness with her, his kindness to Billy, even his icy anger at JoLynn's cruelty. There was an essential goodness in Cain, a clean inner strength that was more compelling to Shelley's senses than any arrangement of male skin and bone and muscle.

"It isn't fair," she said, her eyes almost gold as she looked at him, feeling emotions condense inside her, filling spaces she had never known were empty, filling them until she thought she would overflow.

"What isn't?"

Shelley tried to explain but could say only, "Men aren't supposed to be beautiful."

The last bite of sandwich stopped halfway to Cain's mouth. The color of his eyes went from blue gray to silver as he read the simple truth in her expression. To Shelley, he was beautiful. Slowly, absently, Cain set aside the sandwich, never taking his eyes from Shelley.

"I'm not beautiful," said Cain finally, smiling his crooked smile, making Shelley ache. "Hell, mink, as you pointed out when we first met, I'm not even handsome."

"I was wrong," she said simply, resting her chin on her

crossed arms, looking at Cain with the attention she brought to judging an objet d'art. "Oh, sure. Someone like Brian or JoLynn might have more surface prettiness. But you can't see *into* them. They're . . . muddy. You aren't. You're clean and strong all the way to your soul. That's what beauty is, Cain. The rest is just distraction."

"Then," said Cain softly, reaching for Shelley, "you are the most beautiful woman ever born."

Slowly, gently, Cain lifted Shelley onto the bed and cradled her against his body. There was no passionate demand in his embrace. He just held her, needing to feel her warmth, the stir of her breath against his neck, the feminine strength of her arms holding him in return. His hands moved over her ceaselessly, reassuring him that she was real rather than a dream born out of his own loneliness, a loneliness that had been part of him for so long that he had taken its existence for granted. He wasn't lonely now, though. The difference went through him like a shock wave, changing everything in its wake.

Suddenly Shelley pushed herself slightly away from Cain. "Did I do that to you?" she asked, gently touching his chest. Beneath the thick hair was the shadow of a bruise.

Cain felt her gentle touch and smiled. "Not likely, mink. You'd have to take a hammer to me to leave a dent like that."

"Then what was it?"

"A hammer."

Shelley looked at the line of Cain's mouth and realized that he wasn't teasing her. "What happened?" she asked, her voice tight. The thought of anything hurting him went into her like a knife.

"A slight difference of opinion," said Cain dryly.

Shelley waited.

Cain looked over at her, saw the emotion darkening her

eyes. "Hey," he said, pulling her head down, kissing her lips lightly. "It's OK. No permanent damage done."

Shelley waited.

Cain sighed. "You know the geologist and the engineer I was having trouble with?"

Shelley nodded, waiting.

"I got up there just in time to break up a fight, that's all."

"Someone used a hammer on you?" asked Shelley, her mouth dry.

Cain shrugged. "My own damn fault. I was more worried about the man with the pistol. When I went after the gun, Joe and the woman jumped me. I got the gun away from Ken and blocked most of the hammer blow. Then I knocked some sense into the two men."

A ragged, indrawn breath was Shelley's only comment. "Does this happen often?" she asked faintly.

"No. And if it does, it's usually only with the miners, not the professionals. But Ken was a miner before he was anything else. Two drinks, one flashy woman and *bang*, he's ready to fight."

"Aren't there any police?"

"Were there many cops in the Sahara?" asked Cain dryly.

Shelley closed her eyes, remembering a handful of times when she had sensed tension in the air and her mother had retreated into their tent, taking Shelley with her. Shelley had watched what happened, though, squinting through the slit where the tent flaps didn't meet. She had seen her father talk to angry men with a shotgun in the crook of his arm.

"No police until after the fact, and usually not even then," admitted Shelley, seeing the past with new eyes. "Dad had to take care of things himself."

"It's the same in a mining camp," said Cain. "It's up to the camp boss to keep order. Unfortunately, Ken was the camp boss and the woman was Joe's wife. She was the one with the hammer.''

''Oh, Lord,'' breathed Shelley.

''Yeah. A mess. If she'd been a man, I'd have broken her neck.'' He shrugged. ''As it was, I told her that if she ever came at me again, I'd take her down like any man.''

''What about Ken?''

''He'll be looking for a new job as soon as his arm heals.''

''His arm?''

''I broke it,'' said Cain bluntly. ''I don't like guns, especially when they're pointed at me.''

''And the husband?''

''Joe took his wife back to their cabin. I don't know what happened after that. I don't really care. I didn't see her the rest of the time I was there, which was fine with me. I was too busy trying to get things running again to worry about some troublemaking piece of ass.''

The contempt in Cain's voice was like an icy wind. It was the same contempt Shelley had heard when he mentioned his ex-wife or JoLynn. The same contempt that he had turned on Shelley when they first were introduced.

''You don't like women very well, do you?'' said Shelley quietly.

There was a long moment of silence. Cain's arm tightened around Shelley. ''No, I don't,'' he said slowly. ''Too many of them are on power trips. They want every man they see. No, I take that back. They don't want men. They want men to want *them*.'' The muscles of his arm were tense against Shelley's soft skin as he continued, his voice low and deep. ''I haven't liked women for a long time, until I saw a woman standing in a shaft of sunlight with a snake draped over her arm. She was handling it so gently, and she handled a lonely boy just the same. She had no reason to be gentle, nothing to gain. She was simply a loving kind of woman.''

Cain's mustache and warm lips brushed over Shelley's forehead. ''You intrigued me, mink,'' he said. ''You were strong and vulnerable, civilized and wild, intelligent—and your kiss was a lesson in the kind of honesty I'd given up hoping to find. I knew after I saw you lighting candles on Billy's cake that I had to have you, to find out what it was like to have an honest, loving kind of woman in my bed. Now that I've made love with you, you fascinate me even more. You make me believe in possibilities that I've denied for too many years.''

Cain's lips were as gentle as his words, his warm breath mingling with Shelley's in a slow kiss.

''But I'm not wild,'' she objected finally, softly. ''I'm a homebody.''

''Look out that window and tell me that you aren't wild,'' said Cain.

Shelley looked across Cain's chest to the wall of glass that gave the guest bedroom a spectacular view of the steep hills. The land glowed with a rich, mystic light that called to her senses, urging her to get up and explore, to walk in places where man rarely went. This was her favorite time of day, when the sun was easing its fierce grip on the land. Soon twilight would come, and with it a pungent coolness sliding down hot ravines, the moist exhalation of an ocean breeze reversing the hot Santa Ana winds. Deer would begin to glide out of cover, picking their way through the brush on delicate feet. Raccoons would sneak down to drink from her pool, followed by oppossums. Sometimes there would be the amusing black-and-silver elegance of a skunk strolling by. And always there were jack rabbits freezing at the first sound, sensing the coyotes that moved like tan shadows through the concealing chaparral.

"JoLynn covered up her windows," said Cain, watching Shelley's eyes, "because she is too silly and shallow to respond to something as wild as the sea. You built yourself walls of glass facing away from the city, because you need to see that there is something left untamed in the midst of the concrete and macadam. There is wildness in you, Shelley," he said simply, caressing her with his hard, sensitive hand.

Shelley stiffened beneath Cain's touch, withdrawing from him without moving away. Yet he sensed her withdrawal as surely as he would have sensed a change in his own heartbeat.

"Why do you deny it?" asked Cain, his voice soft and his eyes clear, intent, watching her.

"Because it isn't true," she said, shifting her body restlessly. "I love the hills for their tawny colors and the way light transforms them. They're as superb as any objet d'art." She lifted her troubled, hazel eyes to Cain. "I'm a homebody, Cain. Really I am." Her lips curved slowly, trying to soften her words. "But you, you're a traveling man." *And the most beautiful person I have ever known.*

Shelley's sad smile made Cain's breath catch. "It's not that easy," he said.

"Who said it was easy?" she asked, her eyes brilliant with tears she would not shed. Then, quickly, she covered his lips with her slender fingers. "No, please. We can't change what we are. But we can share ourselves, can't we? For as long as it lasts?"

"It will last forever, Shelley. I love you." Cain's fingertip touched her lips delicately. "And that's another first. I've never told a woman I loved her."

The word *love* vibrated through Shelley, destroying and creating at the same time, changing her. Tears trembled in her eyelashes. She didn't know whether to laugh or cry or run away from the certainty in Cain's silver eyes.

"Cain . . ." Her voice was small, anguished, frightened.

He kissed her very gently. "It's all right. As soon as you know why you're afraid of your own wildness, you'll know that you love me as much as I love you." He sat up and looked down at her slender, womanly body. "I want to make love to you right now, to feel you come apart in my arms, hear you cry out your pleasure and your love for me. But that would only frighten you more." He smiled almost sadly. "So show me your hills, mink. I've never hiked through an objet d'art."

For a moment Shelley simply lay on the bed, watching Cain as he stood and retrieved the clothes that he had shed with such impatience earlier. Finally she got up and dressed clumsily, her hands shaking, her thoughts chaotic.

"Do you have a canteen in that big bedroom closet of yours?" asked Cain.

The casual question surprised Shelley. It was as though Cain had never looked at her with luminous gray eyes and spoken of love. "Yes."

"Knapsack? Hiking shoes?"

Shelley nodded. Cain smiled as though he had just won a bet with himself.

"Know a place where we can picnic in your hills?" he asked.

Slowly, Shelley nodded again, feeling frissons of emotion chase over her. Cain's smile was so beautiful that it made her simply want to stand and stare at him.

"Good," he said. "I'll make some more sandwiches

while you gather the gear. Meet you in the kitchen in ten minutes.''

It didn't take Shelley ten minutes. Everything Cain had asked for was neatly stacked in a corner of her closet, waiting to be used. She went into the hills at least once a week with her knapsack and a cold dinner. She loved to sit quietly, absorbing the stillness, the twilight sliding into night, and the fugitive glimpses of life ghosting through the chaparral.

"I poured the lemonade into the canteen," said Shelley as she came into the kitchen. "If you want something else, I have another canteen."

"Lemonade is fine. Did you pack a flashlight?"

Shelley hesitated, sensing that there was more statement than question in Cain's words. "I always have one in the knapsack."

"Knife? Matches? Compass?"

"And a first-aid kit and a ground cloth that can either reflect or absorb heat," said Shelley dryly. "Did I miss anything?"

"Nope." Neatly, Cain stacked ham onto slices of bread. He gave her a sidelong glance, then returned to making sandwiches. "For a homebody, you sure know a lot about surviving in rough places."

"I learned the hard way. That was before I had a home," she added deliberately.

Cain didn't take the bait. "Got something to wrap these sandwiches in?" he asked.

"Third drawer from the right." Shelley went to the refrigerator. "I've got some fried chicken left from last night."

"Billy must have been off his feed."

"No. I got smart. I cooked enough for five normal

appetites. That way there was enough left for him to take a piece or three in his lunchbag.'' Shelley shook her head and added in an amazed voice, ''I never really understood the expression 'hollow leg' until I saw Billy eat. While he was here, I made a quadruple batch of chocolate chip cookies. Twice.''

She looked up and saw Cain watching her with a gentle smile that made her heart turn over.

''A loving kind of woman,'' he said softly.

''It comes with being a nice, tame homebody,'' said Shelley, but her voice wasn't nearly as contrary as her words. It was impossible for her to argue with Cain when he smiled at her like that. ''I hid some cookies in the red coffee tin on the top shelf of the cupboard over the refrigerator,'' she admitted, closing the refrigerator door. ''I thought you might not have outgrown your taste for them.''

As Shelley spoke she dragged over a kitchen chair. Cain took it from her hands. ''Remember? You have a man in your home now.'' He leaned past her, opened the cupboard over the refrigerator, and lifted out the tin of cookies without even having to stretch. ''This the one?'' Then, before she could answer, he pried open the plastic lid. The scent of chocolate curled against his nostrils. ''This is the one,'' he said, breathing in deeply, filling his lungs. ''Damn,'' he added softly, ''but that smell brings back memories.''

''Good memories?''

''The best. Seth loved chocolate chip cookies. After Mom married him, the cookie jar was always full. Laughter and love and the smell of chocolate.''

Shelley smiled. She wanted to put her arms around Cain and hug him, sharing his memories in the only way she could, telling him with her touch that she was glad to be with him. She didn't realize that she had followed her impulse until she felt the hard warmth of his chest beneath her cheek.

"I'm glad they're good memories," said Shelley, hugging him, feeling him hug her in return.

Cain kissed the top of her head and breathed in deeply again, but this time it was her scent he was savoring. Reluctantly he released her. He watched her pack the knapsack, putting the hard things on the bottom and the soft things on top, shaking the sack gently to see how everything would travel, rearranging a sandwich that wanted to slip beneath the heavy tin of cookies. Every move was sure, skilled, revealing how many times she had loaded up a knapsack and headed for her tawny hills. Cain started to tease her again about being a tame homebody, but stopped just in time. The wariness had only begun to fade from Shelley's green and golden eyes. He would be a fool to call it back, sending her into hiding again.

He lifted the knapsack out of her hands. With deft movements he lengthened the straps so that they would fit over his much wider back and shoulders.

Shelley led Cain into the bronze and scarlet evening. Once they left the landscaped walkways of Shelley's pool and garden, Cain could feel the heat radiating up from the ground. There was a ploughed strip twenty feet wide at the end of her property, a fuel break meant to thwart brush fires from spreading up to the top of the hill and engulfing the necklace of expensive homes. Mourning doves flew up from the chaparral immediately beyond the fuel break. Graceful, darting, leaving a wake of liquid cries, the rosy gray birds flew deeper into the chaparral.

"Watch your eyes," cautioned Shelley as she eased sideways between two competing shrubs. "There's no real trail, just a way I've found into and out of the ravine."

Cain followed Shelley deeper into the steep, brush-choked ravine. With growing admiration he watched her glide through the chaparral, making very little noise despite the roughness of the land and the absence of a trail. She moved with the smooth economy of motion that was only learned through long experience in—and rapport with—the wild. Watching her, Cain smiled, silently enjoying her gift of becoming part of the land, passing through it with no more disturbance than the flight of a bird.

Tame, was she? A homebody? Sure. That's why she was hiking down a steep hillside, moving as gracefully as a dove through dense chaparral that had grown undisturbed for generations. But Cain kept his thoughts to himself.

The ground at the bottom of the ravine was strewn with water-rounded rocks, silent testimony to occasional winter gully washers that tumbled down the ravine. There was no water now. There was only a lessening of heat, for the sun barely penetrated this far down. It was a forest of treelike bushes twenty feet tall. Twilight pooled thickly, redolent with the pungence of chaparral.

"In the winter," said Shelley, turning and speaking very softly to Cain, "if you sit very still, you can watch the animals coming to drink at the seep."

His glance followed the slender line of her finger. Dried moss carpeted an area not much bigger than the knapsack. The dry seep looked like a small, rumpled brown throw rug.

"The seep used to run year round," continued Shelley, her voice still soft, blending with the twilight silence. "The winter before last was dry, though, and this one was worse. The seep dried up. That's why the wild animals come to my pool to drink."

Silent again, Shelley crossed the ravine and began to climb quickly up the far side. She stopped several hundred feet up the hill, where bedrock shelved to make a small clearing in the chaparral. Without a word Cain took off the knapsack and spread the ground cloth. Shelley watched, catching her breath from the last, steep scramble. Then she realized that Cain's breathing wasn't the least disturbed.

"You must do a lot of hiking," said Shelley, not hearing the wistfulness in her own voice.

"A fair amount. Satellite photos are good for narrowing the choices, but nothing beats walking the land. Or scrambling," Cain added dryly. "Mother Nature tucks the most useful minerals in the damnedest places."

"You love them, though. The wild places."

Cain looked up, expecting to see disapproval in Shelley's eyes even though there had been none in her voice. He saw only her acceptance of him. Traveling man.

"Yes, I love it," said Cain. "Just as you love the bit of wildness that you allow yourself."

"What do you mean?"

"This," said Cain, watching the chaparral with eyes the color of twilight. "In some ways, this is as wild as any place I've ever been."

"That's ridiculous," said Shelley, uneasiness lacing her voice. "Los Angeles is all around us."

"Is it? How many people do you think have stood here, right here, since the beginning of time? A thousand? A hundred? Ten?" Softly, "Two, Shelley? You. Me."

"It's not the same as being wild," said Shelley, taking the knapsack and pulling out food, avoiding his eyes.

"How is it different?"

"I don't know," she snapped. "I just know that it is. I can have this and a home too. But then, I don't expect a traveling man to understand that!"

"Shelley," said Cain as his hand smoothed over her

cheek, "home isn't a place, it's an emotion. Like love," he whispered. "Don't hide behind the elegant walls of what you call a home. Let yourself love me. That's the only home either one of us needs."

Swiftly his hand covered her mouth, preventing the retort he saw forming on her lips. "No, not yet. Listen to me, love. Please. Then I won't speak of it again, I promise you." Cain took a deep breath and watched Shelley's face with hungry eyes. "I want to marry you, laugh with you, argue with you, make love with you until for a few incredible moments there's only one of us, not two. I want to spend my life with you. We belong to one another in a way that has nothing to do with when we met or how long we've known each other. I've always known you, always loved you. It just took me years to find you. Too many years. Don't waste any more of our lives. Be with me, marry me, *love me*."

Tears escaped Shelley's eyes and ran warmly over Cain's hand across her lips.

"You don't have to give me an answer yet," continued Cain softly, relentlessly. "In fact, I won't let you. You think you want to say no. You think that loving a traveling man will destroy all your dreams, all that you have, even destroy you." He felt the shudder that went through Shelley. "That's it, isn't it?" he asked. "That's why you're afraid of me and the wildness in yourself. Don't be, little mink. I love you so much. We'll make a home together, in each other's arms." He kissed the hot tears gleaming on her eyelashes, her cheeks. "We won't talk about this any more. We'll be with each other, you'll gild my home—and when you're done, we'll talk again. Say yes, my love," he whispered.

Shelley didn't know whether Cain was asking for her

agreement not to argue now or her promise to love him in the future. She only knew that she couldn't refuse the man whose lips were gleaming with her tears, the man who held her so gently, the man who knew her so terrifyingly well.

Slowly, Shelley nodded her head.

Chapter 10

"THEN WHAT HAPPENED?" ASKED SHELLEY, A CHICKEN wing poised near her lips.

"The Minister of Development told me that his brother-in-law had studied geology and was certain that there were no iron deposits anywhere around. And tin or manganese? Impossible. So there I sat with a sack full of ore samples that could have launched a decent, home-grown metal industry and listened to an idiot tell me that there was no useful ore in his country."

"What did you do?"

Cain shrugged. "I went to the military tribunal that was running the country between elections. I dumped the ore on a colonel's desk, told him that the Minister of Development was a horse's ass and left. Three days later the colonel called me in L.A. Seems that the Minister of Development's brother-in-law—who was the Minister of Trade—was getting a percentage on all steel imports into the country. A local steel industry would have cut into his profits, so the trade minister did his best to sink my recommendations.''

"But the country needed to cut back on imports," protested Shelley. "You said they had a huge trade deficit.''

"The country's needs came in a bad second to the Minister of Trade's greed," said Cain sardonically. "That's the way it often is in the underdeveloped countries. Human need and human greed collide and there's a wild scramble at the money trough. Guess who wins—the needy or the greedy?" He looked at her with gray eyes that were cynical and weary. "I can't tell you how many times I've found resources that might have taken the *under* out of underdeveloped country, and had the find ignored or bungled because a handful of people didn't want any changes.''

"But if the country became richer, wouldn't the people in control just get richer, too?"

"Maybe. Maybe not. Once the tiger of change comes to a country, it's hard to predict who's going to ride and who's going to get eaten. So the leaders evade or strangle the possibility of change, and ninety percent of the population lives somewhere between the Stone Age and the Dark Ages. And the children—" Cain made a defeated gesture with his hand.

"I know," said Shelley softly, taking Cain's hand, understanding his frustration and pain. "It used to tear at me, seeing the children smile despite their fevers and running sores. Simple aspirin was a miracle drug. Penicillin was the hand of God touching them.''

Cain's long fingers interlaced with Shelley's. He held on to her warmth, a gentle anchor in the turmoil of his memories. "There were times when I'd make a find in a particularly beautiful place," said Cain slowly. "After the first flush of discovery wore off, I'd be tempted to keep the find to myself. Mining isn't a pretty process. Then I'd think of the children. I knew that even if I filed an accurate report, there was no guarantee that the children would be better off. I also knew that if I *didn't* file a report, there was no chance at all that the kids would have a life that wasn't nasty, ugly, brutish and short.''

''What a terrible decision to have to make,'' whispered Shelley, her fingers tightening in Cain's. ''The beauty of the land versus the laughter of a child.''

''In most cases there was no real choice,'' Cain said grimly. ''In a few, though, the country was reasonably wealthy or already had enough of whatever mineral I found. When that happened I refunded my fee and walked away. I'd like to show you those places, Shelley. They're as superb now as the day God made them.''

She looked at Cain's face, all but concealed from her in the gathering night. ''Tell me about them.''

''One is tucked into the Andes, eight thousand feet up and one thousand miles from anywhere. Too high for jungle, not high enough for ice. The air is so clear that it's like being suspended in fine, fragile crystal. One sound, one careless movement, and you feel as though the air will shatter around you. The mountains are green and black and wild, and the sky is so blue that there's no other color like it on earth.''

Slowly, almost absently, Cain brought Shelley's hand to his mouth and rubbed his mustache across her fingers. ''I was following a river up to its source,'' he continued. ''The water was a ribbon of diamonds. Pure and cold and brilliant. There was no trail, no sign that any man had ever walked where I was walking. The *indios* in the village below had told me that there was no way up this mountain, no pass into the next range, and that those who dared disturb the sleeping gods never returned.''

Cain paused, his eyes unfocused, remembering. Shelley leaned closer, looking at the pale gleam of his eyes, the dense sweep of his eyelashes, his lips softly curved in a remembering smile. She knew what he was feeling as surely as if she were hearing him speak. There was an aura to the truly untamed places of the earth that was unique. Like the sea and the sun and the stars, the wild places were an enduring core of reality joining man's forgotten past to his enigmatic future. Untamed places humbled and elevated man at one and the same time, teaching him that some things must be taken as they are, untouched, their wildness both a reassurance and a challenge to man's restless soul.

"I was looking for one thing and found another," continued Cain. "A stream-bed pocket no bigger than my knapsack, and gold nuggets so pure I could draw designs on them with my fingernail." Cain's eyes narrowed, squinting into the past and the flashing instant of discovery. "I panned downstream from that point, using a plate from my mess kit, and found only traces of gold. The pocket of nuggets lay just below the influx of a network of tributary streams that drained several mountaintops. The gold could have washed down from any one of them. The nuggets were rounded smooth, so they had come some distance in the water before they were trapped in the pocket I'd found."

Shelley waited, breath held, caught between Cain's words and the rough silk of his mustache stroking her fingers.

"I knew what would happen if I brought back the handful of nuggets I'd found," he said. "A thousand men would descend on that mountain, tearing at it with hydraulic jets. If I could have pinpointed the source of gold, I'd have burned candles for the children at the *indio* church and walked down out of the mountains to file my report. But the mother lode could have been anywhere within a thousand square miles. And,'' Cain said with a shrug, his face hardening into cynical lines again, ''that particular country was already making several billion dollars a year in the cocaine trade, and spending every bit of it on wine, women and weapons. I didn't see how a handful of gold would make much difference to the *indios*. Losing their mountain gods would, though.

''Besides,'' he added softly, ''it was the most beautiful place I had ever seen. I needed to know that it was still there, intact, even if I never had the chance to see it again.''

''Landscapes of the soul,'' Shelley whispered, giving Cain's words back to him. She kissed the back of his fingers gently. ''Thank you.''

''For not filing the report?'' he asked, smiling.

''For being the kind of man you are.''

Cain lifted Shelley and settled her between his legs, resting her back against his chest. ''I wish I'd had you to talk to before,'' he said, kissing her temple. ''I always felt like a stranger in a strange land, totally alone. I'd come out of the mountains or the desert and go to the conference tables and try to make men understand.'' He shrugged. ''They didn't. The ones who knew the wild didn't know the city, and the ones who knew the city were afraid of the wild. The only common ground we had was developing resources so that the next generation had a chance at penicillin instead of disease. A lot of the men didn't even care about that. Not really. They all cared about money, though. Revolutionaries and tyrants, bureaucrats and brigands. Money was the universal language, not children.''

''I wish I'd been there for you to talk to,'' said Shelley, leaning against Cain's warmth. ''I wish you'd been there for me. Nobody knew how I felt. Nobody had lived in the wild and the city and everywhere between. When I'd talk about a desert spring, city people wouldn't understand the miracle of water. When I'd talk about the astronauts, desert people wouldn't be able to comprehend men on the moon. By the time I had stayed long enough to share enough experiences for some kind of friendship to develop despite the differences, Dad would wrap up his project and move on. That's when I began to hunger for a home of my own."

Cain hesitated, then asked softly, "Was it a place you wanted, or people who understood you?"

"That's what home is, a place where people understand you."

"And L.A. is your home."

"Yes." Shelley's voice was soft, certain.

"Who understands you in L.A.?" Cain felt the stiffening of Shelley's body as she rejected the implications of his question: nobody understood her in L.A.; therefore her home was not in L.A. He kissed her hair gently as his arms wrapped around her bent knees, drawing her closer between his legs. "Never mind, love. It's too beautiful to argue. Look out just beyond the houses. The moon is the color of antique gold, like the flecks in your eyes."

Shelley shivered as Cain's lips nuzzled beneath her hair to find the sensitive curve of her ear. It was more than his touch that made her shiver. What he had said was vibrating through her soundlessly, each word a pebble dropped into the still pool of her determination, words setting off ripples that went clear to her soul, threatening her security, threatening her idea of home.

As though at a distance, she heard herself begin to speak.

"When I was seven, we were staying in a tent somewhere in the Negev. There was a moon like that. Fever moon." Shelley's hands tightened over Cain's forearms. Her voice was thin, strained. "We'd only been in that camp two days. We must have picked up the sickness in the city. Dad was out in the field, doing the initial survey. The guide was the only one who spoke English. He was with Dad. Mom and I were in camp. She got sick first.''

Shelley shivered despite Cain's heat surrounding her. His arms tightened and his cheek rubbed reassuringly against her. Her hands moved restlessly over his forearms as though to convince herself that she wasn't alone.

"She was hot when I touched her, as hot as the desert sand. Hotter. Then she started talking and laughing and crying. It scared me. She was talking to grandparents I knew were dead. I didn't know what to do.'' Shelley hesitated, and her fingers closed around Cain's wrist with punishing force. "Then Mom started calling for Dad. I ran out into the night. The sand was the color of tarnished brass and the moon on the horizon looked as big as the world.

"There were two men out tending the pack animals. The men didn't speak English. No matter how much I cried and pleaded, they didn't understand that my mother needed help. Finally I dragged one of the men toward the tent. He refused to come inside. He heard Mom laugh and babble and then scream. He turned and ran.''

Cain's face was grim, but Shelley didn't notice. She was caught in memory. He murmured softly against her hair, rocking her very slowly, holding her until she took a deep, ragged breath and went on talking.

"Years later,'' continued Shelley, "I realized that the man had shown remarkable courage even to walk as far as the tent. He was a Muslim, and in his culture the price of being alone in a tent with another man's woman was death. I didn't know that, then. All I knew was that I was terrified. Mom didn't recognize me. I was afraid to leave her, so I sat next to her, holding her hand and crying until the fever took me, too.''

Shelley's fingers loosened, but she leaned heavily against Cain, pulling his warmth around her like a cape. "Dad came sometime before dawn. The man hadn't just run away from me. He had taken a camel and tracked Dad by moonlight. Dad nearly ran the animals to death getting back to us.''

With a long sigh, Shelley rubbed her cheek against Cain's chin. ''We all survived. But after I woke up, I promised myself one thing. When I was an adult, I would *never* be in a place where if I called for help, my only answer would be an alien jumble of syllables. I would find a place where people understood me, and then I'd never leave.''

Cain hesitated, almost afraid to speak, afraid of pushing Shelley too far on the subject of understanding and security and home. ''How did your mother feel about it?''

Shelley shrugged. ''She just made sure from then on that if we were in Muslim countries there always was a native woman in camp. That way if we fell ill again when Dad was gone, the woman would be able to communicate our needs to the men who remained in camp.''

''A practical woman, your mother,'' said Cain approvingly.

Shelley hesitated, turning the words over in her mind. ''I never thought of it that way. If I'd been Mom, I'd have climbed on the first camel and left.''

''Without your father?''

Sighing deeply, Shelley acknowledged defeat. ''No. She loved him more than anything else on earth. She must have. God knows she put up with enough.''

''I'll bet she loved the desert, too.''

''You're right. The only arguments she and Dad ever really got into were when she wanted to go exploring. Sometimes she and I would sneak away and ride out into the desert just to listen to the silence.''

Cain's arms tightened. "That was a damn fool thing to do."

Shelley laughed. "You sound like Dad. Mom was no fool. She could track and ride like an Arab, and she taught me to do the same. I was safer in the desert with her than I was in a city taxi."

"I think," said Cain distinctly, "that I'm going to enjoy your parents. Where are they now?"

"Some godforsaken strip of coastal Chile where it never rains for years at a time. The Atacama desert. Next to the moon, it's the driest piece of real estate within reach of man."

"Or snake?" suggested Cain, laughing soundlessly.

"Or snake," sighed Shelley. Then, softly, "That's another first."

"What is?"

"I've never talked about the fever moon before. Not even with Mom. I've dreamed of it, though," Shelley said, her fingers tightening over Cain's hard forearms. "I still do. The helplessness terrifies me."

"You have a home now, a place where people understand you. The dream shouldn't be able to touch you."

Cain's voice was reasonable, words like more pebbles dropping into Shelley's stillness, disturbing old certainties, sending questioning ripples throughout her.

"Cain—"

He tilted Shelley's face up to his and changed the subject in the oldest way of all. The ripples that went through her this time had nothing to do with uncertainty, everything to do with the sensual excitement of his mouth joined to hers. She turned slightly, tilting her head against the crook of his arm, giving herself to his touch without hesitation or regret. The honesty of her response was the most potent aphrodisi-

ac imaginable. The kiss deepened and lengthened until both
Cain and Shelley were breathing raggedly, their bodies
straining to be close and then closer still.

Cain's hand moved from Shelley's face to her throat,
caressing her, moving slowly down her body, stopping
short of her breast. She made a small sound and put her
hand over his, silently urging him to touch her.

"It's all right," she murmured, kissing his lips, his chin,
the pulse beating in his throat. "I won't freeze on you
again. I know now that you won't make fun of my body.
Touch me, Cain. I want you to touch me."

Cain's voice was almost harsh, but his hand was very
gentle on Shelley's breast, teasing the hidden, aching
nipple. "I want to do more than touch you. I want to tear off
your clothes and—" His hand trembled as he removed it
from the soft seduction of her breast. "I think," he said
slowly, "that we'd better get out of here. We're liable to set
fire to this dry brush."

"Impossible. Spontaneous combustion is a myth."

"Want to bet?"

Cain shifted, lifting Shelley in his strong hands, arching
her breasts toward his mouth. Her thin cotton blouse and
delicate bra were no barriers to sensation. She felt the
warmth and moisture of his mouth, the hardness of his teeth
and the electric caress of his tongue. She moaned softly and
dug her fingers into his thick hair. Slowly, with a reluctance
that was in itself a caress, he lifted his head.

"I'm not going to bruise your soft body on this granite,"
Cain murmured, kissing the wildly beating pulse in Shelley's throat.

Gently he lifted Shelley from her nest between his legs.
In the moonlight her face was half-gold, half-wild, and her
blouse clung to the breast he had kissed, outlining the
hungry ruby peak. Cain groaned and bent over her un-

touched breast. He didn't straighten again until the nipple
was hard and the cotton clung wetly, outlining her arousal.

"I'm a great believer in symmetry," said Cain, his eyes
silver in the moonlight, admiring Shelley's breasts through
the nearly transparent cloth.

"Is that what you call it?" Shelley asked, her voice
husky and her mouth frankly sensual as she reached for the
buttons on Cain's shirt.

He caught her hands, biting them not quite gently from
her palms to her fingertips. Then he stood, pulling her to
her feet as he did. "Enough teasing, mink. I'm going to
have a hell of a time walking as it is."

"I wasn't teasing."

He closed his eyes. "I know. That's what's driving me
crazy."

Shelley took a step, winced, and rubbed her bottom as
muscles stiffened by sitting on rock complained. "Now that
you mention it, the granite does leave something to be
desired."

"Comfort?" asked Cain wryly.

"Everything," she retorted.

With hands that had an alarming tendency to tremble and
be clumsy, Shelley began gathering things at random and
stuffing them into the knapsack. Every movement proclaimed her impatience to be off the rocky hillside and in
Cain's arms again. Too late, she realized that the flashlight
was at the bottom of the sack. She fished for the light,
muttering imprecations that made Cain struggle not to
laugh. Finally he took the knapsack from her and probed
until he found and retrieved the flashlight.

"I'd claim a kiss as my finder's fee," he said, his voice
deep, "but I don't trust myself."

Shelley's lips parted slightly even as she closed her eyes
and tried not to see Cain's hungry, beautiful mouth. "That

makes two of us who can't be trusted," she admitted,
turning away.

Shelley led the way through the brush, using the flashlight rarely. With each passing moment the rising moon was
shedding its muted golden mask and assuming more of its
normal silver brilliance. A surprising amount of illumina-
tion filtered through the chaparral. Only at the bottom of the
ravine was it completely dark, as though night had run
down the hillside and pooled thickly there.

The sound of the waterfall and the scent of flowers curled
down the dry hillside in wordless welcome. The fragrance
of flowers was as pervasive as the moonlight itself. The
waterfall breathed moisture into the dry air, and the pool
winked silver invitations as Shelley and Cain approached it.
He sat on one of the long cushions that lined the edge of the
pool and rapidly began unlacing his boots. Before Shelley
had taken off one of her hiking shoes, Cain was shucking
off his jeans and underwear.

"Last one in does dishes for a week," he said, smiling
wickedly as he unbuttoned his shirt with flying fingers.

Shelley had just taken off her jeans when Cain issued his
challenge. Without hesitating, she entered the pool in a long
dive. She surfaced, flipped hair out of her eyes, and smiled
up at him.

"No fair," protested Cain. "You're still wearing your
blouse, among other things."

"All you said was 'last one in,' " pointed out Shelley.
"You didn't mention what I should or shouldn't be wearing."

Cain's grin flashed whitely as he conceded defeat.
Shelley's own smile widened, then slowly faded as she
looked at him. He was naked, unself-conscious, moonlight
running down his hard male body like a ghostly caress. If
he had seemed compelling to her senses before, at this

moment he was almost overwhelming. Desire shivered through her, its hot satin petals unfolding deep inside her like a flower blooming in darkness.

"How's the water?" asked Cain, sitting cross-legged at the edge of the pool, watching her.

"Water?" asked Shelley, her voice breathless. As she looked at him she was unable to think of anything but the moment when Cain would slide into her, filling her.

"Water," said Cain patiently. "You know, the stuff you're swimming around in."

"Oh, that."

"Yes, that."

"Water," repeated Shelley.

Cain's laugh rippled through her. "This water, to be precise." He dipped his hand into the water, then made an approving sound. The water and the air differed only in texture, not temperature, and the scent of flowers curled around him. Like the woman floating in the pool, the night was a sensual Eden waiting to be explored. "Beautiful night," he murmured, "beautiful water, beautiful woman. Why do I get the feeling that you're not paying any attention to me?"

"You couldn't be more wrong," said Shelley as her eyes memorized everything about the man sitting by the pool, as naked and potent as the night itself. "Cain—" she said, her voice throaty.

"What is it, love?"

The endearment set off another frisson of warmth, another petal unfolding deep inside Shelley. "Don't you want to swim?" she asked wistfully.

"Do you?"

"Come in and find out."

Smiling, Cain straightened his legs and slipped from the warm air into the equally warm pool, barely disturbing the surface of the water. He pushed off from the side and swam underwater to Shelley. His hands wrapped around her ankles. She took a quick breath, expecting to be pulled under. Instead, his long fingers kneaded up her calves to her knees, then to her thighs, then to the wisp of nylon circling her hips. His fingers burrowed beneath the thin fabric of her panties before sweeping them down the length of her legs.

Cain surfaced a few inches from Shelley, dangling her bikini underwear teasingly from his finger before he tossed the bit of cloth onto the flagstones. Though the water was too deep for her to stand, Cain had no such difficulty. While she clung to his shoulders, he slowly pulled her close, feeling her shiver when his aroused flesh pressed between her thighs. She started to speak, but his mouth closed over hers and his hard tongue searched her mouth intimately. His hands spread beneath her hips, caressing and supporting her at the same time.

"I'd unbutton your blouse," said Cain, biting her neck lightly, "but my hands are delightfully full at the moment."

Shelley's breath stopped as Cain demonstrated just how full his hands were. With a small sound of pleasure, she moved her torso sinuously, increasing the pressure of his touch.

"Undress for me," Cain said, his voice low, coaxing, his long fingers caressing her. He smiled at the surprise on Shelley's face. "Don't be shy, mink," he said, sipping at her mouth with tiny kisses. "I want to see how beautiful you are wearing only moonlight."

A combination of sensual excitement and unexpected shyness made Shelley's hands tremble as she found the first button on her blouse. She pulled at the smooth mother-of-pearl, only to have it slide away from her fingertips. She recaptured it and lost it again. Finally she managed to hang onto the slippery button long enough to worry it through the buttonhole. The second button was even more difficult, for it was not only wet, it was completely underwater. She made an exasperated sound.

Cain walked a few steps backward, bringing both of them closer to the shallow end of the pool. Shelley's body rose a few more inches out of the water, revealing her struggling fingers. He bent and licked her hands, capturing one finger after the other between his teeth and sucking on it lightly. The feel of his warm, slightly rough tongue sliding between her fingers dissolved her, making her almost too weak to breathe.

"If you keep that up," said Shelley shakily, "I'll be hours getting these damned buttons undone."

"There's no hurry," Cain said, his voice deep and certain. He lifted his head and looked into her eyes as his hands explored the smooth strength of her hips and the secrets hidden beyond the deep cleft of her bottom. Shelley gasped as he skimmed her softness. Her eyes were almost black with desire, gleaming darkly in the moonlight. "We have all night," he said slowly. "Literally. All night."

Shelley shivered, but it wasn't due to cold. Cain's eyes were watching her, praising her, promising her pleasures she could not imagine. The last of her shyness fled. Her fingers were more sure now, capturing and pushing buttons through buttonholes one at a time while Cain watched. When the last button was conquered and the tails of the blouse floated out behind her hips, he brushed his mouth over her collarbones and the hollow of her throat, the taut curves of her neck and shoulders.

As he caressed her, he eased backward into more shallow water. With each slow step, less of Shelley was concealed by the warm pool. He kissed each new inch of skin that was revealed until the surface of the water lapped at her sensitive nipples, teasing them into dark, tight peaks. His teeth closed over the lacy edge of her bra, then released it in the instant before he lifted his head and looked into her eyes, waiting, silently asking.

Shelley's fingers moved with odd reluctance to the clasp that lay between her breasts. Her hands were trembling again, her eyes caught in Cain's waiting gaze. His eyes were deep and transparent, asking that she give herself to him in a way that she had given herself to no man, to trust completely that he would cherish instead of ridicule. Finally her fingers surrounded the clasp and opened it. The wet lace clung to her breasts as though the clasp had never been released.

Cain looked into Shelley's eyes, waiting; and then she knew that she would have to remove the lace with her own hands, irrevocably offering herself to him. Cain read the instant of understanding in Shelley's eyes, felt it in the sudden, subtle tension of her body.

"I love you," he said softly, waiting.

With fingers that shook, Shelley peeled away the lace, wholly revealing the creamy breasts beneath, baring herself to Cain in an intimacy that transcended simple physical nakedness.

Strong hands shifted, lifting Shelley until her breasts were free of the warm, clinging liquid. Drops of water gathered and ran down her body. A few drops remained, shining in the moonlight as though she wore a network of diamonds on each breast. Her nipples gleamed like miniature jeweled crowns. With aching slowness, Cain lifted Shelley higher. Trembling, Shelley braced herself against the flexed muscles of Cain's upper arms, watching as his beautiful mouth came closer to her. His lips parted as the tip of his tongue licked diamond drops from each dark crown.

Shelley trembled between his hands, caught in a golden

net of sensuality. She watched Cain caress her, saw the moist gleam of his tongue laving her sensitive nipples, the pale flash of teeth as he caught and held her, then drew her into the heat of his mouth until she shivered and made tiny sounds of pleasure. He released her, only to return to her breasts with gently savage nips that made her arch against him, wanting more, needing more. He watched her through half-closed eyes, savoring the wildness he could draw out of her.

"Love me, Cain," she said, lacing her fingers into his thick hair, drawing his mouth to her breast again.

Cain shuddered and took her between his lips with a barely leashed hunger that made Shelley moan. Then he turned and carried her to the edge of the water. With a swift, powerful motion, he seated her on one of the cushions at the edge of the pool. Her blouse clung wetly to her arms and back and her legs dangled on either side of him, sheathed in warm water from her toes to her knees.

"Soft enough?" he asked, his voice husky.

Shelley nodded, unable to speak. Her hands rubbed slowly along Cain's arms and shoulders, enjoying the feel of his hot, water-slicked skin stretched over taut muscles.

"Good," he said thickly, turning his head, kissing her vulnerable inner thighs, "because I can't wait any longer for dessert."

With a deep groan, Cain sank his teeth sensually into Shelley's smooth flesh. His mustache stroked against her skin as his hands parted her legs with slow, caressing motions. She rubbed her fingers through his hair, tugging gently on his head, wanting to feel his mouth on hers, wanting him to come out of the pool and lie with her on the cushion. Instead, he slipped her legs over his shoulders.

"Cain, wh—?"

The question died in Shelley's throat as she felt Cain's

mouth caress her with an intimacy that she had never imagined. A firestorm of sensations raced through her, turning her body to molten gold. She could say nothing, do nothing, not even breathe, for in that moment her body was wholly his. The flower hidden within her bloomed in a soundless satin rush. She moved helplessly against him, aware of nothing but his hot, endlessly caressing mouth. Each sensuous movement of his lips and tongue and teeth told her that she was exquisite, perfect, a gift from gods who understood all the ways a man wanted to love his woman.

Shivering, crying, Shelley twisted, burning for Cain slowly, slowly burning him alive. She didn't know the exact instant when Cain came out of the water and buried himself within her. She only knew that when the night came apart around her again and again that he was there to cling to, that he was there to drink the tiny screams from her lips, that he filled her satin heat to overflowing and then crushed her to his own body as ecstasy ripped through him, tearing him apart with a pleasure so excruciating it was almost pain.

Gradually, Shelley sensed the moonlight and night condensing around her again. Cain's breath was warm against her cheek, and the weight of him was unbelievably sweet on her body. She ran her hands over his shoulders and back and hips in long, slow sweeps, wordlessly savoring his warmth and resilience. She could hardly believe that he was real, that she was real, that a man and a woman could give each other such transcendent pleasure.

Cain's lips brushed over Shelley's closed eyes, her cheeks, her softly smiling mouth. "What are you thinking, love?" he asked.

"This is a dream," she whispered, tracing his flawless

mouth with the warm tip of her tongue. "You're a dream. Don't wake me, Cain. I'll die if I wake up."

"I've already died," he said simply, kissing her with a gentleness that brought tears to her eyes.

When Cain moved as though to leave her, Shelley's body tightened reflexively, holding him within her. "Don't go. It feels so right to have you like this."

He whispered her name and his love against her lips. Then he gently withdrew. "I'm crushing you," he said as she moved again to keep him inside her. "You can barely breathe."

"I don't care."

"I do. I have so many things I want to share with you tonight, tomorrow, all the nights and days in the world." Cain kissed her, then nibbled at the ticklish spot he had discovered just behind her ear, smiling when she squirmed against him. "I can't do much with you if I mash you flat, now, can I?" he asked reasonably, shifting his weight entirely off her.

"What did you have in mind?" she asked, smiling slowly.

Cain stood, pulling Shelley to her feet in the same motion. "Water sports, among other things."

"Water sports?" she asked.

His agreement was muffled against her neck as his tongue tasted the perspiration drying on her skin.

"Like swimming?" she said.

"Like showers and baths and Jacuzzis and pools and lakes and rivers and oceans," he said, smiling. "Didn't you know? Minks are incredible in the water. Nothing else on earth like them."

"You're thinking of otters," Shelley said.

"No, I'm thinking of one very special mink." Cain's

eyes gleamed down at her as he peeled off the wet blouse and bra that still clung to her. "Come with me, mink. It's time you learned the fine art of back scrubbing."

"And then what?"

"I'll dry your hair and your soft, lovely body," he said, bending down, lifting her into his arms. "I'll carry you to bed. And then I'll kiss every bit of you."

"When do I get to kiss every bit of you?" she asked softly, winding her arms around his strong neck.

Cain's whole body tightened as he read the sensual curiosity and anticipation in his woman's eyes. "Any time, love," he said, biting Shelley's full lower lip with exquisite care. "Any time at all."

Chapter 11

"THE STORM IS JUST BREAKING UP. WE'RE GOING TO TRY TO get out, but I don't know when I'll get to L.A."

Shelley's fingers tightened on the phone. Cain's voice sounded strange, roughened and attenuated by microwave relays trying to punch through an atmosphere alive with static.

"I'll wait for you at the airport," she said.

"It could be dawn before we get this bird back to L.A.," said Cain. "I'll just go straight to my place and crash. I haven't slept much in the last ten days." Then, harshly, "Damn this weather to hell! I love you, mink. I should be with you right now. I miss talking to you, holding you, hearing you laugh."

"I miss you, too," said Shelley, her voice bleak. She had counted on seeing Cain tonight, curling up with him, telling him about the funny things that Nudge and Squeeze and

Billy had done, and the new client who collected stationery from every high-class bordello in the world. "You sound exhausted, Cain," she said softly. "Will you be able to sleep on the plane?"

"Depends on if I lose the toss. Miller sprained his hand, so I'm back-up pilot." Even the static couldn't conceal the sound of Shelley's sharply indrawn breath, her not-quite-squelched protest. "Don't worry, mink," said Cain. "If I'm not up to snuff, I'll ground myself. I didn't live this long by being a fool."

Static intervened, a sound like a thousand claws scrabbling over rock.

"Be careful, Cain," said Shelley urgently. "I—I miss you so much."

"I love you, Shelley."

Slowly, Shelley hung up the phone, fighting an absurd urge to cry. Cain would be home soon. If not tonight, then tomorrow. He would come home to her.

She stood up and pushed away from her desk. Blindly she paced through her shop. She ignored the catalogs that had just come in, their glossy pages brilliant with the lure of the rare and the original. She barely noticed the new shipment from Shanghai, porcelain and jade bowls nested carefully in mounds of packing material. When she had ordered the pieces six weeks ago, she had been impatient to have them arrive, to feel their luminous curves and cool weight against her palms. But when the items had actually arrived this morning, Shelley had had to force herself simply to unpack them to make sure that the shipping manifest agreed with her original order and that nothing was damaged.

Absently she ran her hands over the soothing, sensual lines of the sculpture called *I Love You, Too*. She tried to list all the things that she had to do, but could think only of Cain. He had been gone for ten days, ironing out the last problems in the Yukon camp, packing it up for the winter. He and his men had found a mixed bag of minerals, none of them valuable enough in itself to warrant a full-scale mining operation under the Yukon's difficult conditions. The Canadian government was encouraged, though. It wanted Basic Resources to expand the survey next year, after winter's icy embrace melted beneath the long hours of northern sunlight.

Shelley stroked the sculpture slowly, wondering what it would be like to canoe down rivers and across lakes that had no name, to chip rock samples from river cliffs that had never known the touch of man, to smell the fragrance of cedar and see the mysterious aurora whisper across the face of an unknown sky. She wondered if Cain would find another landscape of the soul in the Yukon's vast primeval forest. And if he found that landscape, would he bring it back to her with words, share it in the peace of his voice and the transparent depths of his eyes? Had he really missed her one tenth as much as she had missed him? Would he stay with her this time, or would he go as he had so often gone in the last six weeks, a day here and two days there, a week, an eternity of loneliness.

Traveling man.

Slowly, Shelley loosened her grip on the sculpture's smooth body, telling herself to trust Cain. He was an honorable man, a man of his word. He hadn't pressed her to marry him, to say that she loved him. He had simply, thoroughly, become part of her life. They went to auctions together, sat curled together on her couch and poured through catalog after catalog while they discussed what might or might not fit into his home, and laughed at some of the bizarre *objets* that people actually bought and installed in their houses. But whenever it came to the point of choosing something to go into Cain's home, he changed the subject, distracting her with a touch or a smile or another story out of his past, another landscape of his soul.

Shelley hadn't pressed him on the subject of gilding his home. She was as aware of his deadline for her answer as he was; and she was afraid. *You'll gild my home, and then we'll talk again.*

For the first time in her life, Shelley didn't want to complete a job.

The contractors had finally finished tearing apart Cain's penthouse, with the usual maddening delays. Cain hadn't complained. When the plaster dust and streams of workmen descended, he had packed his suitcases and showed up on Shelley's doorstep. Shelley hadn't complained, either. She had been hoping that Cain would want to stay with her. Without a word she had bypassed the guest room and led him to her own bed. There, beneath the silver radiance pouring through the skylight, they had explored again and again the sensual possibilities of one another's body. Each night they discovered anew the unique peace of falling asleep with their arms and legs interlaced, and waking in a warm tangle of soft kisses and softer words.

Cain's penthouse was finished now. It had been finished for weeks. Painted and tiled, carpeted and polished, the basic lily waited to be gilded. Shelley had moved heaven and earth, performed minor miracles and threatened eternal damnation, paid special handling fees and outright bribes; as a result, Cain's furniture had been delivered while he was gone. Each piece was unique, made to her exact specifications of size and color, fabric and wood. Forest green and tawny brown, sand and teak, rare accents of teal blue like the hidden flash of a wilderness lake, shades and tones of individual colors overlapping from room to room, giving the effect of walking through a civilized but not domesticated landscape.

Yet each time Shelley tried to pin down precisely what Cain wanted in the way of gilding, he had phone calls to make or Billy was coming over or Cain was too tired to look at catalogs or he was too hungry or sleepy or big or small or not there at all. She knew why he was evading the small decisions; she was evading the big one. She had said nothing about marrying Cain, living with him, loving him.

Flame-tipped nails burned just above the sculpture as Shelley's fingers lingered over the gleaming, polished curves of *I Love You, Too*.

"Shelley?" asked Brian.

Her head snapped around. "Yes?"

"Are you all right?"

"Sure. Why?"

"I've been calling you from the back, but you didn't answer. I thought you'd gone home."

The combination of irritation and concern in Brian's voice made Shelley realize that she had been standing by the sculpture for a long time, lost in her own thoughts, her own fears. Abruptly she stepped backward, away from the sculpture's silent, seductive promise.

"Sorry," said Shelley. "I was thinking about one of the jobs I'm working on."

"Remington's house?"

She hesitated, knowing that at some level Brian resented Cain. "Yes," she said casually.

"Any problems?"

"No, not at all."

Brian's shrewd blue eyes narrowed. "Good. It's unusual for you to take so long on a project."

"Cain is an unusual man."

"Shelley Wilde, Queen of Understatement." Brian's voice was tart, but his smile was almost sympathetic. "Any man who can have you walking around in a daze is a hell of a lot more than 'unusual.' He's a candidate for a full page in Guinness. If he gave a postdoctoral seminar on screwing, I'd be the first to sign up.''

"Brian—'' began Shelley grimly.

He held up his hands in mock surrender. "Never mind. I gave up on seducing you a long time ago. I'll stick to women who appreciate handsome, civilized blonds who are dynamite in bed. Did Mrs. Kaolin's jade come in with that last shipment?''

"Speaking of women who appreciate handsome, et cetera?'' asked Shelley wryly, teasing Brian as she always did about his prowess with women. Her sisterly joking helped to keep Brian at a distance without insulting him.

Today, however, it didn't seem to be working.

Brian's smile reminded Shelley once again of a newly fallen angel—white, shining and already more than a bit corrupt. She gave him a long, level look, seeing him as a man for the first time in years. She was very grateful that it had been Cain who had touched the feminine core of her, rather than a man like Brian who valued only the transient sensations of the flesh. In fact, there were times when she frankly did not like her business partner very much. Especially when he looked at her the way he was looking at her now, as though the fact that she was Cain's lover meant that she would be equally eager to sleep with any man.

"You're different, babe,'' said Brian, walking slowly toward Shelley, measuring her with eyes that had known a thousand women and would know a thousand more. "I get the feeling you've learned a lot in the last few weeks.'' He read Shelley's rejection in the narrowing of her eyes and the movement of her body away from him. He shrugged and backed off. "Too bad I wasn't the one to teach you,'' he said, his voice and manner businesslike again.

"Mrs. Kaolin looks like an adequate consolation prize,''

Shelley said crisply. "The white jade is hers," added Shelley, pointing toward the packing box.

She looked around the room as though she were a stranger who had wandered in off the street. She felt odd, dislocated, almost dizzy, as though her familiar world were being slowly, irrevocably tilted on its end and she were sliding. . . .

How had Cain put it? *Stranger in a strange land.*

The sculpture beckoned irresistibly. Shelley took a deep breath and hung on to the wood with both hands. "If Billy calls, tell him Cain's flight was delayed by a storm. We'll pick Billy up tomorrow after school."

"Billy called. That's why I was looking for you. He said his dad arrived today. Something about getting married here rather than in France, and he'd pick up Squeeze as soon as he could. Does that make sense?"

Shelley smiled, hearing Billy's delight in the garbled message. "It makes perfect sense. He's going to have a family again. A real family." She looked around the room, feeling like an outsider. She took a deep breath. "Do you need the small van today?" she asked, her voice strained.

"No," said Brian, watching her with open curiosity. "Are you sure you're all right, Shelley?"

Brian's tone was concerned, almost brotherly.

"I'm fine, Brian. Don't worry." She smiled at him, silently thanking him for going back to their former, sexually neutral relationship. "I'll bring the van back tomorrow."

He hesitated. "Anything I can do?"

Shelley looked at the sculpture. "Yes. Carry this out to the van for me."

"Where are you going?" asked Brian.

"I have a renegade lily to gild."

Brian smiled slightly, shook his head, and carried the

sculpture out to the Gilded Lily's delivery van. Shelley
secured the sculpture in one of the van's many padded
compartments. Then she got in and drove home, trying not
to think about what she was going to do.

It was one of those hot, brilliant autumn days that race
through southern California on the back of powerful Santa
Ana winds. The air was dry, crackling with static electricity. In the distance were two tiny smudges against the
mountains, amorphous banners of smoke proclaiming that
the fire season was in full bloom. With the critical eye of
someone who has weathered many such seasons, Shelley
measured the smoke plumes. One was nearly white, signi-
fying that firemen were already at work pouring water on
flames, damping midnight smoke to pearl gray. The second
plume was still dark, a dry thunderhead growing toward the
mountains. She watched the dark column as she got on the
freeway.

By the time Shelley turned off onto surface streets again,
the smoke was showing billows of white and gray, thinning
before her eyes. She pulled over to the curb as a fire truck
raced by, sirens blasting. Two more followed quickly.
Shelley waited without impatience while a fourth truck
joined the others. As the owner of a hillside home surrounded by chaparral, she had a decided appreciation of the
various city, county and state fire fighters who kept the lid
on southern California's combustible wild lands. Ninety-
nine percent of the time the firemen managed to do the
impossible, holding the fires down to a handful of acres.

That remaining one percent, though, was a preview of
hell; flames a hundred feet high, smoke that blackened the
day, incandescent embers riding the hot winds and sowing
fiery seeds of destruction. That was when the Sierra Deuces
came, heavy-bellied planes flown by certified madmen. The

aircraft swooped down through a blinding chaos of smoke, flying low enough for the pilots to see the nap of the land and the fire that was consuming it. Then, when they were over the worst of the flames and the updraft from the fire raged around, shaking everything, the planes would open their bellies and spew maroon veils of fire retardant. Below them, on the flanks of the fire, hundreds of men would be fighting with shovels, brushhooks, bulldozers and curses to stem the flaming tide. Eventually the fire fighters won and the skies were swept clean again by the very winds that had fed the flames.

A final fire truck blasted down the boulevard. Gradually cars pulled back into the traffic lanes, resuming whatever business had brought them out into the hot day in the first place. Shelley took her place in the shifting steel river of cars. Traffic thinned to nothing as she turned off on the narrow, two-lane road that snaked through the hills toward her home. No smoke stained the sky here, nothing but pouring sunlight and the chaparral whispering dryly while shadows rippled and changed, made and remade by the restless desert wind.

Shelley parked the van in her driveway and went quickly to the front door, key in hand. Nudge appeared out of the shrubbery, yeowing softly, rubbing her supple body against the back of Shelley's knees with unusual vigor.

"Take it easy, Nudge," said Shelley. "You're going to knock me off my feet."

Shelley bent over and rubbed the cat's broad head, then stroked down Nudge's muscular back. Nudge purred and arched against Shelley's hand.

"Cain's right," she said, smiling. "Just like a woman. Or a man," she added, remembering Cain's uninhibited response to her touch, his body tightening until every inch of him was hard, gleaming with sensual heat, and then his deep groan when she had explored him with her curious, hungry mouth.

The key dropped to the flagstones with a small, ringing sound.

"Shelley," she muttered to herself, "if you keep thinking about Cain like that, you're going to drop something that's a lot more valuable—and breakable—than a house key."

The interior of the house was cool but not cold. Shelley's air conditioning was the kind that came from open windows and a built-in system of air recirculation. She descended the stairs in a controlled rush, stripping off clothes as she went. A list of tasks organized itself in her head. First came comfortable clothes. Then came the packing boxes in the garage.

"The gilding is going to begin, Cain Remington," she said, "with or without your help." Then, softly, "I just hope I choose the things you want."

With a feeling of cheerfulness that bordered on insanity, Shelley changed clothes, bounded up the stairs and began gathering boxes from the garage. She piled them in the upper-level living room, along with huge plastic bags full of packing material. She went to a large storage closet that was concealed behind red cedar identical to the rich paneling she had chosen for Cain's home. Inside Shelley's closet were all the *objets* she had collected for use in her own home. With each season, she changed the living room displays, refreshing her eye and keeping her appreciation of the art sharp and new.

Since the day she had agreed to gild Cain's house, she had been adding to her collection, choosing things that she sensed had pleased him. One was the framed Landsat photo of the Sahara that had been in her shop. Another was a

Japanese screen painted with a flying bird and a spray of bamboo; the screen raised simplicity to an art of unsurpassed serenity. There was a group of modern decoys done by a master carver from Maine. The geese were graceful, elegant, simultaneously lifelike and an abstraction of life. The tension between that which was real and that which was not gave the birds enormous power.

Shelley pulled out a tawny piece of eighteenth century Peking glass and set it next to the geese. Out came a Korean Kiri chest for Cain's bedroom, and two seventeenth century Chinese fur storage chests. A deadly, flawless samurai sword was next, followed by an intricately carved Aztec atlatl. Two Najavo rugs were put carefully on the chests. The rugs' purity of design and execution was a perfect complement for the unadorned Asian chests. An Eskimo mask of whalebone smiled serenely as Shelley pulled it into the light. The mask was followed by a black argylite plate carved with highly stylized representations of Haida totems, bear and salmon and killer whale. A nineteenth century brass telescope with a mellow, gleaming finish was added to the collection, followed by a copy of a Tang horse. The copy itself was nearly four centuries old, and extraordinarily alive.

Carefully, Shelley worked her way through the closet's contents. From a special cupboard came framed oils and prints. The prints were Ojibway, a magnificent synthesis of an ancient native appreciation of animal life and a fluid modern abstraction learned in the great art schools of Europe. The oils were California landscapes done by turn-of-the-century American Impressionists. The paintings' sensual colors and textures beckoned like a refreshing breeze.

Shelley hesitated, then added a wildcard, a Charles Maurin pastel of a dancer that she had fallen in love with.

The woman was surrounded by her rippling costume like a butterfly with endless, filmy wings, a sinuous temptress poised amid shifting colors. Abruptly, Shelley stood back, surveying what she had chosen. Without hesitating she went to the various display cases in the living room, removing the pieces that had most appealed to Cain. The fact that they were also her favorites didn't deter her. Cain had been drawn to them. They would be his.

The Balinese dancer, the ivory chessmen and the Eskimo woman were carefully removed. The last item was the bemused opal jaguar with the ruby butterfly resting on its golden claw. Shelley wanted to add St. George and the Dragon, but the painting was currently in Billy's room rather than in her downstairs office. There was, however, the eerie beauty of the alien stars that she had bought while shopping for Billy's birthday. The painting was in her office where the dragon had hung. Soon the universe of stars would hang over Cain's bed.

Shelley stood for a long moment in front of the painting, watching the swirling stars and enigmatic faces, mysterious landscapes unknown to man. The painting haunted her, trying to tell her something about time and space and the tiny, stubborn condensations of energy and matter known as life. Cain had been drawn to the painting as surely as he had been captured by the jaguar and the butterfly. After he had looked at the painting for a long, long time, he had turned to her and said, "Another landscape of the soul. What do you see there, Shelley?" Her only answer had been, "I don't know. I only know that once I saw it, I had to have it." Cain had smiled suddenly, triumph flaring in his clear gray eyes, but he had said nothing more.

As Shelley packed the painting, she wondered what Cain had seen in it, and why he had been so triumphant when she had said that she had to own all the myriad starry possibilities. She decided then that when Cain returned, she would ask him what he had seen in the ageless, unimaginable sky, and why he had smiled at her like a man who has just been given everything he ever wanted.

By the time Shelley had packed, transported, unpacked and arranged the components of Cain's gilding in his home, it was well past midnight. She walked slowly through the rooms, trying to understand her feelings, a paradox of elation and sadness. She was soaring and at peace, exhilarated and serene, content and on the edge of tears. Gradually she realized that she had made a home for the man she loved. Her love for Cain was everywhere she looked, in every color and texture, in every unique piece of furniture, in every carefully chosen objet d'art. She had done everything she could to make a home so exquisite, so compelling, that even a traveling man would not be able to leave it—or her.

Silently, tears running down her face, Shelley stood in the middle of the home she had created, torn between hope and fear. She didn't hear the front door open and close, didn't hear Cain's sudden intake of breath as he saw her. She felt his arms close around her, though, and hung onto him until she ached. The rasp of his stubble across her cheek was more wonderful to her than a silky caress, and the heavy male smell of wool and sweat was more sweet to her than the fragrance of flowers blooming beneath the moon.

"C-Cain," said Shelley, her voice dissolved by tears, "I m-made a home for you."

"I know, mink," Cain answered, his voice as uneven as hers. "When I hold you in my arms, I'm home."

For a long moment they simply held one another. Then, slowly, Shelley's arms loosened. "Come with me," she said, smiling up at Cain. "I want to show you your home."

"I'm looking at it," he said, his luminous gray eyes watching her.

A shaft of disappointment went through Shelley. She wanted to share with him the home she had created, to give him the gift she had thought so long and so deeply about. Didn't he care about his home even a little bit? She was opening her mouth to protest Cain's lack of interest, when the impact of his physical appearance hit her. His face was streaked with dirt, his eyes were puffy and ringed by darkness and his skin was drawn. Even his lips were pale, almost bloodless.

"Oh, Cain," she whispered, forgetting about the gilded home, thinking only of how tired he looked, "what did you do to yourself?"

"Worked triple shifts to get back to you," Cain said, smiling crookedly. "It was worth every minute of it," he added, kissing her lips. "My only regret is that I'm too tired to do much about anything right now." He ran his fingers lightly over Shelley's face, her shoulders, her arms, as though trying to convince himself he wasn't dreaming. "I flew the first leg of the trip and then had to stay awake on the second to make sure Miller didn't need a hand."

Shelley stood on tiptoe to return Cain's gentle kiss. "You're home. That's all that matters." She tugged on his hand. "Come on. I'm going to scrub your back and tuck you into bed."

"Sleep with me," he said, his hand tightening. "I know I'm too tired to be much company, but—"

She stopped his words with a kiss. "I like sleeping with you."

"Even when that's all we're going to do?"

"Yes, my love. Even then."

Cain's hand tightened on Shelley's when he heard her call him *love*, but he said nothing, simply followed her down the hall. The Ojibway prints called to him silently, a handful of lines evoking birds in flight, birds courting, birds raising their young, a raptor soaring in a transparent sky.

"The falcon," said Cain, slowing.

Shelley's face lit with a smile. "You like it?"

"I love it," he murmured, smothering a yawn. "It keeps blurring, though."

"You're asleep on your feet," she said, urging him past rooms furnished with color and love and unique objets d'art. "I'll give you a full tour in the morning."

She felt his hesitation, sensed the surge of adrenaline through his tired body.

"It's finished?" he asked, his voice careful, precise.

"Yes," she said softly. "It's finished." Then, "You can see it all tomorrow. Now it's more important for you to sleep."

"Shelley—love."

She smiled up at Cain, seeing his hunger to know her answer. "You're too tired for anything now, especially talking."

Cain fought the truth for a few moments, then gave in to the exhaustion rising in him like a black tide. She led him through the master bedroom, not giving him time to admire the chests or rugs, the photo of earth-rise over the curve of the moon, the Sahara, tiger-striped by sun and wind, the ancient brass astrolabe, and the universe of stars. He wouldn't have been able to appreciate them anyway. His eyes were heavy-lidded, all but closed.

Shelley and Cain stepped into the swirling turbulence of the Jacuzzi. She bathed him gently, smiling at him, enjoying being with him. He smiled back tiredly, watching her face as she washed days of work away from him. He cupped her breasts in his hands, caressing her simply because she was beautiful to him and he enjoyed touching that beauty. She bent, kissed his hands, then resumed washing him, savoring the solid reality of his flesh sliding beneath her fingers. With closed eyes, Cain gave himself to the dreamy, undemanding pleasure of her touch.

"Wake up," she said finally.

"Mmmmm?"

"Time to go to bed."

Cain yawned hugely, then pulled himself out of the hot water. He grimaced as his back and chest muscles reminded him of mossy rocks and a hard dunking in an icy stream.

"Are you all right?" asked Shelley, seeing the grimace.

"Just stiff."

Shelley dried Cain with a towel bigger than she was but not nearly so soft. He yawned repeatedly, apologizing, until he yawned again and she apologized for him, laughing.

"Face down, sleepyhead," she said, pointing him to-ward the turned-back sheets and giving him a light shove.

Shelley wrapped herself with another towel and hurried to join him. He reached for her sleepily, putting an arm around her hips as she stood by the bed. She bent and kissed his beard-roughened cheek.

"Go to sleep, darling," she murmured. "I'll rub the stiffness out of your back."

With a deep sigh, Cain relaxed against the mattress. Shelley removed her towel and his, then warmed a fragrant oil in her hands. She knelt next to Cain. When her hands began to knead his body, he groaned contentedly. Smiling, she leaned into her work, massaging away his stiffness. She went from his hips to his shoulders and down to his hands. She kissed his fingertips, the palm of each hand, and smiled when his fingers curled into his palms as though to hold the warmth she had given him. Then she began at his toes and massaged upward gently, firmly, until the long muscles of his body were supple again.

"Are you asleep?" she whispered.

Cain's answer was indecipherable.

"Roll over, lazy man," she said softly. "The other side of you has muscles, too."

"It's stiff too," he said, rolling over, smiling.

Shelley's breath stopped, then resumed. "I thought you were too tired."

"I am," he said, reaching for her.

"You could have fooled me," she retorted, evading him. She went to the end of the bed and began massaging his feet again, his calves, the muscular resilience of his thighs.

He groaned when her fingers feathered through the wedge of hair on his abdomen, teasing him by not touching him in the way he wanted to be touched.

"Shelley?" he said, his voice almost rough.

"You're too tired," she answered serenely. With a lithe movement she evaded his searching hands. "Close your eyes," she said. "You'll be asleep in no time."

"Shel—"

The rest of her name was lost in a thick sound as she bent over him, her breasts brushing against his aroused flesh as she massaged him from his hips to the pulse beating heavily in his neck.

"Close your eyes," she murmured, kissing Cain's neck, savoring the race of his heart. "No, don't move. You don't have to do anything at all." Her lips rubbed over the curly brown hair hiding the muscles of his chest. "Let me take care of you, love. Let me show you how glad I am to have you home."

Cain looked at Shelley for the space of several heartbeats before he sighed and closed his eyes, giving himself to her.

Gently, she licked first one dark male nipple and then the other until they tightened into tiny, hard buttons. Long fingers buried themselves in Shelley's hair, caressing her scalp even as her teeth closed on a sensitive male nub. She tugged and sucked gently, enjoying the shiver of response that went through his strong body. Her hands searched over his chest, moving slowly, sensitizing every bit of his skin. Her breasts brushed against him repeatedly, intimately, caresses that made fire shimmer through her as certainly as it did through him.

She slid down his body softly, inevitably, until her cheek was against his hard abdomen and her hair was a dark, silky fire burning between his legs. She moved her head languidly against Cain, watching pleasure course visibly through the man she loved. With a shiver of desire, she kissed his hot skin, caressing him, cherishing him with lips and tongue and teeth. He groaned thickly and moved against her with a slow sensuality that belied the urgency he felt.

When Cain thought he could take no more, he spoke Shelley's name in a low voice, calling to her, telling her how much he wanted her, what her loving touch was doing to him, the need to be sheathed in her liquid fire. His words were as soft and hot and intimate as Shelley's tongue against his naked flesh, words caressing her until the satin flower hidden within her body bloomed and she moaned, needing him.

She settled over him with dreamlike slowness, wanting to cherish and remember each instant of their melding. Smiling, eyes half-closed, she took him wholly into herself, completing both of them in the same moment. She bent to kiss him, and the kiss was as hot and as slow and as deep as their joining. Languidly, she glided over him in rhythms of love and loving that unraveled him. The long, sliding caress of her body made him moan thickly. She moved again and then again, slowly, deeply, using every bit of their mutual hunger, making tongues of fire lick through their bodies. She felt the tension gathering in him, sensual heat and need growing, taking his body, giving it to her. At the last instant he fought to control himself, holding back, waiting for her.

Shelley lifted her mouth from his. She moved slowly over him, holding him tightly, deeply, and she said, "I love you, Cain."

The words stripped him of his last restraint. With a thick sound, he let the aching sensual need take him, giving him entirely to Shelley's soft, sliding heat. She felt ecstasy explode through him in exquisite pulses. For a timeless instant she savored his release, but his pleasure undid her as surely as her statement of love had unraveled him. Moaning, moving slowly, she gave herself to ecstasy, coming apart around him in a shower of satin fire.

Cain's arms held Shelley for long, gentle minutes, supporting her as she lay bonelessly on his chest. When their bodies were again their own, he rolled over, holding her against him. With one long arm he dragged a quilt over both of them. Sleep pulled at him, but he fought against it.

"Tell me again," said Cain, kissing her gently.

"I love you."

"Thank God," he sighed. "I was . . . afraid you . . ." Cain's voice faded into sleep.

Shelley smiled and kissed his chin, then burrowed into his warmth and slept as deeply as he.

She awoke to the feel of his hands stroking her body, and his mouth pulling lovingly on her breast, taking her from sleep into sensuality. With a soft moan she shifted closer to him, the hidden flower blooming, her body ready for him in the hot, endless instant of waking. When his long fingers caressed her, discovering her readiness, he settled between her legs with a single powerful movement. Hands cradling her face, he moved slowly, pressing against her, touching her intimately without taking her. Eyes still closed, she sought him blindly, aching for him until she cried out.

"Was I dreaming, Shelley?" Cain asked almost roughly. His teeth closed on her nipple with exquisite restraint, making her arch wildly beneath him. The heat and moisture of her made his body tighten violently; but even more than her satin warmth, he wanted her trust, her love, her life. "Tell me I wasn't dreaming."

"Cain——" His name was torn from Shelley as fire took her. She felt him slide slowly against her, into her, and then came a slow withdrawal that made her want to scream her protest.

"Do you love me?" said Cain, his voice hoarse, his body sinking into her again, and again withdrawing before the joining was complete.

Shelley's eyes opened, their darkness illuminated only by a sensual flash of gold. "Yes."

Cain waited, poised at the point of taking her, his eyes the hot gray of summer rain. He felt her shift slightly beneath him, felt her legs part even more, felt her thighs move slowly over his, asking for him.

"Tell me, Shelley," he said, his voice rough with passion and restraint. "I have to hear it. I have to know that I wasn't dreaming."

"I love——" She felt Cain moving against her, into her, filling her, and the last word came out in a ragged gasp of pleasure. "—you!"

Shelley saw the emotion transform Cain's face, felt the shudder that went through his powerful body like a shock wave. They watched each other as she whispered her love again, and then again, her words and his sensual movements matched in a litany of need that ended in wordless cries of ecstasy and completion.

After a few moments Cain's lips moved over Shelley's face, savoring the mist of perspiration that he had drawn from her skin. "I love you," he whispered, nuzzling her hair, her ear, the pulse still beating thickly in her neck. "I love you, my woman. I've waited all my life for you."

Shelley smiled and turned to catch his lips with her own. She murmured her love against his beautiful mouth.

"We'll be married as soon as we can," he said, sipping at her lips, her tongue, the soft lobe of her ear. "Three days, right? Isn't that what California requires?" Before Shelley could answer, Cain took her mouth in a deep kiss. "Would you mind honeymooning in Chile?" he asked when he finally lifted his head.

Shelley caught his lower lip between her teeth and gently savaged it. "Santiago?" she murmured.

"For a few days. Then the Atacama."

"The desert?" she asked. "That's where my parents are. Are we going there to see them?"

"It's a big desert, but we'll find them."

"I'd enjoy that, but . . ."

"What?" he murmured, kissing her lips lightly.

"It isn't necessary. We can wait for a few weeks. They'll be in L.A. for Thanksgiving."

"But we won't. Like I said, the Atacama is a big desert. It will take months to do even a cursory mineral survey."

Coolness washed over Shelley. She felt as though her skin had contracted, as though she were drawing in on herself. "What do you mean?"

"Basic Resources won a survey bid for the Atacama," Cain said, smoothing his lips over one mink brown eyebrow, then tracing the eyebrow again with the tip of his tongue. "It's one of the few places in the world where I've never been. I was going to send someone else. I won't have to, now. You love me and you love the desert. Together, we'll listen to the silence, drink the wine of sunset, and make love in the cool hours before dawn when the stars are so close they're like a wave breaking over us.''

The stiffness of Shelley's body became more pronounced. She couldn't believe what she was hearing. She had made a home for Cain, and all he could think about was leaving it.

"What is it, love?'' asked Cain. "What's wrong?'' Then he smiled and shifted onto his side, pulling Shelley over with him. "I'm crushing you again. Sorry,'' he said, kissing her gently. "You're such a wild thing when we make love. I keep forgetting that you aren't nearly as strong as I am.'' He snuggled her head against his shoulder. "By the time we're tired of the Atacama, the Yukon will be opening again. It's a special place, Shelley. Few trails and fewer roads, a forest like the sea, green and endless. There are lakes and rivers with no names because no man has been there long enough to—''

"What about home?'' interrupted Shelley, her voice bleak.

Cain drew back, looking at her tightly drawn features. "When you're in my arms, that's home for me.''

"What about my home?'' she whispered.

"We'll be in L.A. a lot of the time. If you want, I'll sell this place and we'll live in yours.''

"This place?'' said Shelley, her voice rising. She sat up suddenly, throwing off Cain's arms. "This *place* is the home I made for you! But you don't care about that, do you? You can't even be bothered to look at it!'' Rage rippled through Shelley's words, a rage as great as her passion had been. "How stupid can one woman be? *I made a home for a traveling man!* I fell in love with a man who doesn't want one God damned thing but whatever is over the curve of the earth!''

"I want you, Shelley. I love you.'' Then, his voice as

bleak as hers, Cain said, "But you don't love me, do you? Not really."

"That's not true! I love—"

"You love the idea of home, not me," he continued harshly, as though she had never interrupted. He could not bear to hear her say the words again, mocking him because they were not true. "We were born to love each other, Shelley Wilde. Or is it just that I was born to love you?" Cain's eyes closed and suddenly he looked older than he was, as hard as the lands he had lived in. When he opened his eyes, they were the color of winter. "You don't trust me enough to admit that you're hungry for new horizons yourself. Why? What have I done?"

"You don't understand," began Shelley, but all she could add to it was an agonized whisper, "You simply don't understand!"

"Oh, but I do," retorted Cain, getting out of bed in a single, savage motion. "I understand all too well," he said, yanking on his pants, shirt and boots as he spoke. "You don't even love me enough to give up your precious *home* part of the time and travel with me. You don't love me one damn bit."

The hurt and bitterness in Cain's voice broke over Shelley, stunning her. "Cain, I do love you!"

"Like hell you do. The only thing you love is the idea of a home. You're still a child, Shelley. You still don't know the difference between the appearance of a home and the reality." He stood and looked around the bedroom, truly seeing it for the first time. "Nice," he said admiringly, meaning it. "Very nice. And when I leave, it will be as empty as your words of love. But you don't know that, do you? You don't even admit that there's a whole world out there, and the only home that matters is love. Well, I know what's out there," he added softly. "And I'll be damned if

I'll hide in here with you, playing house and waiting for you to grow up.''

When Cain opened the bedroom door he stopped, turned and looked at Shelley with eyes as clear and hard as crystal. ''Send the bill to Basic Resources, *homebody*. This traveling man is hitting the road.''

Chapter 12

"THANK YOU AGAIN FOR TAKING CARE OF MY SON."

Shelley looked at Billy's father. He was tall and had the same dark blond hair and brown eyes as his son. For an instant all she could think of was how grateful she was that Dave Cummings and Cain Remington were stepbrothers. If Dave had resembled Cain in any way, Shelley didn't know if she could have kept her composure. In the three weeks since Cain had walked out of his home and her life, she had learned that there was something infinitely worse than crying out in the night and hearing an answer in a babble of foreign language. Crying out and hearing only silence was tearing at her soul.

"It was my pleasure to have Billy around," said Shelley, her voice husky.

Without really meaning to, she held her arms out to Billy. He didn't need her now that his father was back, but she had missed Billy's exuberance and his quick, curious mind. Billy wrapped his arms around Shelley in a hard hug, smiling with pleasure, silently telling her that he was as glad to see her as she was to see him. Then he stepped back and eyed her with a child's devastating honesty.

"You been sick, Shelley?"

Dave's eyes went from his son to the dark-haired woman with the haunted hazel eyes. "Don't be rude, son."

"I'm not." Billy looked at Shelley more closely. "You should get to the beach more. You're pale."

"Billy," said Dave warningly, reaching for his son.

"That's all right," Shelley said quietly to Dave. She touched Billy's cheek. "I've had a lot of work to catch up on."

"Well, now that Uncle Cain's back, you can—"

Shelley didn't hear the rest. If she had been pale before, she was white now. Cain was back and he hadn't called her. All the endless hours of loneliness and he still didn't understand her, still didn't believe that she loved him.

Or perhaps he had decided that he didn't love her after all.

Homebody. Child. Playing house.

"Miss Wilde?" said Dave, stepping forward, bracing her with his hand. "Are you all right?"

Shelley took a deep breath and smiled wanly at Billy's father. "I'm fine. Just tired. I worked rather late last night."

And the night before, and the night before that—all the empty nights stretching back to the instant when Cain had walked out on her, leaving her crying in the shell of the home she had made for him. Traveling man, loving only the curve of the earth. All those landscapes of the soul calling to him.

A whole world out there.

Was she hiding in here?

Shelley realized that Dave's hand was still on her arm, bracing her. With an effort, she forced herself to breathe evenly, returning color to her pale cheeks.

"How's Squeeze doing?" she asked Billy, her voice strained.

"Great. Thanks for giving me that huge aquarium."

Shelley smiled gently. "He looked better in it than the fish ever did. Give him a squeeze for me. And if having him is a problem, bring him back."

Billy grinned. "No problem. Genevieve kinda likes him."

Dave ruffled his son's hair affectionately. "That's because you taught her how to talk snake."

The boy's tongue moved in and out quickly, imitating a snake. He frowned, dissatisfied with his speed. "No one does it as good as Shelley."

Her smile slipped. Cain had laughed when she had "talked snake" to him, but the laughter had quickly changed to passion as her tongue flicked teasingly over him.

"You're still coming to the wedding, aren't you?" asked Billy.

Shelley hesitated. She had accepted the invitation only because she had believed that Cain would be in the Atacama. But he wasn't. He was here.

"Please," said the boy. Then, "You promised."

"Billy," Dave said quietly, "Miss Wilde is a very busy woman."

Shelley looked at Dave, wondering what Cain had told his stepbrother.

"But she promised," insisted Billy.

"Say good-bye, son. I'll be out in a few minutes."

Billy measured his father's determination, sighed and

said, "Bye, Shelley." Then he called over his shoulder as he shut the door of the Gilded Lily behind him, "See you at the wedding!"

Dave shook his head. "I'm sorry, Shelley—Miss Wilde."

"Shelley," she corrected softly. "There's nothing to apologize for. You have a son anyone would envy."

Dave looked around the shop. "I can see who did Cain's penthouse." Dave looked at Shelley with troubled brown eyes. "I've never seen a place that reflected a man's personality so vividly. And a woman's. There was more to it, though. There was love." Then, quietly, "Why did you leave him?"

For an instant Shelley thought that she would refuse to answer. But the lure was too great. Perhaps Dave knew something that she did not. Perhaps he could help her understand why she was alone. "Is that what Cain told you? That I left him?"

"No. Cain hasn't mentioned you at all. It was Billy who told me about you."

Shelley's dark lashes closed in a futile effort to conceal her pain. "Ask Cain," she said, her voice low.

Dave's laugh was short and harsh. "I'd like to live to see my wedding day. Cain is unapproachable. I've been in some mean places around the world with my stepbrother. He taught me how to measure men, the signs to look for, the subtle animal signals of violence. Cain is a storm looking for a place to break. God help the person who triggers him."

"Cain walked out on me," said Shelley flatly.

Surprise and disbelief widened Dave's eyes, but before he could speak the door of the Gilded Lily burst open and Billy ran in. "Shelley, there's a fire near your hills! I heard it on the car radio!"

Shelley ran out of the shop and stood in the street. Wind gusted, forcing her to squint against the desiccating rush of air. There was no need for clear vision, though. It was all too easy to see the dense plume of smoke billowing from the direction of her hills. The driving force of the Santa Ana wind had leveled off the top of the column, flattening the smoke into a long black flag rippling toward the sea. Even as she watched, the column boiled blackly, pushing against the harsh wind.

Without a word Shelley ran back into the Gilded Lily, grabbed her purse and ran to her car. Dave and Billy were right behind her.

"Anything we can do?" asked Dave.

"No," said Shelley tersely. "They'll have roadblocks out if the fire's bad enough. Only residents will be let through. But thanks."

She drove out of the parking lot with enough speed to make the tires whine. Within minutes she was on the freeway. The view was better from there. She could see that the fire was at least two ranges of hills east and slightly north of her home. That was little comfort, though. It was 9:30 on a hot, dry Saturday morning. The Santa Ana winds would sweep the land for the next ten hours, dying back only after sundown. For those ten hours the winds would blow between forty-five and fifty-five miles an hour, with gusts up to eighty-five—and embers would ride those wild gusts, sowing fire from the mountains to the sea.

The closer Shelley got to her home, the more sirens she heard. Fire engines were pouring in from all over the county, but there were only a few roads into the hills. Traffic thickened and then congealed. People gathered along the roadside, shielding their eyes from the sun and pointing toward the wall of smoke raging against the brassy sky. A pale dusting of ash sifted down. Fifteen fire trucks had passed before Shelley reached the turnoff to her own narrow road. There was a roadblock, a squad car parked sideways across both lanes. She stopped abruptly and rolled down her window.

"Sorry, ma'am," said the deputy sheriff, leaning down, braced against the wind, holding his uniform cap on with one hand. "This is a dead-end road. Too many sightseers blocking it and we wouldn't be able to move equipment or evacuate the residents if the fire spreads."

"I'm a resident," said Shelley, holding out her driver's license.

The deputy read the address on it, compared Shelley's pale face with the picture, and gave her back the license. "All right, ma'am, but listen for a squad car just in case. They've already evacuated the homes to the northeast. They're bulldozing a fuel break between you and the fire, and the planes will be coming any time now. Your area should be safe unless the wind shifts. But just the same, you listen real good for an evacuation warning, hear?"

Shelley nodded, not believing what she was being told. Evacuation? Impossible. There was some ash and smoke in the air when the wind shifted, but the fire wasn't that close. She didn't argue with the deputy, though. She had no intention of being kept from her home. If just one random ember landed on her cedar shake roof before she was there to put out the spark, she would lose her home.

And her home was all she had left.

A gust rocked Shelley's car and nearly tore off the deputy's hat. Shelley waited impatiently while the deputy got in his squad car, backed it out of the way and waved her through. There were no fire trucks on the narrow, winding road. They were concentrated around the next development in the hills northeast of her home, where the fire threatened houses with each hot gust of wind.

The only traffic Shelley saw as she drove up the hill was an erratic stream of cars heading down. The cars were stuffed to overflowing with clothes and paintings, stereos and potted plants and pets, whatever each person thought was too valuable to risk losing. Some of the cars had made several frantic trips, unloading possessions at friends' homes in the flatlands beyond the reach of flames.

Shelley pulled into her garage, grabbed a wrench and ran to the front sidewalk. There, set in concrete, were the emergency shutoffs for gas and water. The water valve she ignored. The gas valve she shut off. Nudge appeared at her side. The cat's movements were odd, gliding, intent. Every feline instinct was alert as sensitive nostrils read danger in the hot, sooty wind. She yeowed once, very softly, and patted Shelley's leg with claws only partially sheathed.

"I know, Nudge. It smells like hell. Literally."

Racing through the house, Shelley shut windows and doors before she changed into jeans. She hesitated, then hauled out Nudge's car carrier. With firm motions, she stuffed the cat into the cage and carried it out to the car. She didn't want Nudge to get frightened and run off to the hills if the wind shifted, bringing more smoke.

Moving quickly, running through the list in her mind, Shelley went to the garage and tripped the circuit breaker, shutting off electricity in the house. She hauled a ladder out of the garage and leaned it against the overhanging eave. Then she turned the hose on full force, dragged it up the ladder and onto the roof. The rainbird sprinkler attached to the hose chattered wildly as she scrambled up onto the dry shake shingles, scattering water all around. She hooked the sprinkler stand over a roof vent, adjusted the head for a circular pattern and stood back, ignoring the cold stream of water lashing across her with each sweep of the rainbird.

From the rooftop she looked up the street to her left,

where the cul-de-sac described a graceful loop. Beyond the single curving row of houses, two ridge lines to the northeast, fire raged. It looked like a red-fringed, black blanket being shaken savagely over the tawny hills.

The sound of a large propeller plane throbbed through the air. Shelley squinted, caught a flash of pewter, and spotted a Sierra Deuce dropping out of the blue-gray sky. After circling the fiery ridge lines a few thousand feet above the flames, the aircraft slanted down. With a last silver flash, it vanished into the smoke. Unconsciously holding her breath, Shelley watched until the plane finally emerged again. Somewhere, hidden within the smoke, thousands of gallons of fire retardant had rained down, quelling for an instant a hungry patch of flames.

The wind veered suddenly, blowing hard directly toward Shelley's house rather than at a diagonal which would steer the fire past it. Her heart slammed suddenly as she saw the black blanket ripple toward her, smelled the acrid air and saw ashes drift down into the steep canyon across the street from her. If the wind kept blowing from that quarter, it would drive the fire across the empty brushland toward her, rather than at a tangent leading to the sea.

Across the street and beyond the green terraces of the hilltop homes, bulldozers labored on the ridge and in the canyon below, scratching lines of raw earth across the potential paths of the fire like huge mechanical shamans drawing god signs in the dirt. Suddenly the wind shifted again, returning to its original direction. The blanket of smoke retreated a bit. Shelley wondered if the blanket had shaken off any of its red-hot fringe, embers leapfrogging fuel breaks and fire lines, tiny flames licking secretly deep in the sun-bleached chaparral, fire pooling and running together until it leaped fully grown onto the back of the gusting wind and rode to new ridges, new hillsides, new homes.

Her home.

A cold dash of water across Shelley's back brought her out of her trance. Cautiously, she negotiated the slanting roof back to the ladder. She went to the garage and pulled out another lightweight ladder and hauled it through the redwood gate and down the steep flagstone steps until she came to the second rooftop level of her home. She propped up the ladder, turned on another hose and sprinkler, and dragged it up on the middle roof. She waited long enough to make sure that the sprinkler covered as much as possible of the shake shingles, then she went down the ladder again.

By the time Shelley had a sprinkler going on the lowest roof overlooking the pool, she was drenched. Once she moved away from the sprinklers, though, the hot wind dried her with frightening speed. She went to the built-in sprinklers in the yard and turned them all on. The water pressure was low. Most of her neighbors had left sprinklers running when they fled.

The wind gusted, whipping Shelley's hair across her face. A fine mist from the pool's waterfall swirled over her. Eagerly she turned her face to the dampness. Then she ran down the last steps to the pool pump and filtration system discreetly hidden among rocks and greenery. She turned the pump on to its full capacity. Instantly the waterfall tripled in size, becoming a roaring torrent that poured down over a third of the pool and flung curtains of mist into the air.

"Every little bit," said Shelley, voicing hope and prayer in one.

When she looked to the southwest, toward the chaparral where she and Cain had walked, she could hardly believe that a fire burned anywhere. The sky was nearly clear in that quarter. No more than the most tenuous veil of smoke had filtered there from the fire behind her. Flowers bloomed in windrows of color, sending fragrance into the sun-filled air.

Yet when Shelley turned around, smoke reached toward her house like a hand with sooty fingers and glowing nails.

The wind shifted in a single, long moan that swept her hair straight back from her face. Holding her breath, Shelley waited for the wind to shift back. And waited. And waited. Ashes drifted down, ashes as big as her palm, ashes still burning at their edges. They cooled as they touched the earth. The waterfall pounded behind her, a thunder to equal the wind, sound drowning everything as the wind blew and blew, not veering again, blowing straight from the fire to her home.

Shelley went up to each roof and moved the sprinklers, watering a new portion of the desiccated cedar shingles. Ash fell, streaking her arms. Some of the ash was still warm, and only a third of each roof had been wet down even a little. It would be half an hour or more before all the roofs had been sprinkled even lightly. As she watched, heat and sun drew steamy evaporation from the shingles, drying them, making them vulnerable to fire.

A squad car drove slowly down the street. A calm, oddly distorted voice blared out of a speaker. The first part of the message was lost to the wind. Shelley didn't need to hear the words, though. She knew the officer was telling people to get in their cars and get down the hill. As the car came closer, the words sharpened into clarity.

"If the wind keeps blowing out of the east, the fire lines could be breached," continued the calm male voice. *"There is no need to panic. This is a precaution only. There is plenty of time to evacuate. Just get in your cars and drive slowly, carefully, down the hill."*

Shelley stood on the lowest roof and listened to the

evacuation directions being repeated as water and ashes ran down her face. She looked around. The roof was only partially wet. She couldn't leave yet. Too many of the shingles were still tinder dry. Besides, the evacuation was just a precaution. The fire was still at least one ridge line over. The wind would shift again. Santa Ana winds always shifted. She couldn't leave her home at the mercy of a random ember.

The squad car turned at the cul-de-sac and went down the street again, sending the evacuation orders echoing between the smoky, wind-swept houses.

"No," Shelley whispered. *"This is my home."*

She looked around frantically. To the southwest, over the ravine behind her house, the sky had dimmed. Overhead it was smoke-darkened, getting worse with each minute. Ashes rained down and with them came tiny glowing embers. The wind blew directly from the east, and it blew hard enough to make her stagger. Grimly, she climbed to the next level of the roof. The shingles were slippery where the water had fallen, crackling dry where the sprinkler couldn't reach. She dragged the sprinkler to another place. Cool, bright water streamed over the roof.

The wind veered slightly, backing toward the north again. For the next twenty minutes it blew less fiercely. Shelley went from roof level to roof level, trying to cover as much of the shingles as possible, barely getting the cedar damp before she dragged the sprinklers over to wet down another part. She no longer heard the Sierra Deuces as they made their heart-stopping passes over the flames, or noticed the palm-sized ashes floating down, cooled by a descent from thousands of feet.

Forty minutes later Shelley stood on the middle roof level, looking southwest. Sky that had been pure and blue was now the color of slate. She turned away and began climbing up to the roof that looked out on the street and the fire burning down from the north and east. Each time she had climbed from roof to roof, she had promised herself that it would be the last time and then she would go down the hill. She told herself that she was not being foolish. There was plenty of time. Even if flames had jumped the line and settled onto the next ridge over, fire burned very slowly going downhill, and there was a fuel break cut through the canyon bottom. Surely there was enough time to move the sprinklers just once more. Surely there was time to soak the roof and save her home.

Surely the wind had not been blowing from the east for the last twenty minutes.

Coughing as smoke raked her throat, Shelley climbed to the peak of the roof. As she reached for the sprinkler, she saw over the peak for the first time in thirty minutes—and she froze. The hell-glow of the fire was everywhere. Flames twenty feet high, thirty, higher, flames twisting and dancing over the land in terrible beauty. A vast, eerie crackling sound filled the air, as though the day itself were burning.

Motionless, barely breathing, Shelley listened to the voice of wildfire raging through chaparral toward the necklace of hilltop homes where she stood.

Wind gusted fiercely. Wildfire answered with an explosion of flame. Fire consumed the air, the sky, the chaparral, everything but the land itself. Even before the first embers rained down, scorching her, Shelley knew that she had been a fool to stay. The fire hadn't slowed meekly on the downhill side of the ridge to die along the fuel break. Flames had leaped the canyon itself, wildfire riding the searing wind, chaparral exploding in a firestorm that neither sprinklers nor prayers could turn. Spot fires burned on both sides of the winding road leading down the hill. In some places spot fires had already met and blended in small previews of the flaming hell to come. Numbly, held in the thrall of the advancing holocaust, Shelley watched tongues of fire lick across the road, cutting her off from the safety of the flatlands below.

A high scream rose up from the road, a sound like canvas endlessly ripping. Something flashed darkly, a shadow racing between flames several miles below, a black motorcycle accelerating through tight corners, its rider crouched half off the seat as he leaned into the curves, keeping the bike upright by using his own body as a counterweight.

Abruptly, Shelley's numbness shattered into real fear. Not for herself. For the man racing death to be with her.

"Cain! Go back!" The cry tore at her throat, but the sound was nothing next to the consuming voice of the fire. *"No!"* shouted Shelley. *"Go back, Cain! Go back while you still can!"*

But even as the words were torn away by the wind, fire leaped the road behind Cain, in front of him, all around him, caging him in flames. Shelley screamed, a long sound of anguish that was torn from her soul. Time slowed, crawled, stopped, until the only thing that still moved was the wild leap of advancing fire.

Shelley stood rigid, as frozen as time itself, her scream lost in the awful voice of wind-driven fire.

A black motorcycle burst out of the flames, its rider flat over the handlebars, its engine revving in a single sustained shriek of maximum power. Adrenaline swept through Shelley, freeing her. She scrambled off the roof and down the ladder as embers fell all around, burning her. Down the street a cedar roof blossomed into flame with a terrible soft sigh. Tiny fires burned on her neighbor's roof. Glowing ashes drifted down, leaving shriveling plants in their wake.

Shelley ran to the driveway, yanked open the car door, and pulled a trembling Nudge out of her cage. As Shelley turned around she heard the motorcycle's distinctive cry coming closer, dimming the voice of fire. The sound changed suddenly, tires rather than engine shrieking as Cain sent the bike into a long, controlled skid that ended in front of her house. He hit the ground running, letting the bike crash and slide on its side across the pavement.

Fifty feet away, a neighbor's roof sighed and gave itself to the fire.

"The pool!" shouted Shelley, then realized Cain couldn't hear her. His helmet was on, black visor down, the plastic pitted and tarnished by fire.

Cain grabbed Nudge's scruff in one hand and Shelley's arm in the other and ran through the front yard. Suddenly the air was hot, steamy with the sprinklers' artificial rain, yet the back of Shelley's blouse was dry. She heard the fire behind her, felt it reaching for her. Cain kicked the gate open. They raced side by side down the flagstone steps through air that was a mixture of steam and smoke and ashes too thick and too hot to breathe.

Cain didn't wait until the steep path reached the level of the pool. He grabbed Shelley beneath her arm and literally threw her from the steps at the head of the waterfall. He followed in a long leap, taking the squalling cat with him. A thunder of water closed around them, absorbing the initial lethal burst of the firestorm that was breaking over Shelley's home.

Beneath the water Shelley opened her eyes on a world gone the color of flames. Instinctively she headed for the flagstone grotto behind the waterfall. Cain swam alongside, moving powerfully despite his boots, helmet, leather jacket and a fistful of frantically struggling cat. Cautiously, remembering the fierce heat that she had felt in the instant before water covered her, Shelley surfaced behind the waterfall. The water was a seething, translucent, sooty orange wall shielding her from the rest of the world. The air was hot, acrid, steamy—but breathable. The firestorm had passed over.

Cain heaved the dripping cat up onto the stone lip of the pool. Nudge hunkered down, ears and fur plastered to her body, and snarled like the outraged feline she was. She lashed out with unsheathed claws, but Cain had already snatched back his leather-gloved hand. Bracing himself on the side of the pool with one arm, Cain fumbled with his helmet fastening. The buckle opened and he swept off the helmet. He grabbed Shelley and pulled her close. She clung to him, unable to speak, her arms locked around his neck.

"I don't know whether to kiss you or strangle you," said Cain, his voice raw. "If you ever do something that stupid again, I'll kill you myself!"

Before Shelley could answer, Cain's mouth closed over her lips. She didn't object. It was what she wanted more than anything else on earth. He was alive, and so was she. It was more than she had expected when she had seen the fire sweep over him. When he finally lifted his head, she tried to speak, then coughed harshly on the smoke that had penetrated even the waterfall's protective wall.

Cain's hand fastened on Shelley's collar, ripping apart her blouse in a single motion. He used the soaking strip he had torn off to cover her mouth and nose. While Shelley tied the cloth behind her head, Cain struggled out of his gloves and leather jacket. The jacket showed both the dull scars of fire and the pale scars left by Nudge's raking claws. When Cain began coughing, Shelley yanked off another piece of her blouse and tied it over his face. As she finished, a brilliant flare of orange lit the ash gray water. The roof was collapsing, sending fire raining down.

Suddenly reality crashed around Shelley, telling her that everything she had worked for since she was nineteen was gone. She had given up everything for her home, including the man she loved. She had lost her home anyway, and had nearly killed Cain and herself in the process.

With a low moan Shelley closed her eyes, not wanting to see even the molten reflection of her dying home. Gently Cain gathered her into his arms and held her while her childhood dream of security burned to ash around her.

After a long time the last fiery colors ran down the waterfall into the pool and did not return. Cain waited a while longer, holding Shelley, feeling the shudders that ran through her body with each breath she took. When his eyes no longer smarted from smoke, he pulled the soaking cloth away from his face and hers. Gently he kissed Shelley's forehead and took her arms from his neck, putting her hands on the lip of the pool.

"Can you hang on?" he asked, his voice rough from smoke.

Shelley nodded. Cain took a breath, eased through the waterfall, and looked around. The waterfall drowned the first words he spoke. It was just as well. The words were as ugly as the smoking debris of Shelley's home. All that was left were random, ruined walls and the cement foundation. The rest was no more than ashes riding on the back of a wild desert wind.

Grimly, Cain went back under the waterfall.

"It's safe now," said Cain, meeting Shelley's eyes. Then, bleakly. "There's nothing left to burn."

She bit her lip and nodded. She had expected nothing else.

Even so, it was a shock to come out from behind the waterfall and find a landscape gone black, nothing left but ashes and wind. So much beauty engulfed and then reduced to soot and memories.

The black vision blurred beneath Shelley's helpless tears.

"Listen to me," Cain said urgently. He touched her cheek with fingers that trembled. "I'll build it for you again. Every stone, every flower, every wooden beam and piece of tile. Everything. You'll have your home again if it's the last thing I ever do. I promise you. You will have your home again."

"Hold—me," Shelley said, turning toward Cain, trying to control the sobs wracking her body. "Just—hold me."

Cain lay on his side, watching Shelley sleep. She was pale but for the traceries of red where burning debris had touched her. When he had washed the soot from her fair skin, each scarlet mark had been like a knife scoring his body, telling him how close he had come to losing the only woman he had ever loved. His fingers tightened in her silky hair as he bent to brush his lips over her cheek. Shelley stirred. Still asleep, she curled more closely to him, snuggling against his warmth. His arms drew her closer, and he breathed deeply of her sweetness. Her eyelashes trembled, then opened. Cain saw the joy that came as her eyes focused on him, and then he saw the shadows as memory returned.

"I'll make another home for you," promised Cain quietly. His hand smoothed gently over Shelley's hair, comforting her as he would a child. "It will be all right, Shelley. You'll have your home again."

"Do you still love me?" she whispered.

Shelley watched Cain with eyes that were older, darker, even more beautiful than Cain had remembered.

"Not even hell's own wildfire could destroy my love for you," he said, watching her.

"Then I'm home," said Shelley simply. "Wherever I am, when I'm with you I'm home."

Cain's arms tightened and he looked at her as though he

wanted to see through to her soul. "Are you sure, Shelley? I want to marry you, but not like this. Not because you've lost everything else. That would be unfair to both of us." He closed his eyes, afraid that if he looked at her, he would take her despite the knowledge that they would both regret it later. "When you have your home again, then we'll talk about us."

Slowly, Shelley shook her head. "I'll never have my home again," she said, her voice both soft and certain. "Its most important ingredient is gone."

"The art," said Cain, defeat making his voice thick, harsh. "Why didn't you try to save it? Some of it would have survived a dunking in the pool."

Shelley shook her head, sending silky tendrils across Cain's shoulder. "The art wasn't what made my house a home. Love made it a home. My love. But when you left, you took my love with you."

Cain's eyelashes closed, veiling his eyes. A muscle moved tightly along his jaw. "Then why didn't you come with me?" he asked, his voice raw.

"I didn't understand, then. You gave me one kind of fire, Cain, and it burned through all the barriers I had built up against trusting someone else with my life. When you left, I thought that our fire had destroyed me." Tears came as Shelley remembered her pain and her loneliness. "It took another kind of wildfire to burn through reality and show me what is enduring and what is not," she said, her voice husky. "Love is like the naked land. It is real. It is enduring. The structures we build on it might burn or crumble or disappoint us. Love remains, though, like the land beneath the ashes. We can build again."

Shelley took Cain's hands and kissed them, loving each callus and scar, each lean and graceful finger. "I lost a lot of things when my house burned," she said, "beautiful things, irreplacable things. But still *things*. When I saw you coming up the road and the fire burning everywhere—''

Shelley's voice broke as her arms closed around Cain with a grip that even he would have had trouble breaking. ''When I saw that fire explode over you,'' she said, ''I would have given everything I've ever had or hoped to have just to know that you were alive. Everything. My home. My art. Even my life.''

With a hoarse sound, Cain buried his face in Shelley's hair and held her as though he wanted to take her into his soul.

''That's the way I felt when Dave called and told me there was a fire near your house,'' said Cain finally, his voice husky with emotion. ''You weren't at the evacuation center, you weren't at the Gilded Lily, and those bastards at the roadblock wouldn't let me through. I knew you were up there. I knew you wouldn't leave your home. But everywhere I looked there was fire. I went crazy, Shelley. I had to know you were alive.''

''How did you get past the police?''

''A trail Billy and I discovered,'' he said, smoothing his cheek against Shelley's hair. ''I cut over to the road as soon as I was past the squad car.''

''You shouldn't have,'' she whispered. ''If you had been killed—'' Shelley didn't finish. She couldn't. She simply held Cain until she stopped trembling. ''I love you. I'll go with you wherever you want, whenever you want. Just let me be with you.''

''That's why I came back, why I raced the fire. I had to be with the woman I loved.'' Cain kissed Shelley's forehead, her eyelashes, the hollow beneath her cheekbone, the corner of her mouth, the pulse beating in her throat. ''I stayed away as long as I could, trying to lose myself in the Atacama. It should have been easy. It's a wild, harsh land.

Stone and sand and wind, a sky so empty it makes your soul ache just to look up at it. Dry rivers run down to a cold sea. Desert without end, thousands of square miles where nothing grows.''

Cain's lips returned to Shelley's mouth. When he spoke again, his breath washed sweetly over her. ''One day I found a tiny spring no bigger than my hat. The water was cool, pure, miraculous. A single flower grew at the spring. The flower was fragile and yet fierce, radiant with the force of life. I sat and watched that flower. When it began to wilt beneath the brutal sun, I took off my hat and shaded the petals until the sun went down.

''And then I walked out of the Atacama and flew back to the only thing I've ever found that was more unexpected and beautiful than that flower. You.''

Gently, thoroughly, Cain found again each texture of Shelley's mouth, each taste of her warmth, the unrestrained sweetness of her tongue caressing his. ''You don't have to give up your home to live with me,'' said Cain softly against her lips. ''I came back to stay with you.''

''But I want to see your world,'' said Shelley, her fingers working into the chestnut warmth of Cain's hair. ''I'm not afraid anymore.''

''What were you afraid of?'' asked Cain. ''Me?''

''No. Me. I have a wanderlust as deep as yours.''

Cain's gray eyes kindled triumphantly. ''I knew it! But I was afraid you'd never admit it.''

''How did you know?''

''The painting,'' said Cain, looking up at the universe of stars that Shelley had hung above his bed. ''Those infinite possibilities would have terrified a true homebody.''

''You're right,'' she whispered. ''I just couldn't admit it, because I needed security even more than I needed to roam. It's different now. You're the only home I need or want.''

Cain whispered her name and his love against Shelley's mouth. Long fingers stroked her neck, her shoulders, her breasts. Her breath caught, then raced as she flowered beneath Cain's loving touch. She turned to him, her palms sliding down his body until he tightened and groaned, moving against the sweet pressure of her hands. His own hands moved caressingly down her body, finding and touching the unexpected spring within her, feeling the satin flower bloom for him.

"Shelley?" he asked hoarsely.

"Yes," she whispered, pulling Cain's beautiful mouth down to hers as he moved over her. "Show me the landscapes of your soul."

"That will take a lifetime," he said, taking her mouth even as he filled her body with his own.

Shelley moaned softly, moving with him, loving him. "Then I wish we had more than one life to share."

"Maybe we do," murmured Cain, gathering her closer with each heartbeat, each shared movement. "All those stars, a universe of possibilities. . . ."

Together Cain and Shelley explored the most compelling of those possibilities, the shimmering landscape of the soul known as love.

WIN

a fabulous $50,000 diamond jewelry collection

ENTER

by filling out the coupon below and mailing it by September 30, 1985

Send entries to:

U.S.
Silhouette Diamond Sweepstakes
P.O. Box 779
Madison Square Station
New York, NY 10159

Canada
Silhouette Diamond Sweepstakes
Suite 191
238 Davenport Road
Toronto, Ontario M5R 1J6

SILHOUETTE DIAMOND SWEEPSTAKES
ENTRY FORM

☐ Mrs.　　☐ Miss　　☐ Ms　　☐ Mr.

NAME _____ (please print) _____

ADDRESS _____ APT. # _____

CITY _____

STATE/(PROV.) _____

ZIP/(POSTAL CODE) _____

RTD-A-1

RULES FOR SILHOUETTE DIAMOND SWEEPSTAKES

OFFICIAL RULES—NO PURCHASE NECESSARY

1. Silhouette Diamond Sweepstakes is open to Canadian (except Quebec) and United States residents 18 years or older at the time of entry. Employees and immediate families of the publishers of Silhouette, their affiliates, retailers, distributors, printers, agencies and RONALD SMILEY INC. are excluded.

2. To enter, print your name and address on the official entry form or on a 3" x 5" slip of paper. You may enter as often as you choose, but each envelope must contain only one entry. Mail entries first class in Canada to Silhouette Diamond Sweepstakes, Suite 191, 238 Davenport Road, Toronto, Ontario M5R 1J6. In the United States, mail to Silhouette Diamond Sweepstakes, P.O. Box 779, Madison Square Station, New York, NY 10159. Entries must be postmarked between February 1 and September 30, 1985. Silhouette is not responsible for lost, late or misdirected mail.

3. First Prize of diamond jewelry, consisting of a necklace, ring, bracelet and earrings will be awarded. Approximate retail value is $50,000 U.S./$62,500 Canadian. Second Prize of 100 Silhouette Home Reader Service Subscriptions will be awarded. Approximate retail value of each is $162.00 U.S./$180.00 Canadian. No substitution, duplication, cash redemption or transfer of prizes will be permitted. Odds of winning depend upon the number of valid entries received. One prize to a family or household. Income taxes, other taxes and insurance on First Prize are the sole responsibility of the winners.

4. Winners will be selected under the supervision of RONALD SMILEY INC., an independent judging organization whose decisions are final, by random drawings from valid entries postmarked by September 30, 1985, and received no later than October 7, 1985. Entry in this sweepstakes indicates your awareness of the Official Rules. Winners who are residents of Canada must answer correctly a time-related arithmetical skill-testing question to qualify. First Prize winner will be notified by certified mail and must submit an Affidavit of Compliance within 10 days of notification. Returned Affidavits or prizes that are refused or undeliverable will result in alternative names being randomly drawn. Winners may be asked for use of their name and photo at no additional compensation.

5. For a First Prize winner list, send a stamped self-addressed envelope postmarked by September 30, 1985. In Canada, mail to Silhouette Diamond Contest Winner, Suite 309, 238 Davenport Road, Toronto, Ontario M5R 1J6. In the United States, mail to Silhouette Diamond Contest Winner, P.O. Box 182, Bowling Green Station, New York, NY 10274. This offer will appear in Silhouette publications and at participating retailers. Offer void in Quebec and subject to all Federal, Provincial, State and Municipal laws and regulations and wherever prohibited or restricted by law.

If you enjoyed this book...

Thrill to 4 more Silhouette Intimate Moments novels (a $9.00 value)—ABSOLUTELY FREE!

If you want more passionate sensual romance, then Silhouette Intimate Moments novels are for you!

In every 256-page book, you'll find romance that's electrifying...involving... and intense. And now, these larger-than-life romances can come into your home every month!

4 FREE books as your introduction.

Act now and we'll send you four thrilling Silhouette Intimate Moments novels. They're our gift to introduce you to our convenient home subscription service. Every month, we'll send you four new Silhouette Intimate Moments books. Look them over for 15 days. If you keep them, pay just $9.00 for all four. Or return them at no charge.

We'll mail your books to you *as soon as they are published.* Plus, with every shipment, you'll receive the Silhouette Books Newsletter absolutely free. *And Silhouette Intimate Moments is delivered free.*

Mail the coupon today and start receiving Silhouette Intimate Moments. Romance novels for women...not girls.

Silhouette Intimate Moments

Silhouette Intimate Moments™
120 Brighton Road, P.O. Box 5084, Clifton, NJ 07015-5084

☐ YES! Please send me FREE and without obligation. 4 exciting Silhouette Intimate Moments romance novels. Unless you hear from me after I receive my 4 FREE books, please send 4 new Silhouette Intimate Moments novels to preview each month. I understand that you will bill me $2.25 each for a total of $9.00 — with no additional shipping, handling or other charges. **There is no minimum number of books to buy and I may cancel anytime I wish.** The first 4 books are mine to keep, even if I never take a single additional book.

☐ Mrs. ☐ Miss ☐ Ms. ☐ Mr.   **BMM225**

Name _____ (please print)

Address _____ Apt. # _____

City _____ State _____ Zip _____
(   )

Area Code   Telephone Number

Signature (if under 18, parent or guardian must sign)

This offer limited to one per customer. Terms and prices subject to change. Your enrollment is subject to acceptance by Silhouette Books.

Silhouette Intimate Moments is a service mark and trademark.

IMIM-R-A

READERS' COMMENTS ON
SILHOUETTE INTIMATE MOMENTS:

"About a month ago a friend loaned me my first Silhouette. I was thoroughly surprised as well as totally addicted. Last week I read a Silhouette Intimate Moments and I was even more pleased. They are the best romance series novels I have ever read. They give much more depth to the plot, characters, and the story is fundamentally realistic. They incorporate tasteful sex scenes, which is a must, especially in the 1980's. I only hope you can publish them fast enough."

S.B.*, Lees Summit, MO

"After noticing the attractive covers on the new line of Silhouette Intimate Moments, I decided to read the inside and discovered that this new line was more in the line of books that I like to read. I do want to say I enjoyed the books because they are so realistic and a lot more truthful than so many romance books today."

J.C., Onekama, MI

"I would like to compliment you on your new line of books. I will continue to purchase all of the Silhouette Intimate Moments. They are your best line of books that I have had the pleasure of reading."

S.M., Billings, MT

*names available on request